The Two Faces of January

BOOKS BY

PATRICIA HIGHSMITH

NOVELS

Strangers on a Train

The Blunderer

The Talented Mr. Ripley

Deep Water

A Game for the Living

The Cry of the Owl

This Sweet Sickness

The Two Faces of January

The Glass Cell

A Suspension of Mercy

Those Who Walk Away

The Tremor of Forgery

Ripley Under Ground

A Dog's Ransom

Ripley's Game

Edith's Diary

The Boy Who Followed Ripley

People Who Knock on the Door

Found in the Street

Ripley Under Water

SHORT STORIES

Eleven

The Animal-Lover's Book of Beastly Murder

Little Tales of Misogyny

Slowly, Slowly in the Wind

The Black House

Mermaids on the Golf Course

Tales of Natural and Unnatural Catastrophes

The Two Faces of January

Patricia Highsmith

Grove Press
New York

Published simultaneously in Canada
Printed in the United States of America

Library of Congress Cataloging-in-Publication Data
The two faces of January.
Reprint.
I. Title.
PS3558.I366T8 1988 813'.54—dc20 87-30669
ISBN 978-0-8021-2262-9

Grove Press
an imprint of Grove/Atlantic, Inc.
154 West 14th Street
New York, NY 10011

Distributed by Publishers Group West

www.groveatlantic.com

13 14 15 16 10 9 8 7 6 5 4 3 2 1

For my friend
Rolf Tietgens

I

At half past three of a morning in early January, Chester MacFarland was awakened in his berth on the *San Gimignano* by an alarming sound of scraping. He sat up and saw through the porthole a brightly lighted wall of orangey-red color, extremely close and creeping by. His first thought was that they were grazing the side of another ship, and he scrambled out of bed and, still half asleep, leaned across his wife's berth and looked more closely. There were scribblings and scratches and numbers on the wall, which he now saw was rock. NIKO 1957, he read. W. MUSSOLINI. Then an American-looking PETE '60.

The alarm clock went off, and Chester grabbed for it, knocking over the Scotch bottle that stood beside it on the floor. He pressed the button that stopped the alarm, then reached for his robe.

"Darling?—What's going on?" Colette asked sleepily.

"I think we're in the Corinthian Canal," Chester said. "Or else we're awfully close to another ship. We're due to be in the canal. It's half past three. Coming on deck?"

"Um-m—no," Colette murmured, snuggling deeper into the bedclothes. "You tell me all about it."

Smiling, Chester pressed a kiss into her warm cheek. "I'm going on deck. Back in a minute."

As soon as he stepped out of the door onto the deck, Chester ran into the officer who had told him they would pass through the canal at 3:30 a.m.

"Sississi! Il canale, signor!" he said to Chester.

"Thanks!" Chester felt a thrill of adventure and excitement, and stood erect against the chill wind, gripping the rail with both hands. There was no one but him on the deck.

The canal's sides looked four storys high, at least. Leaning over the rail, Chester saw only blackness at either end of the canal. It was impossible to see just how long it was, but he remembered its length on his map of Greece, one half inch, which he thought would be about four miles. Man-made, this vital waterway. The thought gave him pleasure. Chester looked at the marks of drills and pickaxes that were still visible in the orangey rock—or was it hard clay? Chester lifted his eyes to where the side of the canal stopped sharp against the darkness, looked higher to the stars sprinkled in the Grecian sky. In just a few hours, he would see Athens. He had an impulse to stay up the rest of the night, to get his overcoat and stand on deck while the ship ploughed through the Aegean towards Piraeus. He'd be tired tomorrow, however. After a few minutes, Chester went back to the stateroom and crawled into bed.

Some five hours later, when the *San Gimignano* had docked at Piraeus, Chester was pushing his way towards the rail through a grumbling tangle of passengers and porters who had come aboard to assist people with their luggage. Chester had breakfasted in a leisurely way in his state-room, preferring to wait until the majority of the passengers had debarked; but, judging from the number of people on deck and in the corridors, the debarking had not even begun. The town and the dock of Piraeus looked like a dusty mess. Chester was disappointed not to be able to see Athens in the hazy distance. He lit a cigarette and looked slowly over the moving and stationary figures on the broad expanse of dock. Blue-clad porters. A few men in rather shabby-looking overcoats walking about restlessly, glancing at the ship: they looked more like money-changers or taxi-drivers than policemen, Chester thought. His eyes moved from left to right and back again over the entire scene. No, he couldn't believe that any one of the men he saw could be waiting for him. The gangplank was down, and if anyone had come for him, wouldn't he be coming right on board now, instead of waiting on the dock? Of course. Chester cleared his throat and took a gentle drag on his cigarette. Then he turned and saw Colette.

"Greece," she said, smiling.

"Yes. Greece." He took her hand. Her fingers spread, then closed tightly on his. "I'd better see about a porter. All the suitcases closed?"

She nodded. "I saw Alfonso. He'll bring them out."

"Did you tip him?"

"Um-m. Two thousand lire. You think that's okay?" Her dark-blue eyes looked up widely at Chester. Her long auburn lashes blinked twice. Then she repressed a laugh that came bubbling out of her, a laugh of happiness and affection. "You're not thinking. Is two thousand enough?"

"Two thousand is perfect, darling." Chester kissed her lips quickly.

Alfonso emerged with half their luggage, set it on the deck and went back for the rest. Chester helped him carry it down the gang-plank to the dock, and then three or four porters began arguing as to who would get to carry it.

"Wait! Just wait, please," Chester said. "Money, you know. Got to change some." He waved his traveler's check book, then trotted off to a money-changing booth near the gates of the dock. He changed a twenty.

"Please," Colette said, patting a suitcase protectively, and the quarrelling porters folded their arms, stepped back and waited, looking her over with approval.

Colette—it was a name she had chosen for herself at the age of fourteen, in preference to Elizabeth—was twenty-five years old, five feet three, with reddish light-brown hair, full lips, a perfectly straight nose lightly sprinkled with freckles, and quite arrestingly pretty dark-blue, almost lavender, eyes. Her eyes looked widely and straightforwardly at everything and everyone, like the eyes of a curious, intelligent and still learning child. Men whom she looked at usually felt transfixed and fascinated by her gaze; there was something speculative in it, and nearly every man, whatever his age, thought, "She looks as if she's falling in love with me. Could it be?" Most women thought her expression and even Colette herself rather naïve, too naïve to be dangerous; which was fortunate, because otherwise women might have been jealous or suspicious of her attractiveness. She had been married to Chester just a little more than a year, and she had met him by answering an advertisement he put in the *Times* for a part-time secretary and typist. It hadn't taken her more than two days to realize that Chester's business was not exactly on the up and up—what stockbroker operated out of his apartment instead of an office, and where were his stocks on the Exchange, anyway?—but Chester had a lot of charm; he plainly had plenty of money, and evidently the money was rolling in steadily, which meant he wasn't in any trouble. Chester had been married before, for eight years, to a woman who had died of cancer two years before Colette met him. Chester was forty-two, still handsome, graying slightly at the temples, and just a bit inclined to develop a tummy, but Colette was inclined to put weight on all over, and dieting was a normal thing with her. It was easy for her to plan menus that were appetizing as well as low in calories.

"Here we go," Chester said, waving a fistful of drachma notes. "Pick a taxi, honey."

There were half a dozen taxis standing about, and Colette chose the one of a driver who had a friendly smile. Three porters helped them load the taxi with their seven pieces of luggage, two of which went on the roof, and then they were off for Athens. Chester sat forward, watching for the Parthenon on its hill, or some other landmark that might appear against the pale-blue sky. And then he found himself looking at an imaginary Walkie Kar, big as all Athens, red and chromium, with its horrible rubber-lumped handlebars and its ugly, cupped safety seat. Chester shuddered. What a stupidity, what a needless, idiotic risk that had been! Colette had told him so, too. She had got a bit angry when she found out about it, and she was perfectly justified in getting angry. The Walkie Kar had come about like this: in a printer's shop where he was having some business cards made up, Chester had noticed a stack of handbills advertising the Walkie Kar. There was a picture of it, a description, and the price, $12.95, and at the bottom an order blank that could be torn off along a perforated line. The printer had laughed when Chester picked up one of the sheets and looked at it. The company was out of business, the printer said, and they hadn't even paid him for his print job. No, the printer wouldn't mind at all if Chester took a few of them, because he was going to throw them all out, anyway. Chester had said he wanted to send them to a few of his friends as a joke, his heavy-drinking friends, and at first he had wanted to do that only; and then something—temptation, bravado, a sense of humor?—had compelled him to try peddling the damned things, and by ringing doorbells and making with the old spiel he had sold more than eight-hundred dollars' worth, mainly to people in the Bronx. Then he had run into one of his purchasers in his own apartment building in Manhattan, and, moreover, just as he was opening his own mailbox. The man said his Walkie Kar had not arrived, though he had ordered and paid for it two months ago, and neither had the Walkie Kar of a neighbor of his arrived. When that happened to two people who knew each other, they got together and did something about it, Chester knew from experience; and, since the man had taken a good look at his name on the mailbox, Chester had thought it just as well to get out of the country for a while, rather than move to another apartment and change his name to something else again. Colette had been wanting to go to Europe and they had planned to go in spring, but the Walkie Kar incident had hurried them up by four months. They had left New York in December. Yes, Colette had reproached him pretty severely for the Walkie Kar episode, and she had been annoyed also because she thought the weather wouldn't be as pleasant in winter as in spring, and she was right, of course.

Chester had given her a new set of luggage and a mink jacket by way of making it up to her, and he wanted to do everything he could to make the trip a happy one for her. It was Colette's first trip to Europe. So far she had liked London best, and, to Chester's surprise, liked London more than Paris. It had rained more in Paris than in London; Chester had caught a cold; and he remembered that every time he got his feet wet or felt rain sliding down the back of his neck, he had thought of the God-damned Walkie Kar, and he had reminded himself that for the wretched bit of money he had got out of it, he might have caused, might still cause, Howard Cheever (which was his current alias and the name that had been on his mailbox in the New York apartment building) to be exposed to a thorough investigation, which could mean the end of half a dozen companies on whose stock sales Chester depended for his living. Europe was safer than the States just now, and Chester MacFarland, his real name, was a name he hadn't used in fifteen years; but he was guilty, among other things, of defrauding through the mails, which was one of the few offenses the American Government could extradite a man for. It was remotely possible that they would send a man over after him, Chester thought, if they ever made the connection between Cheever and MacFarland.

The taxi-driver asked him something over his shoulder in Greek.

"Sorry. No capeesh," Chester answered. "The main square, okay? The centre of town."

"Grande Bretagne?" asked the driver.

"Well . . . I'm not quite sure," Chester said. The Grande Bretagne was unquestionably the biggest and best hotel in Athens, but for that very reason, Chester felt wary about stopping there. "Let's take a look," he added, though he didn't think the driver understood. "There it is," he said to Colette. "That white building over there."

The white edifice of the Grande Bretagne had a formal, antiseptic air in contrast to the less tall and dirtier buildings and stores that stood around the rectangle of Constitution Square. There was a government building of some sort far to their right, a Greek flag flying from a pole on its grounds, and a couple of soldiers in skirts and white stockings standing guard near the doors.

"What about that hotel?" Chester asked, pointing. "The King's Palace. That looks pretty good, don't you think, honey?"

"Okay. Sure," Colette said agreeably.

The King's Palace Hotel was across a street at one side of the Grande Bretagne. A bellboy in a red jacket and black trousers came out on the pavement to help with the luggage. The lobby looked first-rate to Chester, maybe not luxury class, but first-rate. The carpet was thick underfoot, and, judging from the warmth, the central heating really worked.

"You have a reservation, sir?" asked the clerk behind the counter.

"No, no, we haven't, but we'd like a room with a bath and a nice view," Chester said, smiling.

"Yes, sir." The clerk pushed a bell, then handed a key to the uniformed boy who came up. "Show them six twenty-one, please. May I have your passports, sir? You can pick them up when you come down."

Chester took the one that Colette drew from her red leather case in her pocketbook, pulled his own from his inside breast pocket, and pushed them across the counter to the clerk. It always gave him a little throb of mental pain, a small shock of embarrassment such as he felt when a doctor asked him to strip, whenever he pushed his passport over a hotel counter or had it taken from his hand by an official inspector. Chester Crighton MacFarland, five feet eleven, born in 1922 in Sacramento, California, no distinguishing marks, wife Elizabeth Talbott MacFarland. It was all so naked. Worst of all, his photograph, so untypically for a passport photograph, was a very good likeness, showing receding brown hair, aggressive jaw, good-sized nose, a rather stubborn, thin-lipped mouth with a moustache above it—an excellent portrait of him, depicting all but the color of his blue, staring eyes and the ruddiness of his cheeks. Had the clerk, Chester always thought, or the inspector been shown the same picture of him and told to keep his eyes open for him? This moment in the King's Palace Hotel was not the time to learn, because the clerk pushed the passports to one side without opening them.

A few minutes later they were comfortably installed in a large, warm room with a view of the white, geranium garnished balconies of the Grande Bretagne and of a busy avenue six storys down, which Chester identified on his map of Athens as Venizelos Street. It was only 10 o'clock. The whole day lay before them.

2

At that moment, in a considerably cheaper and shabbier hotel around the corner on Kriezotou Street, sometimes called Jan Smuts Street, a young American named Rydal Keener was pressing the button for an elevator on the fourth floor. He was a slender, dark-haired young man, quiet and slow in movement. There was an air of melancholy about him, melancholy turned outward rather than inward, as if he brooded not on his own problems but the world's. His dark eyes seemed to see and to think about whatever they looked at. He appeared also very poised, not at all concerned with what anybody thought of him. His insouciance was often taken for arrogance. It did not go with the worn shoes and overcoat he had on now, but his bearing was so confident that his clothes were the last thing people noticed about him, if they noticed them at all.

It was an even bet every morning whether the elevator would come or not, and every morning Rydal played a game with himself: if the elevator came, he would have breakfast in the Taverna Dionysiou in

Niko's street, and if it didn't come, he would buy a newspaper and have breakfast in the Café Brasil. Not that it made a bit of difference one way or the other. He would buy four newspapers, anyway, in the course of the day, but in the Taverna Dionysiou he knew so many people, he was always talking too much to read anything, and in the Café Brasil, a fancier place, he never knew anyone, and so always took a newspaper with him for company. Rydal waited patiently, walking in a slow circle over the threadbare carpet in front of the elevator shaft. No annunciatory rattle from below or above showed that anyone had heard or heeded his ring. Rydal sighed, threw his shoulders back, and stared with serious attention at an extremely dark and obscure painting of a country landscape that hung on the wall of the corridor he had just walked through. Even the sky was a sooty black, as if the picture—surely no artist in the world, however bad, would paint a hillside and sky so smutty you could scarcely see where one ended and the other began—had over the years accumulated the dirt of the atmosphere, absorbed the very breaths of the Greek, French, Italian, Serbian, Yugoslavian, Russian, American and whatever people that had passed back and forth in that corridor. Two sheeps' backsides, dingy tan, were the brightest spots in the composition.

The elevator was certainly not coming. He might have rung again, could eventually have got service if he kept ringing, but his game was over, and he no longer cared to ride. He would go to the Café Brasil. Rydal walked slowly down the first short flight of carpeted stairs. There were two holes, each the size of a large foot, in the carpet, and Rydal wondered if anybody had ever tripped in them and fallen. They would have fallen against a cement vase, phony third-century B.C., which stood on a Victorian flower stand of cast iron. Rydal went by a mirror some ten feet long on the wall, crossed a small, meaningless foyer where there was another opaque painting and a pot of dried out ferns, and took some stairs that led down in another direction. On the next floor, a tall and somewhat angular woman in tweeds, not a bit masculine but flat and sexless as something out of a 1920 British fashion drawing, pressed the elevator button with a confident air, then returned Rydal's gaze with calm, greenish eyes. Rydal's eyes lingered on hers a little too long for the look to be merely one that one gives a stranger encountered in a hotel hall, but that was another game Rydal played, and the Hotel Melchior Condylis was just the place to play it. The game might be called Adventure. It depended on meeting the Right Person, male or female. Something would take place when his eyes met the eyes of the Right Person, there would be a shock of recognition, one of them would speak, they would have some kind of Adventure together—or there wouldn't be anything in the eyes, and absolutely nothing would happen. This woman was certainly an odd and fascinating type, but nothing really happened in her eyes. The Hotel Melchior Condylis was full of odd and fascinating-looking people. It was not a place for the well-heeled, not a place the average American would be drawn to, but it had almost every other nationality staying in it, as far as Rydal could see. There was an East Indian couple now, and an elderly French couple. There was a young Russian student whom Rydal had tried chatting with in Russian, but the Russian acted as if he were suspicious of him, and their acquaintance had not progressed. Last month there had been an Eskimo travelling with an American oceanographer, and they were both natives of Alaska. There was the predictable sprinkling of Turks and Yugoslavs. It was amusing to think of little points all over the world where people who had been to the Melchior Condylis would mention its name, in one or the other of twenty-five or thirty languages, and perhaps recommend it (or *could* they really, except for its cheapness?) to their friends as a place to stop in Athens. The service was awful, worse than non-existent, because it was often promised when it did not come. The corridors and stairs of the place had to Rydal the anticipatory air of a stage when all the props are in place and before the first actor makes his appearance. Not one item in the rooms—Rydal had been in three of them—the corridors or the lobby was wrong for its character, and its character was that of an old, tired, Mitteleuropa stable hack.

Rydal found the elevator operator, who also doubled as porter, reading a newspaper on the wooden bench by the door and picking his nose.

"Good morning, Meester Keener," said Max, a black-moustached man in an ancient grey uniform behind the desk.

"Morning to you, Max. How are you?" Rydal laid his key down.

"You want lottery ticket?" Max asked with a hopeful grin, holding up a sheet of tickets.

"Um-m. Am I feeling lucky today? Not particularly. Not today," Rydal said, and went out.

He turned left and walked towards Constitution Square and the American Express. There might be a letter for him at the American Express, there most likely was a letter, because this was Wednesday and he'd had no mail Monday or Tuesday, and he averaged two letters a week. But he decided to wait until afternoon before going in to ask. He bought yesterday's London *Daily Express* and an Athens newspaper of this morning, gave a wave to Niko, who was shuffling about in his gym shoes a few yards away on the pavement in front of the American Express Travel Agency, his figure beige and more or less round under the sponges that hung on strings all over him.

"Lottery?" Niko yelled, swinging up a ticket sheet.

Rydal shook his head. "Not today!" he yelled back in Greek. It was evidently a great day for lottery tickets.

Rydal went into the Café Brasil, climbed the stairs to the second-floor bar where one could also get breakfast, and ordered a cappuccino with a jelly doughnut. The news in the paper was dull today. A small train wreck in Italy. A divorce case against an M.P. Rydal rather enjoyed murder stories, and he liked the English best. He smoked three Papistratos after his coffee, and it was getting on to 11 when he went out. He thought he would drop by the National Archaeological Museum for a little while, then buy a present for Pan—Pan's birthday was Saturday, and he was giving a party—in some haberdashery or leather shop in Stadiou Street, have lunch in the hotel restaurant, then work on his poems in what was left of the afternoon. Pan had said something about going to a movie tonight, but the date might not come off, and Rydal didn't care if it didn't. It was obviously going to rain, and the Athens paper predicted it also. Rydal enjoyed loafing in his room and working on his poems when it rained. Out on the pavement, he was inspired to call at the American Express now instead of this afternoon, so he walked through the arcade that brought him out on another street more or less parallel to Constitution Square, where the American Express mail office was located.

There was a letter from his sister Martha in Washington, D.C. Another slight reproach, Rydal supposed. But it wasn't. It was actually almost an apology to him for having "spoken a little sharply in December". She had written, not spoken. Rydal's father had died in early December, Rydal had been notified by a cable from his brother Kennie two days before the funeral, he could have flown home, but he hadn't. His father had suffered a heart attack, and died within four hours. Rydal had delayed, undecided, for twenty-four hours, and had finally wired Kennie in Cambridge that he was sorry to hear the news, and that he sent him and the rest of the family his love and sympathy. He did not say he was not coming, but that was evident, since any mention of his coming was left out. Kennie had not written him since, but Martha had, and she had said, "Considering the family is so small, just you and I and Kennie and his wife and children, I think you might have made an effort to get here. After all, he was your father. I can't believe that your conscience doesn't bother you. Are you going to nurse a grievance even after the object is dead? You would be happier, Rydal, if you could be bigger about it—and if you'd come and stood by with the rest of us." Rydal remembered the letter almost verbatim, though he had thrown it away as soon as he had read it. Now his sister wrote that she understood that he had his grievances

> ". . . which, as you know, I've always considered rather warrantable. But don't be bitter, if you can help it. You once told me you understood the uselessness of hatred and resentment. I hope it's true now more than ever, and that you're finding some kind of peace over

there. Somehow I like the idea of your being in Athens rather than Rome. . . . When do you think you'll be coming home?"

Rydal refolded the letter and pushed it into his overcoat pocket. Then he walked out of the American Express office and turned in the direction of the arcade again. He was not going to be in Athens much longer. The Right Day would come, and he would take the plane for Crete, have a look at the Palace of Knossos and the Iraklion Museum of Cretan antiquities, and then fly home. Then he would see about getting a job in a law firm, he supposed in New York. He had about eight hundred dollars left in traveler's checks and a little cash. His money had held out quite nicely over the two years he had been away. His dear grandmother's ten thousand. His grandmother had been the only one in his family who had believed in him at the time of the crisis with his father. She had made her will then, and had died when Rydal was twenty-three, midway in his year of army service. He had made up his mind then what he was going to do with it: go to Europe and stay as long as it lasted. His father had wanted him to get started right away in a law firm, and even had a position in a junior capacity arranged for him with Wheeler, Hooton and Clive on Madison Avenue (his father had known Wheeler), but Rydal hadn't and didn't want to start work with any firm that had any connection with his father. *You're late enough,* said his father, mostly in regard to his not getting out of Yale Law School until he was twenty-two, so unlike the precocious and scholarly Keeners, but his father's sending him to reform school for two years hadn't helped, and he had not entered Yale until he was nineteen. His father had graduated from Harvard at nineteen,

Kennie at twenty, Martha from Radcliff at twenty also. All Phi Beta Kappa. Rydal was no Phi Beta Kappa.

Rydal found himself standing in front of the Café Brasil's glass doors in the arcade, awoke to the present and remembered he'd just been there, then went on through the arcade in search of Niko. Yes, he'd buy a couple of lottery tickets today, after all. There was Niko, still shuffling and stomping in the cold in his gym shoes. Niko had bunions, and sneakers were the only kind of shoes he felt comfortable in. Rydal smiled as he watched Niko approach a well-dressed gentleman just emerging from the American Express. Lottery tickets or sponges, which would you like, sir?

Then Rydal came to a stop. The man talking to Niko looked remarkably like his father. The blue eyes were the same, the jutting nose, the color of the moustache. This man was about forty, heavier and ruddier, but the resemblance was so astounding Rydal had an impulse to ask the man if they were related, if his name were possibly Keener. The Keeners had some English cousins, and this man could be English—but his clothes looked American. The man put his head back and laughed, a hearty laugh that carried to Rydal and made him smile, too. Niko's hand jerked back under the sponges, but Rydal had seen a white flash that might have been pearls on his palm. The ruddy-faced man in the dark overcoat had declined whatever Niko had offered, but was buying a sponge. Rydal folded his arms and waited quietly near the newspaper kiosk on the corner. He saw the man push a second bill into Niko's not unwilling hand, saw him wave and heard him call, "So long!" as he walked away.

He was walking towards Rydal. Rydal kept looking at him, seeing even in his walk his father's confident stride. The sponge bulged his overcoat pocket. In his left hand he carried a new-looking *Guide Bleu.* He glanced at Rydal, looked away, then looked again, walking past him now, but turning his head so as to keep him in view. Rydal stared back, and it was no game now, he was not waiting for a sign, he was simply fascinated, spellbound, by the man's resemblance to his father. The man at last looked away from Rydal, and Rydal followed him, walking at a slower pace. The man glanced over his shoulder at Rydal, hurried his steps, ran off the curb at Venizelos Street, then slowed at the wrong place—in front of an oncoming car—as if trying to give the impression he was not hurrying. Now he had passed the Grande Bretagne, and Rydal had expected him to turn in there. Rydal kept him in view, but already his interest was flagging. What if he were an English cousin? Who cared? The man went into the King's Palace Hotel, whose front door was set at an angle on the corner, and he looked back—Rydal couldn't tell if he saw him or not—before he went in.

It was that last looking back that roused Rydal's suspicion. What was the man afraid of? What was he running from?

Rydal walked slowly back to Niko and bought two lottery tickets. "Who was your friend?" Rydal asked.

"Who?" asked Niko, smiling and showing his lead-framed front tooth, next to it a gap.

"The American who just bought a sponge," Rydal said.

"Ah. I don't know. Never saw him before this morning. Nice guy. Gave me extra twenty drachs." Niko shifted and the sponges swayed. The broad, dirty-white gym shoes, all that was visible of him below the panoply of sponges, did slow ups and downs like the feet of a restless elephant. "Why you ask?"

"Oh, I dunno," said Rydal.

"Plenty lettuce," said Niko.

Rydal smiled. He had taught Niko the word lettuce, and a lot of other slang words for money, a subject Niko was very interested in. "But you couldn't get rid of the hot stuff to him?"

"Reed?" asked Niko, puzzled.

Niko knew "hot stuff," but not "rid." "Couldn't sell him any jewelry?"

"Ah!" Niko waved a barely visible hand among the sponges, laughing with a sudden and uncharacteristic embarrassment. "He think it over, he say."

"What was it?"

"Pearls." After a glance to either side of him, Niko pulled a hand out and displayed a circle of pearls, a two-row bracelet on his wide, soiled palm.

Rydal nodded, and the pearls disappeared again. "How much?"

"To you—four hundred dollars."

"Ugh," Rydal said automatically, though they were worth it. "Well, good luck with the rich American."

"He be back," said Niko.

And Niko was probably right, Rydal thought. Niko had been a fence or a messenger for fences since childhood, and he could size people up. Then Rydal realized that there had been something vaguely dishonest looking about the ruddy American, even in the few seconds Rydal had seen him talking to Niko. Rydal could not quite say what it was. At first glance, he looked a jolly, talkative type, open as a child. But he'd certainly had a furtive manner as he walked towards his hotel. The man probably would come back and buy the bracelet from

Niko, and what honest or even reasonably cautious person would buy real pearls from a street peddler of sponges? Perhaps the man was a gambler, Rydal thought. It was a funny incongruity, to look so much like his father, Professor Lawrence Aldington Keener of the Department of Archaeology at Harvard, who had never dreamt of doing anything faintly illegal, a veritable pillar of respectability, and to be possibly a gambler, a crook of some sort.

It was three days before Rydal saw the ruddy American again. Rydal had forgotten about him, or if he had thought of him once in that time, had supposed he had moved on somewhere; and then, one noon, Rydal ran into him at the Benaki Museum among the costume exhibits. He was with a woman, a young and quite chic American woman, almost but not quite too young to look like the man's wife. From the way the man solicitously and affectionately touched her elbow now and then, the good-natured way he strolled about and chatted with her as she looked, with obvious pleasure, at the embroidered skirts and blouses on the glass-enclosed dummies, Rydal thought that they were either married pretty recently or were lovers. The man carried his hat in his hand, and Rydal could see the shape of his head now, high at the back like his father's head, the hair above his temples receding as his father's hair had receded, like an ebbing tide following the contour of a shore. His voice was deep and resonant, a bit more taut than his father's. He chuckled easily. Then, after perhaps five minutes, the woman looked directly at Rydal, and Rydal's heart stopped for an instant, then beat faster. Rydal blinked and looked away from her, but looked at the man, who, seeing him, frowned slightly, his lips parted in surprise. Rydal turned, slowly walked to a case full of jeweled scimitars and daggers, and bent over it.

Less than a minute later, the man and woman were gone. The man certainly thought he was trailing him, watching him, Rydal thought; he'd made the man uneasy, and Rydal had an impulse to go to the King's Palace Hotel, wait for him, just to assure him he meant him no harm and that he wasn't and hadn't been shadowing him. Then that struck him as, after all, uncalled for and a bit silly, and Rydal decided to do nothing about it. Rydal walked slowly out of the museum, feeling suddenly lonely, sad, and vaguely discouraged. He knew now what had struck him about the young woman, but it was irritating and disturbing that his heart had known before his brain, or his memory. She had the same sexy comehitherness, the same soft, plumpish charm that his cousin Agnes had had at fifteen.

"Son of a bitch," Rydal whispered as he walked down a broad avenue. "Son of a bitch," to no one, and with no one in particular in mind.

The woman had blue eyes, anyway, and Agnes's were brown. Agnes's hair was dark brown, and this woman's was reddish. But there was something. What was it? The mouth? Yes, a little bit. But most of all just the expression in the eyes, he thought. He hadn't fallen for it since, Rydal assured himself. But had he seen it since? No, he hadn't. Well, it was a funny thing, a man who looked like his father's twin brother, in the company of a woman who had called up Agnes to him, straight and fast as a light turned on in his face, or a knife that laid his heart wide open. It had been ten whole years ago. He had been fifteen. So much had happened in the ten years since. Now he was supposed to be a mature man. He remembered Proust's remark, that people do not grow emotionally. It was a rather frightening thought.

That night, the night of Pan's party in his family's house over by Hadrian's Library, Rydal drank a few more glasses of ouzo than he needed, and found himself thinking of the ruddy-faced American—his father twenty years ago—making love in bed to the plump woman whose reddish hair and blue eyes kept changing to Agnes's brown hair and brown eyes. But the soft red lips were the same. Rydal was inclined to be ill-tempered at the party. He tried to be very careful in the last hour to make up for a cutting remark he had made to Pan's girl friend. The next morning, with a slight hangover, he wrote a four-line poem about "the marble ghost" of his boyhood love.

Monday, he went by bus for the fifth or sixth time to Delphi and spent the day.

The memory of the pink-cheeked American and his beddable wife still nagged at him. He was exaggerating the resemblance, he was sure, especially the resemblance of the woman to Agnes. He decided that he should see them once more, look at them straight on from a distance of just a few feet, and he felt that something would happen, the spell would be broken, the illusion dispelled. If he asked their hotel clerk, he would find out they were Mr. and Mrs. Johnson from Vincennes, Indiana. Or Mr. and Mrs. Smith of St. Petersburg, Florida. They would never have heard of anybody named Keener.

3

Chester had been reassured on his third day in Athens by a letter that came from his man in Milwaukee, Bob Gambardella. It said, in part:

> Dear Mac,
>
> No news is good news and that's the way it is. Seven new subscribers this week and the proceeds as usual deposited, less my commission. Shall be expecting your dividend instructions shortly on Canadian Star's semi-annual. . . .

It meant that Bob had had no trouble as yet from the police. This was the second letter from Bob, and he'd had one in Paris from Vic, his salesman in Dallas. The police hadn't come around to Vic or Bob asking them if they knew a Howard Cheever or a William S. Haight or, thank God, a Chester MacFarland. Wm S. Haight was the name Chester stamped on his dividend checks as Treasurer of the Canadian Star Company, Inc. Seven new subscribers was quite good, Chester thought, considering he had written Bob last month not to make any effort to get new people until further notice. Bob might have taken in fifty thousand dollars from the seven people, perhaps more. Certificates were issued to the stock buyers, dividends were paid in modest but regular amounts, and if the stock never did quite get on the Canadian exchange in the newspapers, so long as the stockholders got their dividends, why should they complain? Bob and Vic, when talking a prospect into buying, always said they were letting him in on a new thing that was going to be listed in a few months, when the stock would certainly start skyrocketing. So it went, too, with Unimex, Valco-Tech, Universal Key—sometimes Chester could not remember them all. Once in a while, if a stockholder asked too many questions in his letters, Chester would instruct one of his representatives in Dallas, St. Louis or San Francisco to get on the telephone to the man and offer to buy his stock for more than he paid for it, and to give a pitch for some new stock. Nine times out of ten, the suspicious people would hang on to their old stock and buy the new also. Physically, the land on which the Canadian Star stock was founded did exist, it was simply worth very little, and very probably had no uranium in it. It was up in northern Canada—Chester or his boiler-room men could tell the customers just where to look for it on the map—and they made it sound as if uranium was going to come pouring out as soon as the engineers made a few more calculations as to where to dig. Actually, on the back of the stock contract, some very fine print near the bottom stated that the land was "being explored at present", and it did not say for what. And the stock company could not be prosecuted for its intentions or hopes, which were certainly to find uranium.

The Unimex Company was a non-existent offshore oil concern around the Texas and Mexico border. It had brought in over a million dollars on stock Chester offered over the counter at eight dollars per share. Chester had certified financial statements showing Unimex's assets to be worth six million dollars, and he had even had New York brokers sent to inspect certain sites in the Gulf of Mexico, which, however, were owned by other people. Chester had bought a very small abandoned site, but he laid claim to a hundred square miles around it. Unimex and Canadian Star were now Chester's chief sources of income.

After a few days in Greece, Chester found that he breathed more easily. He enjoyed the strange meals at tavernas, the little oily dishes of this and that, washed down with ouzo or a bottle of wine that usually neither of them liked, though Chester always finished it. Colette bought five pairs of shoes, and Chester had a suit made of English tweed in a fraction of the time and for less than half what it would have cost him in the States. Still, it was a habit, a nervous habit, for him to glance around the hotel lobby to see if there were anyone who looked like a police agent. He doubted if they would send a man over for him, but the F.B.I. had representatives abroad, he supposed. All they would need was a photograph, the collected testimony of a few swindled people, and, by checking with the passport authorities, they could discover his name.

In their six days in Athens, Chester and Colette had gone twice to the Acropolis with their *Guide Bleu,* had taken a bus to see the sunset at Sounion and Byron's famous signature in one of the marble columns of the ruined temple there, had done the main museums, gone once to the theatre—just to go, because they hadn't understood a thing about the play—and had made their plans for the rest of the country. The Peloponnesus was next, with Mycenae and Corinth, for which they planned to rent a car, and then Crete and Rhodes. Then back by plane to Paris for another week or so before going home. They were apartmentless in New York now, did not want to live in Manhattan again, and they planned to buy a house either in Connecticut or northern Pennsylvania.

Around six o'clock of the evening before their departure for Corinth and Mycenae, Chester went out of the hotel for a few minutes to buy a bottle of Dewar's. When he walked back into the lobby, he noticed a dark man, in a grey overcoat and hat, standing with his hands in his overcoat pockets near one of the cream-colored columns that supported the ceiling. The man had thick black eyebrows, and Chester could not be sure the man looked at him, but he thought so. Chester looked away, glanced around him quickly, and noticed the young man in the dark overcoat he had twice seen before, standing now near the door and smoking a cigarette. Agents, Chester thought. His eyes had been drawn to the man in the grey overcoat as a result of conditioning, he knew; though because he had felt so secure the last couple of days, his habit of glancing around the lobby had left him. He'd suspected that the younger man was an agent, and now he was sure. Chester went casually over to the hotel desk and gave the message he had intended to give when he came in:

"We'll be leaving tomorrow pretty early. Can you make up our bill so we can settle it tonight? That's MacFarland in six twenty-one." His voice lowered involuntarily, but only a little, on "MacFarland".

As Chester walked on to the elevator, the older man moved, following him. The elevator arrived and the door slid open, and, being closest, Chester went into the elevator first. The man followed, removing his hat. Chester kept his on.

"Six, please," said Chester.

The boy running the elevator glanced at the man.

"Seex," said the man.

A Greek, Chester thought. He felt perhaps one degree better. The man had a thick, somewhat Semitic nose, black and grey hair, and his face was pock-marked. Chester got out at the sixth floor and the man followed him. Chester was just raising his hand to knock on his door, when the man said:

"Pardon me. You are, I think, Richard Donlevy?"

The name meant Atlanta to Chester. The Suwannee Club. "No," said Chester blankly.

"Or—Louis Ferguson?"

That was Miami. Chester shook his head. "No. Sorry."

"You are travelling with your wife, yes? May I have a few words with you in your room, sir?"

"Why? What's all this about?"

"Perhaps nothing," the man said with a smile. "I represent the Greek police. I should like to ask you a few questions."

Chester looked down at the billfold the man had opened. In a window of it was an authentic-looking card covered with Greek print and signatures, and, in heavy black letters in the middle of it, GREEK NATIONAL POLICE. If he refused to talk to him, Chester thought, it might make matters worse. "All right," Chester said indifferently, and knocked.

The door opened at once, but only a crack. Colette was in her dressing-gown.

"Excuse me, dear," Chester said. "I'm with a gentleman who wants to talk to me a moment. May we come in?"

"Why, of course," said Colette, but her face had gone a little pale.

They went in. Colette wrapped her dressing-gown closer about her, and stepped back near the chest of drawers.

The Greek agent bowed to her. "Madam. Forgive my intrusion." He turned to Chester. "May I ask under what name you are registered here?"

Chester drew himself up and frowned. "What's this about? What right have you to ask me that?"

The man pulled from his overcoat pocket a small looseleaf notebook, opened it to a certain page and extended it to Chester. "This is not you?"

Chester's heart stumbled. It was a photograph of himself, fuzzy from enlargement but still recognizable, laughing, with a highball glass in his hand. It was from a group photograph of the dinner guests at the Suwannee Club maybe three years ago, when he'd been Richard Donlevy, with more hair and no moustache then, and he'd been selling some kind of stock. Selling what? He'd forgotten. Chester shook his head. "That's not me. I see some resemblance, but . . . I don't know what you're trying to say."

"It is in regard to various—how do you say—investment matters in the United States," said the agent, still calm and pleasant. "I have not the details with me, and it is not my place to say them now, if I knew. I am only working in cooperation with the American authorities, who suspected you were in Europe."

A chill of panic passed over Chester and did not quite leave him. They were on to him in the States. Someone had tried to put up his stocks as collateral or something like that, and had been told they were phony. Or perhaps it was even the Walkie Kar. He looked at Colette and saw his own fear leap to her face for an instant, then she controlled herself and gave him a quick smile. "But you're looking for somebody with another name, you told me," Chester said.

"Various names. It does not much matter. You will please to come with me, anyway, to answer some questions, will you?" the man asked with an air of being very sure that Chester was going to come with him.

"No. Why should I? It's your mistake," said Chester, taking off his overcoat.

Colette came forward, lifted the notebook in the agent's hand, studied the picture, and said, "Why, that's not my husband."

"Madam, under what name are you both registered here? It is the easiest thing in the world for me to find out. I shall simply call down and ask who is in room six twenty-one."

Colette looked at him, and said in her high, young voice, "I don't think that's any of your business."

"I would like you to know that I am armed. I should not like to have to take you away at gun-point." The Greek agent's black eyebrows came down in a puzzled way as he looked at Chester.

Chester shrugged, not moving from where he stood. He was glancing around the room, however, as if he might find a weapon in some corner with which to defend himself.

The Greek walked quickly towards the telephone.

Chester darted for the bathroom.

"Stop!" the agent said. "I have a gun!"

Chester glanced behind him, saw the man running towards him with a gun pointed, and calculated that he wouldn't use it. He leapt to the tub edge and yanked the window up. It was sticky and moved only about eight inches.

"Chester!" Colette cried.

The man pulled at Chester's jacket tail, and Chester looked over his shoulder, raised his left foot and kicked backward, catching the fellow in the pit of the stomach. He got down from the tub edge, and, before the man could straighten up, Chester hit him on the back of the neck. The man's forehead banged against the rim of the basin. Chester swung him up again, hit him on the jaw and knocked him into the tub. He started to pull him up for another blow, and realized he was out cold.

Chester stood with his fists clenched, panting.

"My God!" Colette was standing in the bathroom doorway. "You're all right, darling?"

Chester nodded. He picked up the agent's gun, which had fallen on the bathroom floor. A drinking glass had been knocked down, and there were pieces of glass on the tiles. Chester kicked one nervously with the side of his shoe.

"I'll clean that up," Colette said.

"Got to get him out of here," Chester murmured, "before that other agent—there's another one downstairs."

"Really?" Colette gasped. "Let's see. The balcony?"

There was a balcony outside their windows that ran the length of the hotel. "No. He's going to come to in a couple of minutes. I'll think of something. Start packing us up, will you, honey? We've got to get out of here tonight."

Colette hurried out of her dressing-gown, pushed it into a suitcase and grabbed the skirt of a dark suit that was hanging over a chair.

"I've got it!" Chester said, and took one of the man's limp arms.

"What?"

"There's a store-room down the hall." Chester heaved the man across his shoulder. "Red light over it. Saw it one night when I was looking for a loo and you were in the tub. Uff! Guy's heavy." Chester staggered across the room with him. "Take a look in the hall. See if there's—"

Colette nodded and quickly opened the door an inch or two. "Someone at the elevator."

"Damn," Chester said, and tightened his hold on the man's wrists. "He's going to come to before I can—" But that tub was hard, Chester realized, and so was the basin. In fact, the fellow could be dead. With this thought, Chester's strength ebbed, and he let the man down gently to the carpet. He was about to say something to Colette about feeling for a pulse, when Colette said:

"It's okay now. Nobody in sight."

Chester summoned his strength and hoisted him again. Dead or not, he thought, the store-room was the best place for him. If he were dead—Well, Chester had never seen him before. Someone else had killed him. The man had never knocked on his door, never said a word to him. Chester went on towards the door with the little red light over it, praying it would be open as it had been before.

Then, from around the corridor corner in front of him, the other agent appeared, and stopped short in surprise. Chester stared at him, paralyzed. The young man's mouth had opened slightly, and Chester saw the start of a faint smile—of satisfaction, sarcasm? Chester expected him to pull a gun. His right hand hung empty, his left carried a newspaper. The young man advanced.

"Where're you taking him?" Rydal asked, with a quick glance up and down the corridor.

"I was—" Chester went suddenly limp, and the dead weight slipped to the floor. "That room," Chester said, motioning weakly to the door with the red light over it.

The young man dropped his newspaper, bent quickly and took the Greek under the shoulders and began to drag him towards the store-room.

Chester stared.

"Didn't he have a hat?" Rydal asked, and, at Chester's frightened nod, "Better get it."

Chester opened the store-room door—it was unlocked—then ran back to his room. Colette had unlatched the door and was standing right behind it. "Honey, get me his hat. It's there by the telephone."

Colette got the hat from the telephone table and handed it to him.

Chester trotted up the hall with it. The door under the red light was half open, and he heard a clatter of buckets. "Here." He handed the hat to the young man.

"The man's dead?" asked Rydal.

"I don't know."

"I think he is." Rydal, with rather shaky hands, pulled out quickly the contents of the man's inside pockets, and the billfold that was buttoned into his hip pocket, and stuffed them into his own. "Was there a gun? He's got a holster here."

"I've got it," Chester said. Dead, he thought, his hands twitching. He watched the young man shove the feet farther in, so the door would close, and then the door shut on the first man he had ever killed, a man with a lolling, bleeding head, seated among buckets and mops and dirty grey rags.

Rydal pulled Chester by the arm, back towards his room, and scooped up his newspaper as they passed it.

Chester drummed on the door with his fingertips. It was a strange way for an agent to behave, he thought. Did he want to protect the hotel patrons from the sight of a corpse?

Colette opened the door and drew in her breath.

Chester went in quickly.

Rydal followed him, automatically giving a little bow of greeting to the woman. He did not care for the sight of blood, and he was beginning to feel a bit airy in the head. "My name . . . my name is Rydal Keener," Rydal said to both of them. "How do you do?"

"How d'y'do?" Chester mumbled.

"My husband hit the man in self-defense," Colette said quickly, looking straight at Rydal. "I saw the whole thing happen."

"Don't say anything, Colette," Chester said.

"But . . . allow me to tell you," Rydal said, and was ashamed of the "allow me" as soon as it was out of his mouth, "that I'm not a police agent."

"Not a—Then why—?" Chester said.

Rydal didn't know why. It had been such a fast decision, it was no decision at all. "I'm just an American tourist. You can consider me a friend." It was odd talking to them; it made him feel very odd. Or was it the blood drops on the pale-green carpet? "You'd better wipe up those blood spots while you can," he said to the man.

Helpless himself, Chester motioned for Colette to do it.

She went off to the bathroom and returned at once with the sponge Chester had bought for her. "I've wiped it all up from the bathroom," she said. She got down on her hands and knees and began scrubbing away.

Her derrière looked perfectly round under her straight black skirt. Rydal looked at her instead of at the blood spots. Then he moved quickly to the door, opened it cautiously, and looked out into the corridor.

"Hear something?" Chester asked.

"No. I wanted to see if there was any blood in the hall. There probably is, but it doesn't show on the black carpet. Now," he said after he had closed the door again, (But now, what? The man was looking at him, blank and expectant.) "the thing to do is get out of this hotel before that fellow's missed—at his headquarters or whatever."

"Yes. Or found," Chester said. "Well, we're nearly packed and ready, aren't we, honey?"

"Two more minutes for the stuff in the john," said Colette. "You get your razor and things, Ches. I've practically got this finished. Toss me a towel, will you?"

"A towel?"

"A towel, so I can dry this."

Colette sounded very practical. She was certainly cool-headed. She looked up and saw Rydal looking at her and smiled at him, then adroitly caught the towel Chester tossed across the room to her. "What a mess," she said, bending to her work again.

Rydal remembered the papers he had stuffed into his overcoat pocket, and pulled them out. There was a chunky notebook, and he flipped through it. There were many photographs, and he found Chester's at once. He walked closer to Chester, who was putting things into a suitcase. "This is you?"

Chester looked embarrassed, but he nodded.

The comment, in Greek, said that he was wanted for fraud and embezzlement. There were several different names under the picture, in Greek and English characters. "Which of these names is yours?" asked Rydal.

Chester held the notebook's edge and looked over the names, looked a little wildly. "None of them. My name's—I'm Chester MacFarland." There was no use in hiding it, Chester thought, because the fellow could just ask the hotel desk who was or had been in room six twenty-one.

"Chester MacFarland," Rydal repeated softly.

Chester gave a nervous smile. "Heard of me?"

"No . . . no." The Greek agent's name, Rydal saw, was George M. Papanopolos.

"Uh . . . we were going to Corinth tomorrow. I don't suppose you know if there's a train or bus there tonight, do you? We were going to rent a car tomorrow, but—"

"I don't happen to know, but I can call down and ask the desk to find out," Rydal said, moving towards the telephone.

"No, wait!" Chester spread his hands. "Your calling—from this room—"

"Well, it just occurred to me," Rydal said to Chester, and the woman, too, who was now standing in the middle of the room, looking at him, "since nobody saw me come up, I can just as well say I've been here with you all afternoon. Or at least a few hours." The man looked blank still, so Rydal said, "I didn't take the elevator up. I saw it went to the sixth floor, so I took the stairs up. I don't think anybody noticed me. I mean, in case that man is found before we get out—I'll provide an alibi." The words seemed to come out of him from nowhere. He was offering to perjure himself. And for what? For whom? A man whose look of a gentleman didn't go very deep, Rydal could see now; a man whose clothes were well cut and tailor made, but whose cuff-links were flashy; a man whose over-all manner looked dishonest, because he was dishonest. "Take your choice. I'm not insisting," Rydal added. "I mean, whether I call downstairs or not."

"Yes. Do call. That's fine," Chester said. He looked away from Rydal's eyes.

Rydal picked up the telephone and, without thinking, began to speak in Greek, asking about trains and buses to Corinth. The woman, after closing a couple of suitcases, returned to staring at him curiously, unself-conscious, apparently, as a child. Rydal hung up and said, "The last bus left at six. No train until tomorrow. You could perhaps rent a car at this hour, but it's an odd time to be starting off for Corinth. The view along the sea is considered the best part of the trip. Kinetta Beach, you know."

"Hm-m. Yes. Kinetta Beach," said Chester. He looked at his wife.

"You're very kind," Colette said to Rydal. "Kind to endanger yourself for us."

Rydal had no reply. He noticed the bulge of the gun in Chester's jacket pocket for the first time. It occurred to him that the MacFarlands were going to need different passports at once. By tomorrow, anyway. Niko was the man for that.

"What about Crete?" Chester asked. "We did want to go to Crete."

"That I happen to know about," Rydal said. "There's a plane out every morning and a boat a little earlier every morning, but nothing at this hour."

"Are you part Greek?" Colette asked Rydal.

Rydal smiled. "No." He was trying to think, and he was thinking only that he was very bad at this kind of thinking. His mind should be working like lightning, conjuring up the exactly right, brilliant thing for them to do. Niko's place as a hideout? Rydal somehow didn't *want* them there. But why not? Get Colette and Chester into a taxi with their luggage and drive to Niko's. Niko's wife Anna would be there now, and would be agreeable to anything. But their apartment was so unspeakably sordid, and they'd all have to be in one room. "Anyway, the thing to do is get out of here right away. Are you ready for a porter?"

"Yes, but where do we go?" Chester asked.

"To another hotel in Athens. I know one. The Dardanelles, about ten or fifteen streets from here. It's medium-sized and sort of out of the way. Just for tonight. Then tomorrow—I'd suggest Crete rather than the Peloponnesus, because it's bigger and farther away."

"Oh, wonderful! Crete!" said Colette, as if it were a bright and unexpected spot on a holiday tour.

"Just tell the driver—Hotel Dardanelles?" Chester asked.

"Yes. Well, if the bellboys from this hotel are listening, tell the driver the railroad station, then switch it after you take off. You'd better tell the hotel here that you're taking a night train to—to Yugoslavia, something like that."

"I get you, I get you," Chester said, embarrassed that he hadn't grasped the point a little more quickly. Chester frowned. "You really think that's best, another hotel in Athens?"

"I do, definitely. With luck, the Greek agent won't be discovered until early tomorrow morning, when the help start their cleaning.

If the hotel here thinks you've taken a train, the police'll check the trains and the borders before they check the hotels in the city."

"Yes. You're right," Chester said. Then his lips bared over his set teeth. "Oh, my God, the passports! The God-damned passports!"

"Yes, I thought of that," Rydal said, moving towards the door. "I think I know how something can be arranged."

"How?" Chester asked.

"If I can see you tonight, I'll explain it. I shouldn't take up any more of your time now. I'll call on you tonight at the Dardanelles around ten. How is that?"

Chester hesitated, then said, "All right."

"Oh, it's so exciting!" Colette said, rising on her toes, her hands clasped under her chin. She pursed her lips as if to throw Rydal a kiss.

"Till tonight," Rydal said, and went out.

Alone, Chester and Colette stared at each other, he frightened and blank, she smiling dazedly.

"I'll call for a porter," Chester said, and went to the telephone.

Colette watched him as he spoke. Now she was frowning a little, biting her underlip as she did when she thought hard about something. After he had hung up, she said, "Ches, what did he mean about that Greek agent not being found till tomorrow morning? When he comes to, isn't he going to—"

"Honey, I think that guy's dead," Chester said in a low voice. He saw Colette's lavender eyes widen.

"Really? Do you *know*?"

"I think he is. There really wasn't any time to make sure," Chester said, frowning.

"And does . . . does this fellow know it?"

"Yes," said Chester firmly.

"My God."

"Yes." Chester stuffed his fingers into his hip pockets and walked forward between the beds, then made a lunge for his Scotch bottle, whose neck was sticking up out of an antelope duffel bag. "Yes, and we'll pay for it. We'll pay plenty."

"What do you mean?"

Chester was getting the second, unbroken glass from the bathroom. "I mean he'll want some money for keeping quiet. Wait and see. Fortunately, we've got it. It just mustn't go too far."

"Oh, do you think he's really like that?" she asked, still breathless with the shock of death. "He looks—Well, he doesn't look like a crook. He's an American."

"And not too well-heeled. Wait and see, wait and see. Why else do you think he came in here like this? I'd go to some other hotel, except he's probably downstairs on the street ready to follow us." Chester waved his glass, then drank it off, half Scotch and half water. "Why else do you think he came in here like this?"

4

Rydal walked from Niko's apartment to the Hotel Dardanelles in Aeolou Street, walked slowly, but even so he was early, and he lit a cigarette and lingered a block from the hotel, staring into the window of a closed and unlighted pharmacy. The marquee of the Dardanelles had only half its lights on. The street was unusually quiet, Rydal thought. It was a quiet that gave him the feeling something had already happened, was finished, rather than that something was going to happen. A skinny, reddish dog went trotting by, its taut, pointed face thrust anxiously ahead, as if it were fleeing from something. Rydal knew what could have happened. The Greek's body could have been found hours ago, say just before seven, the trains and buses out of Athens—certainly no more than two or three of each—could have been checked, no MacFarlands found aboard them; the hotels could have been checked and the MacFarlands picked up. The police might be in the hotel this minute, talking to the MacFarlands, getting an admission from Chester that he killed the Greek, because whatever his coolness might be in defrauding, murder seemed to unnerve him. And he, for no particular reason, was going to walk right in on it. Chester would be glad to see him, if the police were there. Chester would say, "Oh! Why, here's the young man who was with us all afternoon," and would that reverse Chester's story of a few minutes before? With a sudden sink in his heart, Rydal realized that, if Chester chose, he could say that he, Rydal Keener, had been tugging the corpse along the hall when Chester came out into the hall and saw him, and that Rydal Keener, knowing the Greek agent was after Chester, had forced Chester to keep silent about his murder. His motive? They couldn't possibly pin any on Rydal. No, don't worry about fantasies, Rydal thought. He threw his cigarette down. It was one minute to ten by his Hamilton pocket watch, which was more reliable than his wristwatch.

Rydal glanced around in the lobby of the Dardanelles for anyone who looked like a police type. Besides the young man behind the desk, there was only one other person in the lobby, a fiftyish woman in a black fur-trimmed coat and hat who looked like a German. "Would you call up Mr. MacFarland? I'm expected," Rydal said, and watched the young man's face. It was calm.

The young man plugged a pin into the switchboard and said with a heavy Greek accent, "A gentleman to see you, sir."

Chester's deep, brisk voice buzzed back over the wire.

"You can go up. Room thirty-one, sir," said the young man.

There was an elevator, but Rydal took the black-and-white tile stairs. Room 31 was evidently on the second floor, as Rydal saw 28 on a door as soon as he reached the landing. The old floor carpet was vaguely green, the single light tiny and yellowish. It was shabbier than the Melchior Condylis. Rydal knocked on 31.

After a few seconds the door was quickly but only partly opened by Chester.

"Good evening," Rydal said.

Chester blinked. "You're alone?"

"Yes." Rydal saw the fear ebb from Chester's face. Chester had thought he might arrive with the police, Rydal realized, or perhaps with a friend who would back him up with physical force, if necessary, in order to extort some money.

"Come in," Chester said.

Rydal went in. "Good evening," he said to Colette, who was sitting in an armchair, her arms relaxed on the chair's arms, her legs crossed. A pose of deliberate calm, Rydal felt. "So, no trouble leaving the hotel?" Rydal said to Chester.

"No, no." Chester rubbed his moustache with a forefinger, and looked at his wife.

"I must say this is a picturesque hotel you sent us to," Colette said, smiling.

Rydal glanced around the room. It was dingy, the furniture cheap, and that was that. "I suppose it's only for tonight. I came here to talk to you about passports. I can get two for you by tomorrow noon, I think. I've just spoken to a friend." He meant to sound polite and businesslike, but Chester seemed taken aback at his blurting.

"Oh. Well—Wouldn't you like to have a seat?" Chester asked, pulling up a straight chair. "Want me to take your coat?"

Rydal started to remove it, then said, "No, that's all right, thank you." He unbuttoned his overcoat, and sat down in the chair.

"Considering the heat situation here," Colette said, "we all ought to be sitting around in our coats. Darling, could you get me my mohair?"

"Certainly, dear." Chester went to the closet, which had shelves in it, and brought Colette a large black and white mohair stole.

Rydal watched her drape it gracefully and quickly around her shoulders and tuck her hands under it, out of sight.

"You were talking about passports," Chester said, sitting down in another straight chair. From somewhere he had picked up a half-finished highball. "How about a drink?"

"Not just now, thank you," Rydal said. He took one of his own cigarettes and lit it. "I can get two passports by tomorrow noon for five thousand dollars apiece. That's not expensive. The man who is arranging it will expect—say, another thousand. The ten thousand goes to the man who'd obtain them and who can fix them."

Chester glanced at Colette, then looked back at Rydal. He seemed about to speak, but he took a slow draught of his glass instead.

"I'm not trying to sell you these passports unless you want them," Rydal said, beginning to feel uncomfortable under Chester's obvious suspicion of him. "But by tomorrow morning, it seems to me, the police are going to be looking for Chester MacFarland. Even though your name wasn't on the picture in the agent's notebook, they'll have copies of that picture. Someone may know the agent was specifically looking for you this afternoon. You were on the sixth floor of that hotel and so is the agent's body. They'll just ask the hotel employees which man on the sixth floor resembled any of the pictures in the agent's notebook. Then the fact you checked out when you did—"

"Um-m." Chester leaned forward, took out a pocket handkerchief, and blew his nose.

"It does sound as if he's right, Ches," Colette said. "You were saying something about our getting out tonight, but imagine being stopped on the Yugoslav border, for instance, and asked to show our passports, and being told the police want to see us." She gestured with her left hand as she spoke, and Rydal noticed her diamond, a good big one in an engagement ring, whose value seemed guaranteed by the platinum wedding ring behind it.

Was Chester MacFarland hesitating over the money, Rydal wondered? Five thousand for an American passport was ridiculously cheap, even though Niko's friend's work on it would probably be pretty sloppy, too. Rydal glanced at his watch.

"In a hurry?" asked Chester.

"No. Well, yes, I have an appointment at ten-thirty. My friend will wait, but I didn't want to make him wait too long. It's Niko, the one who can arrange to get the passports." Rydal was sitting on the edge of his seat now. He passed his hand over his forehead. He was beginning to feel angry. He could have made a speech to the effect he wasn't going to get a cent out of the deal, and that he wanted Chester to know that, but something kept him from it. "The purpose of my meeting Niko tonight is to give him the photographs out of your present passports so he can pass them on to his friend. The photos and a first installment on the price, which I think ought to be five thousand. But that's entirely up to you." Rydal stood up and crossed the room to an ashtray, an ugly, standing ashtray beside Colette's armchair.

"Chester, darling—don't you see his point?" Colette looked up at Rydal. "I do."

Rydal turned quickly away from her. He looked at Chester, impatient and frowning now, then looked at the door and thought that in five more seconds he'd walk through it and never see them again, speak to Niko and tell him it was all off, and pay out of his own pocket for Niko's long-distance calls to Nauplion, where his friend Frank was.

"Yes. I guess I do," Chester said. "We need passports and that's that." He was like a man cornered into a bad bargain, cornered and resigned.

"You may have a better source for them. If so, don't take mine. Not that it's mine, I just know the people," Rydal said.

"I have no better source," Chester said.

"Darling, I think he's doing us a big favor!" Colette said, standing up. "And I don't mind saying thank you." She looked at Rydal, her hands close under her chin now, holding the scarf. "Thank you."

Rydal smiled despite himself. "You're welcome."

"What do you want, extra little photographs?" Colette asked, going to her pocketbook on the bureau.

"No, the ones from your passports now. The perforations have to be matched," Rydal said. "It's easier."

"Oh, of course. How stupid of me. I saw a movie where they did that. I hate this photograph, but I guess I'm stuck with it. This trip around, anyway." She handed Rydal her passport. "You can probably get it out better than I can."

"Yes." They were tightly glued in, Rydal knew. Chester was reaching for his, in his inside jacket pocket.

"Good thing I asked the clerk to let me have these things back when we came in from dinner," Chester said as if to himself. "I told him we were checking out early tomorrow morning."

"Yes, that's another thing," Rydal said. "The plane to Crete leaves at ten forty-five. I think that's the best thing for you to take. Unless you've any better ideas." Rydal took the passport Chester was holding out.

"No, no, Crete sounds fine," Chester said, spreading his hands palms down, pacifically. He looked very worried.

Rydal's mouth twitched a little in contempt. Glancing at Colette, he saw that she had seen it. She wasn't stupid, Rydal thought. "And the money. Have you five thousand in cash?"

"Got it in traveler's checks," Chester said.

Rydal shook his head. "I don't think many people will be wanting to handle traveler's checks signed Chester MacFarland after tomorrow."

Chester nodded, with absurd seriousness, glanced about, then went to a new canvas and leather suitcase in a corner of the room. He carried the suitcase into the bathroom, and closed the door.

Rydal knew exactly what he was doing, getting some greenbacks from a compartment, probably sewed into the suitcase lining and probably sewed in by his wife. Rydal kept his cash in the lining of his suitcase, too. He had eight American tens and about ten singles left there now. Chester probably had a fortune. Colette was looking at him sidewise, standing behind the armchair, dancing her fingertips along its back.

"Where're you from in the States?" she asked.

"Massachusetts," he said.

"I'm from Louisiana. But so long ago, I haven't any accent, I think."

She had a faint Southern accent, and Rydal had noticed it. He said nothing, only stared at the back corner of the armchair by the floor, as if he awaited the appearance of her black suede pumps and her shapely but quite solid ankles there. Then they appeared, and Rydal's eyes moved upward from the ankles to her calves, to the swell of her hips, her breasts, and fastened on her eyes, as Chester opened the door.

Chester looked from one to the other of them, then set the suitcase on the floor with a thud. His hand was full of new green bills. "So—here we are," he said.

"Would you like to come with me and meet Niko?" Rydal asked in a polite tone.

Chester was wary. "Where?"

"I'm meeting him on a street corner not far from Syndagma. Near Constitution Square. Maybe you know Niko. He sells sponges out in front of the American Express."

"Oh." Chester smiled, weakly at first, then his smile became real, with a twinkle. "Yes, sure I do. Bought a sponge from him. I like him."

Why, Rydal wondered? For the things they had in common, maybe, a mutual crookedness. "We'd better take off and catch a taxi." Chester was still half holding out the money to him. Rydal ignored it, looked at Colette and said, "Good night."

"Good night," she replied. She had a pleasant but quite high-pitched voice, and her final consonants came out sharp and clear.

"How long do you think this will take?" Chester asked, pushing the greenbacks into his jacket pocket.

"Oh, less than an hour. Forty-five minutes at most, if you take a taxi back," Rydal said.

Chester looked at his wristwatch and said, "Back a little after eleven, honey." He put both hands on her sides, above her waist, and kissed her uplifted lips.

Then Colette looked at Rydal, and Rydal turned to the door.

There was silence between them as they went down the stairs, silence in the first block they walked before Rydal, who had been trying all the while, hailed a taxi that stopped. Silence in the taxi.

Rydal was inspired to be both open and above board and knowledgeable and sinister, but the result of this was silence, too.

Niko was waiting on the corner where he said he would be, slowly tramping up and down, due to impatience or the cold. They were seven minutes late, Rydal saw by his wristwatch.

"Ah, yes, there we are, the fellow in the gym shoes," said Chester, beaming with recognition, letting Rydal pay for the taxi.

"Kalispera," said Niko as they approached.

"'Spera," said Rydal, and he continued to speak in demotic. "What's up with Frank in Nauplion?"

"Oh, he can do it, just like I said," said Niko.

"May I present Mr. Chester MacFarland, who has already purchased a sponge from you," Rydal said, motioning to Chester.

Niko said, "Enchanted and highly honored." And, to Rydal, "Between sponges and passports there is no difference to a true Greek."

"Well said. Mr. MacFarland has both his and his wife's passports with photographs."

"What's happening?" Chester asked. He was plainly enjoying the business, rocking on his heels and looking at Niko with amusement as if Niko were merely a tool, an underling whom he could please with a good tip.

Rydal gave Niko the two passports, and said to Chester, "Now you may give him the five thousand dollars."

Chester sobered a little and, his pink jowls folding over his white starched collar, swung his overcoat open and got the money from his jacket pocket. He handed it to Niko.

Niko accepted it with a nod, moved under the light of a streetlamp, and began to count the money.

Rydal folded his hands behind him and looked up at the street-lamp. Chester glanced over at the opposite pavement, where a young man and woman were walking with arms about each other, paying them no heed at all. Niko was about fifteen feet away. After he had counted the money, with an air of handling such sums every day, he ambled back, wiping a running nose with a finger, and said to Rydal, "Okay. And five thousand on delivery and—eight hundred for me, okay?" The only English word in it was "okay".

"I thought a thousand for you," said Rydal, smiling.

"Okay," said Niko gaily, and his lead-framed tooth gleamed dully, the gap beside it black as night.

"What time is Frank getting here?" Rydal asked.

"Seven in the morning," Niko replied positively.

"Can he finish the passports by ten-thirty tomorrow morning?"

Niko spread and waggled his hands, then shook his head. "No. Not that fast."

"What are you asking him?" asked Chester.

"If he can get the passports to us by the time you have to catch the plane. The answer is no. But you don't have to show passports going to Crete."

"I know," said Chester. But his blue eyes were a bit wider. "When *can* he get them to us?"

"By plane the next day, I'm sure. Thursday," said Rydal. He said to Niko, "We've got to have them by Thursday, okay? You take the plane and fly with them. The ten forty-five plane to Iraklion, okay?"

"Okay," said Niko.

It would probably be his first plane trip, Rydal thought. "And you take your fare from the thousand you're paid, okay?"

"Okay," said Niko.

"If this language consisted in 'okay'," Chester said, "I'd be okay." He was reaching in his wallet for another bill.

Rydal started to stop him and didn't. If he wanted to tip, if it made him feel better—

"What about those pearls," Chester said. "You know, those pearls, the bracelet you showed me."

Niko knew the word pearls. He jumped as if he had received an electric shock. "Wants to buy the pearl bracelet?" he asked Rydal in Greek.

"Depends on how much. Let's see it again," said Rydal.

"It's home. You saw it," Niko said.

"I know, but what're you asking? Go and get it, you'll sell it, I just want to know how much."

"Fifteen thousand drachs," said Niko.

"Five hundred dollars?" said Rydal skeptically. "Let's see the pearls again, Niko."

Niko held up a thick, dark finger. "Twenty minutes." Then he checked the snaps on his American army waist-length jacket pockets, where the money and passports were, and dashed off at his top-speed gait. His feet splayed, it was neither a walk nor a trot, and he gave the impression of walking on the inside of his ankles.

Rydal folded his arms, held his head high, and waited until a dumpy little figure of a woman had passed by with a small, stuffed shopping bag. "So you're interested in the pearl bracelet?"

"Yes. For five hundred," Chester said. "They looked real to me."

Rydal nodded. They were real, and a bargain at five hundred. Soon they would be around Colette's plump, slightly freckled wrist.

She would give Chester a big kiss and a bit more for that bracelet, Rydal supposed. "By the way, I don't know if you understood our transaction," Rydal said. "You'll give Niko five thousand more when he delivers the passports Thursday in Iraklion. Niko asked eight hundred for himself. I suggested a thousand for him. That'll cover his telephone calls, his ticket to Crete and back and . . ." Rydal paused.

"And?"

"Since Niko's now your confederate, I think it's better to have him a bit overpaid than underpaid or merely adequately paid," Rydal said somewhat stuffily.

Chester's smile was naïve and understanding. "I agree. I know what you mean."

They were silent for a few seconds. Rydal expected the question, "And how much are you getting or what would you like for yourself?" But the question didn't come. Rydal turned up the collar of his overcoat against the fine mist that was drifting down. The edges of his collar and lapels were getting threadbare, he could feel it with his cold fingertips. He sensed Chester's awkwardness, his lack of courage about mentioning money, possibly his stinginess, and, for all his threadbare clothes, Rydal felt quite superior to Chester MacFarland.

"We've time for an espresso somewhere," Rydal said. "Shall we get out of this fog?"

"Sure. Fine."

Rydal found a café around the corner that was full of small, mostly empty tables. Rydal was hungry, and could have eaten one of the white plates of yoghurt or tapioca that were displayed behind the glass counters, but he ordered only espresso black, and Chester a cappuccino.

"How will he know where to meet us in Crete?" Chester asked.

"You can meet him at the airport in Iraklion Thursday around one in the afternoon. That's the simplest," Rydal said. "The plane comes in between one and one-thirty. Niko'll be going right back to Athens."

"Um-m." Chester watched the waiter's hands serving them glasses of water, then their two coffees. "You think the passports'll be passable," he said, and gave an apologetic or nervous smile.

"Yes, I'd say so. I've never seen any of Niko's friend's work, but he seems to get business," Rydal replied, as if they were discussing the merits of a tailor. He looked calmly at Chester.

Chester's large, manicured hands were restless on the edge of the table, as if he hadn't enough to do with them between smoking a cigarette and lifting his coffee cup. His pale blue eyes were slightly bloodshot. He gave off an aroma of Scotch, mingled with some unsweet, masculine toilet water or after-shave lotion. Rydal tried to imagine Chester with his father's brown beard along his lower jaw and rising up near his chin to join his moustache. It was easy to imagine Chester with his father's beard. It was easy to imagine that Chester was his father, at forty or so, without the beard, because his father hadn't started the beard until he was forty-odd. Rydal realized that Chester's resemblance to his father was the main reason why he had so suddenly and spontaneously helped Chester with the corpse in the corridor this afternoon—if one could assign a reason to an act of such unreason. It implied, Rydal thought, a lurking respect for his father. He did not like that thought.

"You've been in Athens quite a while?" asked Chester.

"Two months or so."

Chester nodded. "Picked up the language, eh?"

"It's not difficult," said Rydal, and shifted in his chair, remembering his father introducing him to Greek at the age of eight, or maybe even younger, at any rate after he had reached a "reasonable proficiency" in Latin, and then, at fifteen, demotic Greek, in preparation for the European tour that his father intended to make in the late summer with his wife and three children. It would have been Rydal's second trip to Europe, but it never came off, because he met Agnes that spring. He felt Chester's eyes on him, more intense now, and involuntarily Rydal leaned to one side and glanced into the mirror which covered the wall just behind Chester. His short, dark hair was combed, a bit shiny with damp, no smudges on his rather pale face, his eyes and mouth serious and composed as usual. Chester was probably thinking he was a very reserved type for a crook, or someone who drifted on the fringes of criminals. It was of no interest to Rydal what Chester thought. "You're in the investment business?" Rydal asked suddenly, lighting a cigarette.

"Well—" Chester's fingertips lifted from the table and hovered in the air. "I am in a sense. I arrange business for several other people. Adviser, you might say," Chester added heavily, as if he had just found the word. "Stocks. You know."

Rydal thought he knew. "What kind?"

"Oh—" There was a long hesitation. "Matter of fact many of them are pretty secret just now, not on the market yet officially. One stock, for instance, is being launched on an invention that hasn't yet even been completed. Universal Key. Works on a magnetic principle." His voice was gathering conviction. He looked Rydal in the eye.

Rydal nodded. Chester was getting onto home ground now, and Rydal could imagine how he operated. He was a con man, and probably a very good one, the kind who convinced himself, fell himself under the spell he wanted to throw over a prospective customer. Rydal sensed that he lived in an unreality. No wonder the reality of the corpse this afternoon had given him a jolt. "Well, I'm not exactly in a position to buy any," Rydal said.

"No. Well." Chester smiled easily. "Position to buy any. I was going to mention . . . uh . . . a little reimbursement for your trouble in arranging these passports. What would you—"

"I didn't mean financial position," Rydal said, putting on a smile also. "I meant I'm not interested in stocks, and don't know anybody I'd be passing secrets on to." The reimbursement situation was making Chester nervous, Rydal saw. Chester wanted it over with, wanted to know if he were in for blackmail or not. Rydal took a deep breath and sighed, and finished his coffee. He looked at his wristwatch. They were due to meet Niko in five minutes.

"Well, in regard to reimbursing you, what do you think would be fair? I'd like to give you something. Or . . . have you arranged that with Niko?"

"No," Rydal said casually. "Thanks very much. No need for reimbursement."

"Oh, come now. I don't mean to insult you . . . didn't mean to, but surely . . ." He was like a man protesting to get the bill and not really wanting it.

Rydal shook his head. "Thanks." He lifted a finger for the waiter, and reached for his money to pay the tabs which had come with the coffees. "To be businesslike, you should wait anyway to see if the passports are satisfactory. All I've done for you is deprive you and your wife of your passports and five thousand dollars, you might say."

"Oh!" Chester smiled. "No, let me get this. You got the taxi." Chester put his own money down and left a hundred per cent tip. "You also did me a great favor in the hotel," Chester said more quietly, "by offering to give me an alibi, if the police arrived." He had been looking down at the ashtray, and now he looked up at Rydal. "If you'd like to come to Crete with us, I'd be glad to take care of expenses. That's the least I can do. Give you a small trip and—especially if you're still willing to provide that alibi, in case I'm questioned." It was an effort for him to get the words out. He brushed away some beads of perspiration on his pinkish brow.

Rydal was considering. He had been planning to go to Crete soon. But that was no reason, no reason he was interested in Chester's offer. Would it be wise or unwise? The unwisdom was plain, the wisdom not, yet Rydal sensed its presence. He was drawn towards Chester in a way he could now only attribute to curiosity. And he was attracted to his wife, though he hadn't the slightest intention of trying to start an affair with her. The situation had its dangers, but was *that* crude attraction really it? He had hoped for adventure in the lavender dusks of Athens, in the rosy-fingered dawns that touched the Acropolis, and he hadn't as yet found it. Was he destined to find it in the liquor-rosy face of a con man who looked like his father? Rydal smiled to himself.

"Well? Need some time to make up your mind?"

"No," Rydal said. "No, just thinking. Yes, I'd like to go, I think. But I was going to Crete, anyway, and I have the money to pay my way."

"Oh. Well, we'll see about that, but—you'll come with us tomorrow morning?"

Rydal nodded, wordless, somehow afraid to utter another syllable of assent. "We should be getting back to Niko."

5

When Chester returned to the Hotel Dardanelles a little after eleven, he found Colette in bed with tears in her eyes. The night-lamp by the bed was on. She lay on her side facing the door, her head cushioned on her bent left arm.

"Honey, what's the matter?" Chester asked, kneeling on the floor beside her.

"Oh, I don't know," she said in the high, childlike voice she always had when she cried. "It's just—all of a sudden it all crashes down on me. On *us*."

"What do you mean, honey?"

She wiped her right eye quickly. "That man is dead, isn't he?"

"Yes, I think so. I'm sorry. But if it had to be . . . an accident like that, and it certainly was an accident, it's lucky for us, because if he'd waked up in a few minutes, we'd never have got away. This way—"

"I can't understand how you're so cool about it," she interrupted.

"Well, I've got to be. I'm *not* cool about it, but I've got to keep cool, if I—if we get out of this, honey. You don't want me to lose my nerve, do you?"

"No-o," Colette wailed, like an obedient child.

"Well, then. I'm doing what I have to do. We'll get the new passports Thursday noon in Crete. I'm meeting the fellow at the airport as soon as he steps off the plane. And look. I brought you something." He stood up and took the pearl bracelet out of his suit-jacket pocket. He held it under the light for Colette to see.

She looked at it a few seconds, then, without lifting her head, extended her right hand to touch it. Her fingers turned it slightly on his palm, then she said, "It's very pretty," and drew her hand back under the bedclothes.

"Ho-ney . . ." Chester was at a loss for a moment. "Real pearls and I got them for a song. Five hundred bucks American. Come on. One little smile for me tonight?" He took her soft warm face between his thumb and fingertips.

Usually she smiled, usually she expected a kiss. Now her eyes were troubled and almost frowning. "This'll go on your record, won't it?"

"What?"

"That you killed that Greek man."

Chester released her, and sat on the bed, puzzled. "It'll go on the record of Chester MacFarland, I suppose. MacFarland's not connected with *me* yet." He looked at her as if he'd just made the most logical statement in the world. "MacFarland . . . well . . . We'll have a new name Thursday, you and I." He waited for her to say something, and when she said nothing, he got up and started to take off his overcoat.

"Chester, I'm worried," she said, like a child who wants its daddy to sit down by it again.

"I know you are, dear, but you'll feel better tomorrow. I promise you. Rydal's getting tickets for us, I gave him the money, and all we have to do is to be at the terminal at ten o'clock."

She was silent, and Chester saw that her eyes were still open, staring into space ahead of her. Chester put on his pajamas—he'd had a bath in tepid water in the tiny tub before dinner—and touched up his face with his battery rotary razor. He had a heavy beard, and it was a double bed tonight. As he knocked the water out of his toothbrush, he said in a cheerful tone, "By the way, that fellow's coming with us tomorrow. What do you think of that? I think he'll be rather helpful."

"To Crete?" Colette asked, lifting her head for the first time.

"Yes. I offered him the trip, if he wanted to go. He wouldn't take a cent for what he's done, or so he told me. He may be getting something from the thousand I'm paying his friend Niko. Anyway, he's coming; and it has the added advantage," Chester said in a lower voice, walking closer to Colette, but concentrating on drying his hands on a face towel, "that if we're questioned at all by the police, Rydal can say he was with us all this afternoon and that we never saw that Greek agent, but—" Chester broke off, having realized that the alibi would be unnecessary after Thursday, when they were no longer the MacFarlands and had different passports.

"Didn't want any money from you. Isn't that nice of him? See, your suspicions weren't right at all," Colette said, smiling. She was sitting up in bed hugging her knees now.

"No. Except—" Chester was beginning to think he was a fool, inviting a potential blackmailer—he was still a potential one—for no really good reason to stick with them. After Thursday, Chester could conceive of no possible service Rydal Keener could render. And why hadn't Rydal pointed that out? He was a very intelligent young man, Chester was sure. He looked at his wife's brightened face. All sign of tears was gone now. Chester moved towards his Scotch bottle on the bureau top. "Like a nightcap with me?"

"No, thanks. What I'd really like is a big glass of cold milk."

"Want me to try?" Chester put the bottle down and started for the telephone.

"Um-m, no," Colette said, shaking her head. She was staring in front of her again, and thinking of something else. "I hope he's getting something out of that thousand."

"Why?"

"Because I think he deserves it. He also needs it. Did you notice his shoes?"

"Yes, I noticed them." Chester sipped his drink and frowned. "I just realized that we don't really need him after Thursday. Not unless something happens that we can't get the passports and we have to say our own were stolen or something like that. He offered to say he'd been with us all afternoon, you know."

Colette gave a faint laugh, no more than her breath against her upper lip, and Chester felt she had realized this minutes ago. Chester often felt that Colette's brain was better than his, better in the sense of being more direct and therefore quicker.

"Well, he speaks Greek, so that's bound to be a help," she said. "Besides, he's a very nice fellow, you can see that."

"Can you? I hope so. Shall we turn the light out now?"

"Yes. He told me he was from Massachusetts."

"Oh, and so what? I know a lot of crumbs from Massachusetts."

"Well, he certainly doesn't look like a crumb!" She snuggled into the curve of his arm, her head against the swell of his chest.

"You were talking about his shoes."

"Oh, the hell with his clothes," Colette said. "You can see he's got nice manners. He may come from a poor family, but it's a good family."

Chester smiled indulgently in the darkness. It was one of the things he'd never argue with Colette about. She was essentially a Southerner, he supposed. A pipe began to clank mysteriously in the bathroom. Then an angry voice shouted something that sounded as if it came through several walls, and was answered by a woman's shriller voice.

"Kee-rist! I hope that doesn't keep on all night," said Colette.

"Hope not." She was in a better mood, and the fact the young man was coming with them had picked her up, Chester realized. He had thought he might have to do some persuading to make her agree to his coming. It was funny. Then he stiffened a little, remembering the way they had been looking at each other when he walked in from the bathroom with his suitcase tonight. So. Maybe. Maybe that was why the young man hadn't pointed out that his services as an alibi-provider wouldn't be needed for very long. Chester squirmed a little. The young man now had him by the short hair, too, if he wanted to stay on. Maybe he was after bigger money than a few hundred dollars or a thousand.

"S' matter, darling? Am I heavy on you?"

"You're never heavy on me," Chester said. He was uneasy. He was thinking, as he had been thinking off and on all evening, that the Hotel King's Palace employees might find the body as early as 5 a.m., the police might have the trains and buses checked by 7 a.m., and start on the Athens hotels. They could be picked up at 8 a.m., before they were even out of the Hotel Dardanelles. Or was he feeling over-pessimistic because it had been such a long, horrible day? He had ordered a beefsteak for dinner and hardly been able to touch it. And Colette said he was acting *cool* about it! He lay awake a long time after Colette had fallen asleep, until his arm grew cramped, and he gently pulled it through the little gap her neck made at the bottom of the pillow, and turned over.

Chester awoke first at 7:30 and ordered breakfast. "*American* coffee and toast and marmalade. Buttered toast . . . Oh, all right, butter on the side, yes. . . . No, the milk aside from the coffee. Not in the coffee. Understand? . . . No, I never said anything about French coffee. *American* coffee. . . . All right, if the milk comes in it, it comes in it. Just make it quick, will you? And have our bill ready, if you will." He hung up. "Whew!"

Colette was awake. "Trouble, honey?" She smiled and sat up, ran her fingers through her hair and stretched her arms up, her fingers splayed and arched backward, like her spine. She took a quick bath, shrieking at the coolness of the water, while Chester shaved at the basin. "Draw one for you, dear?" she asked as she washed the tub out with her sponge.

"Thanks. Not taking time this morning."

He did not sit down for his grey-colored coffee, and did not eat any of the round rusklike stuff that passed for toast, though Colette got through several of them, dunking them quickly to soften them, then spreading them liberally with orange marmalade.

"Smell this butter, Ches," she said through a laugh, holding up the butter plate to him. "Smells just like a wet sheep."

Chester sniffed, agreed with her, then went on about his business, which at that moment was sneaking a fortifying drink in the bathroom. Colette didn't like him to drink in the early morning.

They were at the Olympia Airlines by a quarter to 9. Rydal had told him he would purchase the tickets in the name of Colbert. Chester checked their luggage, and was not required to give a name, though he was asked which flight he was on. Chester said the Iraklion flight at 11:15 (the time had been set back a half hour, he had seen on a black board). Then Chester went out into the street with Colette. He wanted to take a little walk, to get out of the airline office, which was such a likely spot for the police to look for Chester MacFarland, he thought, though the airport itself was an even more likely spot.

The time dragged. Chester checked an impulse to go by the American Express, as he had been doing twice daily, to see if he had any mail. He couldn't claim Chester MacFarland's letters now. And he couldn't sign Chester MacFarland to any of the five or six thousand dollars' worth of traveler's checks in his suitcase. He wondered if Rydal Keener could come up with an idea as to how to get rid of them without taking a total loss?

"Darling, look at those shoes!" Colette said, dragging him by the arm towards a shop window.

Chester stared into a window full of reddish-brown shoes, all very pointed and arranged in concentric semicircles, so that they all seemed to be pointing at him. "Yes. Sure there's time," he said automatically to her question, and then he saw her dark-clad figure in the mink stole take a jolt, bend sideways, as the door resisted her.

She came back opening her arms, her pocket-book swinging out. "Closed, the fools! They could've made a sale. Nine-thirty!" She was lively as a little bird.

Chester was secretly glad the store had been closed. He steered her back towards the danger spot, the Olympia Airlines office.

"There he is," said Colette, pointing with a hand sheathed in a light-grey suede glove. Then she waved.

Rydal saw her, and gave them a wave back. He was walking towards them on the pavement, carrying a brown suitcase. He held up a finger, apparently wanting them to wait where they were, then disappeared into the Olympia office. People were getting out of taxis in front of the place now, and porters were bustling about with luggage.

"He's going to get our tickets," Chester said.

"Oh. Well, we've got to go in some time." She tugged at his arm, then stopped, waiting for him to move. "Shouldn't you give him some money for the tickets?"

"Gave him some last night for ours. In cash," Chester said. "He's buying his own." Chester walked towards the airline office doors, his feet almost dragging.

They found Rydal among a crowd of twenty or thirty people who were standing about beside their luggage in the office. Rydal greeted them with a lift of his head, and Chester and Colette made their way towards him, stepping around suitcases and laden porters.

"Good morning," Rydal said, and with a nod at Colette, "Mrs. Colbert."

"Good morning," Colette said.

Rydal glanced around at the people, then said to Chester, "They found him this morning around seven."

"Yes?" asked Chester, his scalp tingling as if he had not been prepared at all. "How'd you hear?"

"There's a radio in my hotel lobby. I waited for the nine o'clock news, and there it was." He looked at Colette.

His coolness was almost like contempt, Chester felt. No skin off his nose what had happened, of course, no skin at all. Yes, definitely, Rydal Keener had a cocky, top-dog manner. But now was no time to worry about it. After tomorrow noon, if the fellow asked five thousand dollars to disappear, fine, pay it, and say good-bye.

"Here's your ticket," Rydal said, handing it to him.

"Where's hers?" asked Chester.

Rydal glanced around the babbling crowd, and said in a low voice, "I thought it was better to buy your wife's and mine under Colbert, and yours under another name, Robinson. She and I ought to sit together on the plane, and you should sit alone. Don't worry about the names. You probably won't be spoken to. No passports involved, you know."

Chester was vaguely piqued, and not able to say anything for a moment.

"If they're looking for you now," Rydal went on, "on planes, for instance, they'll be looking for a man with his wife. I thought it might be a slight advantage this way, that's all."

Chester nodded. It made sense, and the flight was only a two-hour affair. "Okay. That's fine," said Chester.

"Looks like the bus is loading now. Did you check your luggage over there?"

Chester went off and claimed his and Colette's luggage.

Then they boarded the bus, and, as it happened, all had to sit separately. The long bus tooled smoothly past the National Gardens and made a curve around the tumbled and standing columns of the Temple of Olympian Zeus, where Chester had taken snapshots of Colette, and an Italian stranger had taken snapshots of both of them with Chester's camera only yesterday morning. The film was still in Chester's Rolleiflex, and he supposed he would get it developed in Iraklion, leaving them in a name he did not yet know. The back of the seat in front of him pressed against his knees. He looked down at something rolling under his shoe, and found a pale, flesh-colored, cheap-looking fountain pen. A ball-point. Made in Germany, it said on the barrel. Trying it on the back of his hand, he saw that it wrote, in blue ink. Maybe it was a little sign of good luck.

At the airport they had time for an espresso at the small bar which also served liquor. Chester ordered a brandy with his coffee. He was nervous. The loud speaker kept bawling things out in Greek, French and English, plane departures and arrivals and weather conditions and calls for people, and he was half expecting an announcement of the discovery of the body in the Hotel King's Palace. Rydal left his coffee to go and buy a newspaper. It was all very confused and noisy. Only Colette looked calm, sitting with her legs neatly crossed on the high stool at the bar counter, looking about at the people seated in the deep leather chairs among tall potted plants, behind newspapers, behind thin screens of cigarette smoke. Rydal came back, scanning a Greek paper as he walked, bumping into one or two people.

He shook his head at Chester and smiled slightly, offered Colette a cigarette, which she declined, then finished his coffee.

They boarded the plane, Rydal and Colette going ahead, Chester following, with four or five people between them. Immediately upon leaving Athens they were over water, and then over a woolly, level field of clouds, the blue sky lost. Chester thumbed through his *Guide Bleu,* trying to concentrate on the pages on Crete. The maps of Knossos looked undecipherable and uninteresting today. Behind him, he heard over the roar of the plane's engine a man and women laughing and talking in Greek. Farther behind him and across the aisle, Rydal sat with Colette. He wondered what they were talking about. Pleasantries, probably. Colette had her moods. He had never seen her so disturbed as last night, yet it had passed in a matter of minutes. *Murder.* Well, that was certainly a bad thing, and it was really a wonder she hadn't been more upset than she was. It was a second-degree murder, Chester reminded himself, even merely manslaughter. Certainly. Unpremeditated and an accident. No, they couldn't give him a life sentence for that! What disturbed him was that they were on his trail at all, and that the death of the Greek agent hadn't solved anything, had only made the situation worse, had gained them only a few hours' time, nothing more.

Chester took his flask, which he had providently filled, from the duffel bag between his feet, pocketed it, and went to the men's room at the back of the plane. Colette sat with her head back against the white-aproned pad on the back of her seat, her eyes closed. Rydal stared out the window.

The passengers had barely finished a snack of cold cuts, when they landed. The Iraklion airport presented a simple, barren picture: a flat field along the water, a building like a long, low box, a few empty American Air Force buses and a handful of blue-uniformed American Air Force men standing about. All the passengers were soon on a rather shabby bus heading, presumably, for the city. There were one or two stops at what Chester took to be villages or farm communities, and then, at a spot that looked no bigger or more important, all the passengers started to get off. They stepped out into a dusty, creamy-pink street which sloped down towards the white-capped sea, three or four streets away.

"'Otel Iraklion! Cheap! 'Ot warter!" said a dirty-looking fellow, whose only badge of authority was a worn-out visored cap that said Hotel Iraklion on its band.

"No," said Rydal, who was attempting to corral their luggage. All the luggage was being unloaded haphazardly from the top of the bus.

"'Otel Corona! Two blocks up! Thees way!"

"'Otel Astir! Best in town!" A young dark-haired chap in a beige bellboy uniform saluted Chester, and started to pick up two pieces of luggage near Chester's feet.

"That's not mine!" Chester said quickly, and walked towards Colette and Rydal. A strong breeze was blowing from the sea. The sunshine was bright, glassy-bright and cold also. "What do we do now?" Chester asked, but, seeing that Rydal was occupied with identifying their seven pieces of luggage plus his own, Chester began helping him.

"Let's let this crowd clear away," Rydal said. "Then we'll get a taxi—oh, down to the waterfront, I suppose."

The crowd was thinning out. Taxis were puffing up, taking people and luggage away. Successful bellhops were tottering off under mountains of suitcases, their possessors straggling behind them.

"Got a hotel in mind?" asked Chester.

Rydal lifted his head and looked towards the sea, his profile pale and sharp against the blue sky. He fitted a cigarette between his lips. "Our problem is that we can't go to a hotel," he murmured. "No passports, you know." He glanced at Colette.

"How wonderful!" she said, swinging her arms out. "We'll just walk around the rest of the day. And tonight!" she added, with enthusiasm.

Rydal shook his head thoughtfully, still looking towards the port. Then he looked the other way, up the street of pinkish and cream-colored three- and four-story buildings. A booted man was flogging a donkey before him. On either side of the donkey baby goats in slings sat upright and gazed with serene eyes at them, snug as papooses on a mother's back.

"Aren't they *dar-rling!*" Colette said, starting towards them.

"Colette!" Rydal lifted his hand.

She came back.

"There'll be more," Rydal said. He turned to Chester. "I don't know anybody here we might stay with. We'll just have to sit it out tonight. So the best thing to do is save your energy, I'd say. And, number one, let's get rid of the suitcases."

"No use you suffering," Chester said. "You've got a passport you can show at any hotel."

"Yes," Rydal said vaguely. "Let's see if we can check the luggage in some restaurant down by the water." He crossed the street and spoke to the driver of a taxi parked at the opposite curb, a taxi that had been left behind by the mainstream and had been waiting for them to make up their minds what they would do.

They all piled into the taxi, luggage at their feet, on their laps and on the taxi roof. The trip was very short, down to the sea, and Rydal stopped the driver after they had gone a few yards to the left: there was a restaurant with a sign in the shape of a fish hanging in front of the door. Rydal came out a moment later, and said the proprietor would be glad to check their suitcases.

"I think we ought to have something here," Rydal said. "Lunch or a drink, anyway."

They stayed in the place more than two hours, drinking ouzo and eating tiny plates of radishes, horseradish and onions first, then a lunch of broiled fish and underdone homefried potatoes with which they had a couple of bottles of sharp-tasting white wine. But they tipped well, and the proprietor by this time was willing to keep their luggage overnight. Rydal told Chester that he had given the man a story about all of them spending tonight with a friend in town, a friend with whom they had been staying, and about their having missed the plane back to Athens today, and about not wanting to burden their friend by dragging all the suitcases back to his house in the hills. Chester would carry the duffel bag out, that was all. They would pick up the luggage tomorrow afternoon around 1. Then they wandered up the main street, the street on which the airport bus had stopped.

The Iraklion Museum of Antiquities was open. Here they killed another hour or so, gazing at statuary and amphorae and jewelry, and while Colette went to powder her nose, Rydal told Chester what he had heard on the radio.

"Well, George Papanopolos's death was due to a fractured skull. Very brief announcement. They didn't mention your name, but they told the name of the hotel and how long the man had been dead. About twelve hours."

A cool chill ran down Chester. This was fact. It had been on the radio. Thousands of people had heard it. "It'll certainly be in the papers today, though."

"Yes, in Athens," Rydal said. "The papers probably come here by boat, a day late. Oh, it may be in the Crete papers this evening. I suppose they've got an evening paper. In that case, your name might be mentioned. I mean MacFarland."

Chester nodded and swallowed. MacFarland. Something to hide from. He'd feared it since the minute he filled out the application for his passport in New York. Why hadn't he finagled a phony birth certificate? *Chester MacFarland.* It was he. It was awful.

"Then, of course, Crete has a radio," Rydal went on. "The news is probably coming in now, all right, maybe with a description of you."

"Well—" Chester had another spasm of fear. "The photograph that agent had is years old. Doesn't look much like me now. I'm heavier now, with a moustache. Maybe I ought to shave it off," he added.

Rydal's dark eyelashes blinked calmly. "Here comes your wife. They'll ask the hotel personnel for a description of you. Don't shave your moustache off. You might grow a beard. That might change you more than shaving off the moustache."

They had tea and inedible pastries at a large, cheap café opposite the museum. They braced themselves in its warmth for a walk along the mole in the harbor at sundown. There it became too cold for them to wait for the sundown, and anyway the mole, paved with loose stones, was not suited for Colette's high-heeled pumps. At the cocktail hour, they tried the Hotel Astir's restaurant. There was no bar proper, and they were served cocktails in the restaurant, where a field of white-clothed tables flowed out from theirs and disappeared in three unilluminated corners, empty miles away from them. Chester was growing tired. He had slept badly last night. He ordered two drinks more than Colette or Rydal had. The conversation of Rydal and Colette bored him and also annoyed him. Silly chatter. Colette was talking about Louisiana, about her trips twice a year there while she had been going to boarding school in Virginia, about holiday parties and her attempt to organize a dramatic society in Biloxi for three years running, only to have it fail for lack of popular interest. Rydal commiserated. Rydal answered her questions about Massachusetts, said his school had been Yale, but he was not elaborating on any of his answers, Chester noticed. Then Rydal excused himself, saying that he wanted to go out and find an evening paper, and that he would be right back.

"I'm not sure if I can stay up all night," Chester said.

"Oh, darling! Drink some coffee. Don't have Scotch if you want to stay up all night. Look at me. One drink and I've just ordered coffee, too. I think it might be exciting to stay up all night in Crete, don't you? Our first night here?"

Chester rubbed his fingertips along his jaw. The stubble made a scraping sound. Should he grow a beard? What about the passport picture, his current very good one? What good would a beard do? Was Rydal giving him a bum steer? "I think I'd like another Scotch."

"Oh, darling," Colette said, disapproving.

"If I don't—Well, never mind, I've got the flask right here. Better Scotch and a lot cheaper," he added petulantly. He spiked his nearly empty glass of Scotch highball.

Rydal was back with a newspaper, and Chester started to ask him to let him see it, then saw it was in Greek. With a serious, confident air, Rydal sat down, folded the paper so that he could see an item on the front page, and began reading. "It goes like this." He glanced over his shoulder—his back was to the room—then read in a quiet voice: "The body of George Papanopolos, thirty-eight, was found this morning in the . . . the cleaning room of the King's Palace Hotel by Stefanie Triochos, twenty-three, a girl of cleaning in the employ of the hotel. Papanopolos, a detective of the National Police Force, was found to have died from a fracture of the skull. It is suspected that he was the victim of Chester Crighton MacFarland, forty-two, an American wanted for um-m . . . embezzlement of investments, investment funds," Rydal corrected himself, "and that he had been on the quest of MacFarland when he entered the hotel. MacFarland had been occupying a room down the corridor from the closet of cleaning utensils in which the body of the detective was found. Traces of blood were found on the bathroom floor and the carpet of the room in which MacFarland and his wife Elizabeth . . . Elizabeth?" He looked at Colette, who nodded nervously, "—had stayed and also on the carpet of the hall leading to the closet of cleaning utensils." Rydal paused and took a sip of water without looking at his attentive listeners. "MacFarland checked out of the hotel shortly after 7 p.m. last evening," Rydal continued in a quiet, impersonal voice, "saying to one of the hotel personnel that he was catching a night train in the direction of Italy. A . . . an official investigation of trains and buses and airplanes failed to reveal . . . to reveal that you were on them," Rydal finished, looking across the table at Chester, then at Colette.

Colette was silent, her hand tense on the table, her red nails digging into one red thumbnail. Her eyes, when she looked at Chester, were frightened, and a little reproachful, he thought.

"There's more," Rydal said. "Authorities therefore believe MacFarland is still within Grecian borders and that . . . he may have tried to assume another identity. George Papanopolos leaves behind him, et cetera."

Colette looked at Rydal. "Go on. Leaves behind him?"

Rydal cleared his throat and read, "A wife Lydia, thirty-five, a son George, fifteen, a daughter Doria, twelve, two brothers Philip and Christopher Papanopolos both of Lamia, and a sister Mrs. Eugenia Milous of Athens." Rydal laid the paper down.

Chester met Rydal's eyes, but he felt he met them dumbly, that his spark was gone. He sat up a little in his chair.

"Not bad news," Rydal said. "They didn't mention a lead on Crete, and they didn't even give a description of you. It's really as good as it could possibly be, under the circumstances."

"But he's dead," Colette said. She rubbed her forehead with her fingertips.

Chester poured another drink for himself, then tipped the flask upside down and let it all run out. He wanted to get high, even a bit drunk. Why not? What was he supposed to do, sit up all night mulling over the mess he was in, all night long awake without even the temporary oblivion of sleep? "If it's good, let's have a drink on it."

Rydal declined at first, then accepted his offer.

Eleven o'clock found them in a huge barn of a restaurant which seemed to be also a nightclub of a simple sort, right on the seafront. Chester did not know how he had got there. Some time, hours before, he thought they had had dinner somewhere, but he wasn't sure. Now Colette and Rydal were dancing on the tiny dance floor that looked half a mile away from where he sat, though the orchestra was so loud, and so rotten, it hurt his ears. Chester stared sullenly at a near-by table, a large round table at which a whole family of Greeks sat, papa and mama and grandma and all the kiddies. The kiddies were in their party best, and several minutes ago Chester had staggered over and chucked one of the little girls under the chin (it had been on his way back from the men's room, a filthy hole), and he had been rewarded with a cold, uncomprehending stare. Then Chester had realized he was in Greece and not in America, not in some pizzeria on Third Avenue in Manhattan, and that the little girl had not understood a word he said, and that her family, which had glared at him, had probably thought he said something terrible to her. Chester fell asleep.

He was awakened by a tapping on his shoulder. Rydal stood beside him in his overcoat, alert and smiling, saying, "They're closing. Got to take off."

Worst of all, there wasn't a taxi. Chester walked between Rydal and Colette, partially supported by both of them, needing their support and feeling ashamed of it.

"It's the worst hour," Rydal was saying. "It's rough."

Chester heard them discussing him for a few seconds, discussing what would be "best for him", and, though he didn't like it, he thought why not let them worry over him, because wasn't it *he* who had the God-damned load on his shoulders, *he* who'd gotten into trouble trying to protect his wife as well as himself? And who'd asked Ryburn—what was his name?—to come along, anyway? A hard, brutally hard bench, a hard, cold stone bench jolted him awake. He was sitting on it. He looked to his left and saw Colette beside him, snuggling her head against Rydal's shoulder, getting ready to fall asleep. Rydal smoked, looking straight ahead, the duffel bag between his feet. Chester thought they were in the little square by the Iraklion Museum, where they had been that afternoon, but he wasn't sure. Maybe that dark café across the way was where they'd had tea. The dawn was showing signs of coming, showing signs.

It was the worst hour, as the fellow had said. Nothing was open, that was plain. *Damn them all, damn everybody for not being open!* Chester thought, and was too tired to say it. Colette was holding hands with Rydal, Chester saw. He smiled a little, superiorly. Nobody could take Colette away from him. Just let them try, see how far they'd get. Chester closed his eyes.

He woke up from the cold, he didn't know how much later, but the dawn hadn't made much progress. Now both Colette and Rydal were asleep, holding hands, their heads tipped towards each other, bracing each other. Chester stomped up and down the pavement, his teeth chattering, every muscle rigid with chill and trembling. For hours, it seemed, he watched the progress, watched cynically and bitterly the progress of the opening of the café across the street. First the opener or the proprietor arrived on a bicycle, started to unlock the padlock on the door and didn't, got into a long conversation with the milk-deliverer, also on a bicycle, shared a mutual cigarette with him, swapped several jokes, slapped the milk-deliverer's back, took off one shoe and stood in a stockinged foot while he explained something apparently of great interest about the sole, put the shoe back on again, and then the milk-deliverer propped his foot up on the handlebars and began to discourse on his own shoe. It was 6:17.

At 6:32, when the doors of the café at last opened, Chester shook Rydal awake roughly and with pleasure, saying that the café across the way was open and that they could now get some hot coffee.

6

Of all man's capacities, Rydal was thinking as he rode on the airlines bus towards the airport, memory was the most eerie, pleasant, painful, no doubt at times the most deceptive. All night, awake, dozing, or sleepwalking, he had been half in the present, half in the past. Dancing with Colette had stirred the old desire that he had felt for Agnes, that he had not really felt since. And yet Colette was *not* like Agnes, not at all. Colette was shallower, he thought—in a way. No, that wasn't right. Who could have been shallower, more flippant and unfeeling than Agnes when she said good-bye to him? There was an example of memory being deceptive again, simply because ten years ago he had attributed to Agnes all the depth a woman's soul could possibly contain. Last night the memory of Agnes had been sweet. Colette didn't even look like Agnes. But she flirted rather like her, there was no doubt about that!

Rydal stared into the blazing disc of the sun until he could stand it no longer and had to set his teeth and close his eyes.

Colette was merely playing, enjoying making him feel desire for her, playing for want of anything better to do in the long night without a warm bed to sleep in, to share with her husband, who had passed out. Go a little farther with her, take her up on it, and she'd say no. "Of *course* not, silly boy. Do you think I'd do that to Chester?" Rydal could hear her.

He smiled, thinking of Chester this morning, his teeth chattering against the thick rim of his coffee cup in the café. Chester had huddled by the wood-burning stove in the place, chafing his hands and stomping, but neither the stove nor the coffee had seemed to do much good. Chester was chilled through, chilled by the sea wind and the after-effects of all the Scotch and ouzo he'd drunk, and it would probably take all day to get him back to normal. He had been funny to look at, but Colette hadn't laughed, Rydal noticed. She had been tender and serious and concerned, warming Chester's muffler over the stove, bringing it back to wrap close about his neck. Yes, Colette was a good wife. She'd be an angel to Chester if he got sick.

They were getting to the airport. Rydal glanced around at the six or eight people in the bus who were bound for Athens on the three-thirty plane. Half of them looked downright poor, the other half lower middle class, economically speaking. None was American. None looked like a plainclothes man. Rydal twisted the newspaper gently in both his hands. In this morning's paper there had been a description of Chester MacFarland, *with* the moustache, though the photograph reproduced had been the moustacheless one of the agent's notebook. Rydal had torn the notebook's sheets out, torn them up and dropped them into three different rubbish bins in Athens yesterday evening before calling on the MacFarlands. He could have sold the Greek's credentials to Niko for a couple of hundred dollars, no doubt, but Rydal hadn't had the heart, somehow, to do it. It would have been like selling pieces of the man's flesh after he had died. He'd only been doing his job, an honest man's job, and he hadn't deserved to die. Rydal had thrown the credentials away, torn up, and the billfold also, but he had taken the man's drachmas, a mere two hundred and eighty.

Niko was sitting on one of the wooden benches in the bleak terminal building, his sneakered feet splayed on the floor. His musing smile became a grin when he saw Rydal. He lifted a hand in greeting, and stood up. Rydal nodded, pleased that he had come. It meant he had the passports. Rydal beckoned him towards the door that opened onto the field.

"You got them?" Rydal asked.

"Got them." Niko nodded.

They strolled along the edge of the field, exchanging comments on the weather, slowly passed an American Air Force bus that stood waiting, empty except for its driver. Rydal lit a cigarette, offered one to Niko, then lit his for him, too.

"How are the ages on them? On the passports?" Rydal said, unable to wait any longer to find out this important point.

"Ages?" Niko shrugged. "I forgot. Okay, I think."

A fat lot Niko cared, Rydal thought, and sighed. Niko's hands itched for his money, he itched to be off again to Athens with his thousand dollars American. Rydal slowed to a stop. "Well, let's see them."

They were standing in an empty corner of the field under the wide, windy blue sky.

Niko reached into his khaki jacket, undid a shirt button, and pulled them out. They were faintly, disgustingly warm from his skin.

Niko stepped between the passports and the terminal building at his back, and watched eagerly.

William James Chamberlain, Rydal read. Wife, Mary Ellen Forster Chamberlain. Minors XXX. Height 5 ft 10 in. Hair brown, eyes grey. (The first bad thing, Chester's were pale blue.) Visible marks XXX. Birthplace Denver City, Colorado. Birth date Aug. 15, 1922. And the signature.

"Used to be Chambers," Niko said, pointing with a dirty-nailed linger at the signature. "Frank changed. Changed passport number also."

Rydal nodded. He flipped the other open, and looked for the coloring. Blue eyes, thank God, and felt his heart give a dip of relief. The birth date would make her twenty-nine now, and she'd said last night that she was twenty-five, but that wasn't bad. He looked at her photograph, which he hadn't seen before, and thought, my God, she's giving the same, direct, come-to-me look even to the man who made the photograph! He saw that the stamped-in PHOTOGRAPH ATTACHED DEPARTMENT OF STATE PASSPORT AGENCY NEW YORK that spread over the bottom part of the photograph, and the page fitted neatly, and checked the same thing on Chester's photograph, and found it good, if a bit worn-looking. Both passports were soiled, as if they had been stepped on a few times. Rydal wondered how many filthy hands they had passed through before they had come to his? He flipped them shut and put them into his overcoat pocket.

"Okay?"

"Okay," Rydal said. Then, thinking of something, he pulled them out again. He scanned the last stamped pages in both of them. Good. There was no Greek EXODOS stamp on them, only an EIZODOS, both dated in December of last month. That meant that the former possessors of the passports had entered but not left Greece, at least not with these passports. "Let's walk on," he said, and began walking back towards the terminal building, hands in his trousers pockets. His left hand felt the crisp, folded five-hundred-dollar bills that Chester had given him that morning for Niko. The five thousand dollars was buttoned into the back pocket of his trousers. Carrying such a sum made Rydal a bit nervous, just on principle, he thought, if one could be nervous on principle. If he'd lost it, Chester wouldn't feel it. He remembered Chester this morning, dragging the big brown suitcase, which Rydal had fetched for him from the seaside restaurant, behind the curtain that concealed the hole-in-the-floor W.C. of the café. Chester felt he had to hide, when he went into his cash.

"You got the money?" Niko asked anxiously.

Rydal pulled his left hand out. "Here's yours."

Niko glanced at it and stuffed it away somewhere, like a squirrel.

Rydal turned around. They were not being watched, as far as he could see. He unbuttoned his back pocket, and got the other money. "You don't have to count it. It's ten five hundreds." He saw Niko's hand tremble as he took it.

Niko smiled. "Fine. Zank you."

Rydal smiled. He turned again, back towards the terminal.

"What they give you?" Niko asked.

"Oh-h, I don't know yet," said Rydal.

"He kill a man, no? I see in this morning's paper."

"An accident," Rydal said.

"Sure, but . . . he kill."

Ergo, gouge him plenty, Niko might have added. "We'll see," Rydal said vaguely.

"When you coming back to Athens?" Niko looked up at him, smiling, showing the lead-framed tooth, like an absurd miniature picture frame setting off that masterpiece of bad diet and neglect, Niko's yellow incisor.

Rydal thought of Colette's white teeth, her fresh lips. "I don't know that, either. Have to do a little sightseeing first. I've never been to Crete before."

Niko stuck his underlip out, looked around him at this thing called Crete, nodded and seemed about to make some disparaging yet important remark, but said nothing. Then he giggled. "I never been before, either."

After a moment, Rydal said, "There's your plane loading, I think."

Niko jumped, started towards it as if it were a street-car he was about to miss, checked himself and grinned self-consciously. He was a few yards away from Rydal now. "Hey! Frank say he want to make a date with . . . with the girl!" Niko gestured towards Rydal with a finger.

It took Rydal an instant to know he meant Colette. Rydal put his head back and laughed, and waved good-bye. "My love to Anna!" Then he trotted towards the terminal.

He had missed the bus to Iraklion, so he took a taxi. In the taxi, he closed his eyes and let his head rest against the comfortless seat back. His eyes smarted from lack of sleep.

He found Chester and Colette in the place they had appointed, a modest little restaurant by a round fountain, some six blocks up the main street from the sea. Chester had managed to shave with his battery razor, in some men's room probably, and he looked better than he had when Rydal left him, though his eyes were still pink and squinty from fatigue. They both looked at him anxiously as he approached their table, and Rydal smiled and nodded to reassure them. They had finished lunch, apparently. Their empty coffee cups were on the table, and also a large cloudy glass of ouzo at Chester's place.

"Greetings," Rydal said, pulling out a chair for himself.

"You got them?" Chester asked.

"Yep." Rydal looked up at a solemn, tired waiter who had come to the table. "Just a coffee, please," he said in Greek. When the man went away, Rydal looked to see if the mild interest his arrival had caused in the place had died down—it had—then coolly lit a cigarette and unbuttoned his overcoat. There were only three customers in the restaurant, a fat man reading a newspaper at a table in the rear, and two Greeks who had also finished their lunches and were talking pugnaciously at a table some fifteen feet away. Rydal pulled the passports out of his overcoat pocket and passed them under the table onto Chester's thigh.

Chester glanced over his shoulder nervously, then opened one of the passports, looking at it below the level of the table. His face relaxed. He smiled. He looked into the other passport. Then he nodded. "It's good, isn't it? They look fine."

Rydal nodded. "I think so."

"Want to see, honey?" Chester asked Colette.

"Well . . . not here. I'll take your word. What I'm interested in is a hotel."

"If you'd like to go on now," Rydal said, "don't wait for me to have my coffee. Bring my suitcase with yours, if you will. The man's already been tipped." Their suitcases were still with the proprietor of the fish restaurant, except for Chester's canvas suitcase with his money in it. They had decided to stay at the Hotel Astir, which appeared to be the best in town.

But Chester and Colette said they would wait—"What's ten more minutes now?" asked Chester, but he was smiling—so they waited, livened and cheered by the passports and the prospect of a hot bath. When Rydal had finished his coffee, Chester paid the bill and they left, Rydal and Chester going down the street for their luggage, while Colette waited for them in the lobby of the Astir.

"It might be well for you to practise Mr. Chamberlain's signature as soon as possible," Rydal said. "The hotel will make you sign a registration card, you know."

"Yes. You're quite right. I'll do it now," Chester said, and he looked rather nervous, but he sat down on the low cement parapet beside the sea, pulled out the passport and a small spiral-bound notebook, opened the passport to its second page, and began to copy the signature of William James Chamberlain. He wrote hastily, scratched out with impatience his first two efforts, and surveyed the third at arm's length. He made a fourth and fifth try.

Rydal moved closer. Even seen upside down, Chester's imitation of the signature appeared quite good in his last attempts, much better reproductions than the average person could have made of somebody else's handwriting. But then Chester was no tyro, Rydal supposed.

Chester glanced up at him with an amused smile. Obviously he was proud of his talent.

"Not difficult?" Rydal asked.

"No, not this. It's tall and slim. Scrawls are hard for me. I'll do fine with this."

He was very sure of himself. Rydal kept his mouth shut, and in fact he had nothing to say. It was Chester's risk, not his. Chester tore out the notebook page, stood up and snapped his pen shut and pocketed the passport and the notebook. He flicked the wadded piece of paper over the parapet out towards the sea, and they walked on towards the fish restaurant.

They were at the Hotel Astir with their luggage in a taxi within five minutes. The tall bellboy in the beige uniform helped them out with it. Rydal and Chester asked for rooms at the desk, taking no trouble to hide the fact they were friends; and no doubt, Rydal thought, the whole town knew it by now. It was a good-sized town, but it had a small town's atmosphere, perhaps due to the absence of tall buildings. And there were few tourists at this time of year. That was bad. Rydal wondered if they were going to be challenged today or tomorrow by some wiseacre who wanted to know if Chester were Chester MacFarland? If they'd have to drag out Chester's passport and show his name to shake him off? Rydal wasn't afraid of a plain citizen, but if a policeman asked any questions—

"Sir? With bath, did you say?" The clerk had been trying to get his attention.

"Oh, yes. Please. With bath."

Chester's and Colette's room was 414 on the fourth floor, and Rydal's 408 on the same floor. They all agreed that they would simply clean up and take a nap for the rest of the afternoon.

The bath was delicious to Rydal, the water hot, the tub big and white. Then he put on pajamas, the better to relax and possibly sleep, shaved, and sent his dirty shirt away via the maid to be washed. He got into bed and propped himself up against the pillows and read the newspaper for a while. He re-read the item on Chester. ". . . believed to be still within the country." But they didn't say where in the country they were looking. Maybe all over it. It occurred to Rydal that it might be wiser if they went to a smaller town in Crete. It would be wiser, too, if Chester and also Colette acquired some cheaper and less fashionable clothes. And it would be wise for him, Rydal thought, to clear out of the MacFarland, now Chamberlain, ensemble while he could. There was probably a boat to Athens tomorrow morning. Rydal had bought a one-way plane ticket. A lot would be wiser, a lot that he wasn't yet doing, he supposed. He put the paper down, closed his eyes, and wriggled farther down into the welcome softness of the bed.

There was a light knock on the door. Rydal lifted his head. He did not know how long he had slept. It seemed about fifteen minutes. He got up, fuzzy-headed, and went to the door. "Who is it?" he said through the door. Then he repeated it in Greek.

"Colette," came the whispered answer.

Rydal glanced down to see if his pajamas were properly buttoned—he had no robe—then opened the door.

"Oh. I disturbed you," she said, coming in. She had her mink stole and her hat on, but she took off her hat and tossed it into the armchair. "Chester's snoring away and I didn't want to disturb him, somehow. He needs it, you know."

"Um-m. Where've you been?" Rydal sat down carefully on the bed, conscious of his bare feet, but Colette wasn't looking at his feet.

"Out for a walk. I had a bath, but I didn't feel like sleeping, so I explored this church next door. You know, the one with the arches and the stained glass?"

Rydal nodded. He vaguely remembered a church to the left of the hotel.

"So." She smiled at him, then went to a window and looked out. "What an interesting old building. Looks Italian, doesn't it, with those balconies?"

Rydal turned his head. The building's roof came midway up his window. He saw an iron balcony that looked about to fall out of its anchorage in the pink stone. He said nothing.

She sat down on the bed, not beside him, but on the opposite side, half turned towards him. Then she lay back, so her head was near his hip.

"Tired? You should take a nap," Rydal said somewhat irritably. "In your room," he added.

Her hand moved down his arm to his wrist, and pulled him towards her. Rydal hesitated—two starts and stops—then he swung his legs up on the bed, embraced her and kissed her. Her arms circled him like a delicious cloud. Her breath was warm and fragrant with American toothpaste, probably Colgate's, and trembling with passion which inflamed him, too; but even as he felt it, he was thinking, pay no attention, it's only because it's been quite a while—a month? two months?—since you've had a girl, and this is only a continuation of last night, the kiss she was leading up to last night that you never took.

"Rydal!" she whispered, as if she had just discovered him.

He drew back from her, smiling a little, his heart pounding. It was over.

"Come back," she said, her arms out again.

And as she kicked off her shoes and pushed herself back towards the pillows, Rydal fell on her again. They lay side by side, tight and close, kissing, their eyes closed. It was like it had been with Agnes, always, with Agnes. The wild, blissful kisses like this ten times a day in the house, stolen, and then at night Agnes waiting for him in her bed, waiting for more than kisses. His body remembered. So did his mind. This is MacFarland's wife, you ass.

She was opening her blouse with her free hand. Her other hand pressed the back of his head, holding his lips against hers. Well, the blouse was all right, he supposed, but not the skirt, not the rest of it. His hand hurried for her warm breast, then caressed it slowly. She took his hand and pushed his fingers inside her brassière. After a few seconds of this, Rydal withdrew his hand, and pressed himself up with his right arm, lifting her part way with him.

"What's the matter?" she asked. Her lips looked even fuller now, with her lipstick gone.

Rydal wiped his own lips with the back of his hand. "Thought I'd better stop," he said.

She smiled, amused, the lavender eyes narrowed. "Come on-n. We're young. We're both only twenty-five," she said softly. "We want to. Why not?" She was unfastening the top of her skirt, her eyes still half closed.

Rydal watched her. Why not? His door had an automatic lock and it was locked now. Chester would sleep a long time, probably. Why not? Now. Then Rydal realized he was looking at her with dazed, wide eyes, like a man drunk—which in a way he was. He blinked and said, "No. Thanks."

Colette stopped what she was doing with her skirt. She looked at him with her eyes open now. "Dar-rling—"

That was for Chester, Rydal thought, that word.

"I didn't really mean go to bed. I just meant lie down with me. Come back." She held out her arms.

And he started to, but of what use was any more of that? He stood up and walked to the window, then turned around and looked at her. She hadn't moved, except that her head was turned to him, her arms down at her sides. There was a soft curve below the waist of her black skirt. Her body was rather like Agnes's, he had to admit, with the minor differences that would have to exist between the body of a fifteen-year-old girl and a twenty-five-year-old woman. Colette was waiting for him to make the next move. And she was tense, Rydal saw.

"You didn't mean go to bed with me?" he asked, moving towards her. He sat down and took her by the shoulders. "Why not?"

"Rydal, don't," she said, smiling, but now she wanted free.

Rydal had had no plan when he recrossed the room, but suddenly he wanted her. "All right. Take off the skirt," he said, zipping it down.

She slid up, away from him, and caught her right shoulder as if he had hurt it. "No, I *didn't* mean that," she whispered, smiling, enunciating it clearly. "I really didn't."

Rydal gave it up. But now he wanted her. Now he would have. He stood looking down at her as she put her blouse back on, and he knew that she knew it, too.

She put lipstick on again, and chatted with him as if nothing had happened. Rydal replied to what she said, she stayed perhaps five minutes more, and then she was gone, and he hadn't any idea of what they had said in the last minutes to each other. It was as if someone had taken his head and with a twist of the hand started it spinning. It was still spinning. He flung himself on the bed and closed his eyes. Her scent was on his pillow.

She'd finally refused. Thus did dreary life repeat what had already taken place in his imagination, and not surprise him at all.

7

Rydal awakened at 7 p.m., dressed, and went down for the papers. He found a street vendor some four blocks away, an old man stooped on his heels and huddled under a cape beside his newspaper stacks. Rydal bought, besides the Cretan evening paper, an Athens *Daily Post* of yesterday in English. The *Post* he could have skipped: there was nothing about the Greek agent's death in it. The Iraklion evening paper, however, reproduced Chester's photograph again, and gave a description of him as well as his wife—". . . his young, attractive, blue-eyed and blonde wife, exquisitely attired, who appeared barely in her twenties . . ." The MacFarlands, said the paper, were known to have stayed at the Hotel Dardanelles in Athens on Tuesday night, 9 January, the night of the murder. Their movements after 9 the next morning were unknown.

". . . They may have taken a plane to Corfu, Rhodes or Crete, authorities speculated. The frontiers of Albania, Yugoslavia, Bulgaria and Turkey have been on the alert since Wednesday morning, and it is doubtful if they have crossed the border, unless they were able to obtain false passports in the short time."

Things were becoming a bit hot, Rydal supposed. The police speculating about Crete, and now the MacFarlands were stopping at the main hotel in the main city of the island. Rydal moistened his lips, seeing suddenly the police tapping Chester on the shoulder in the lobby of the Astir, questioning him, Chester summoning him to tell the police they'd been travelling together for days, had been inseparable for days, and they were talking to the wrong man, anyway. Did they want to see his passport? (You bet they did.) Rydal couldn't imagine Chester answering their questions coolly, producing his passport coolly, unless he were at a certain point of drunkenness, a precise degree of drunkenness. Rydal did not fancy perjuring himself now. He felt he was losing his nerve. It didn't seem as simple and easy as it had yesterday, or the evening of the murder when he'd arranged for the passports with Niko.

He paused for a cold bottle of grape soda at a little sweets shop, and drank it standing up at the counter, listening to the staccato voice of a news reporter on the proprietor's static-filled radio. The voice hurried through the news of a London conference, a fiscal measure France was contemplating, the outlook for the weather, and then—slam, bang, bing and tinkle—back to Greek folk music again. Rydal put his empty bottle down and left.

The telephone was ringing when he entered his room, and he felt a start of fear, then realized it was probably Colette or Chester. It was Colette.

"Did you sleep?"

"Yes."

"Chester wants to know if you would like to come in for a drink before we go out to dinner."

Rydal went down the hall to their door with his newspapers, and knocked.

"Come in!" Chester's baritone voice called heartily, but as the door was locked, he had to come and open it. Chester was in a foulard dressing-gown and trousers.

Rydal noticed that Chester's beard—the one he had suggested, low along the jawline—was already beginning to show. "Good evening," he said to them both. Colette had changed her clothes since he had seen her. Now she wore a light grey, nearly white, tweed dress, and she stood by the long, low chest of drawers, one hand on her hip.

"What do you drink, Rydal?" Colette asked. "We have ouzo tonight, too."

"Yes. Just sent down for a bottle," said Chester.

"All right," Rydal said. "Ouzo. Thanks."

They also had ice in an ice bucket.

"I see you've got the papers," Chester said.

Rydal had taken off his overcoat and dropped it across a straight chair. He picked up the Greek paper, then put it down, remembering Chester couldn't read it. "They're speculating—saying you're probably still within the borders," Rydal said, dropping his voice. "They're concentrating on Corfu, Rhodes and Crete."

Chester listened attentively. "Concentrating?"

"Well, it doesn't say what they're doing. Looking, I suppose." Rydal was uncomfortable. He glanced at Colette. She was fixing his ouzo with ice and water, but she had glanced at him at the same time. She looked cheerful and quite at ease. "I don't know what your plans are," Rydal said to Chester, "but I think it might not be a bad idea to go to some smaller town in Crete. Or—you could try to get out of the country right away on those passports. For that, you'd have to go back to Athens, you know, because no plane from here goes out of Greece. At least not at this time of year."

"Yes." Chester looked seriously down at the floor. He already had a drink in his hand. He felt his jaw with his fingertips.

"The beard will help," Rydal said. "Too bad a beard takes so long."

"Oh, mine won't take too long," Chester said, chuckling but not very mirthfully. "I'm one of those people has to shave twice a day."

"Good. In Athens, you might have the passport photo touched up with a beard. You can get that done through Niko."

"Yes, yes, I thought of that," said Chester.

"I detest beards," Colette said, coming towards Rydal with his drink. "Too bad, isn't it?"

Chester only glanced at her, evidently thinking of something else. "Well—"

Colette's fingers brushed the length of Rydal's hand after he had taken his glass. Rydal did not look at her.

"If I don't look too much like a tramp who needs a shave, we might catch that afternoon plane tomorrow back to Athens, eh, Colette? What do you think?"

Colette looked at him. She did not seem in a mood for thinking.

Rydal pushed his palm across his forehead. "I was considering that plane, too. I'd like to see Knossos tomorrow morning, then take the afternoon plane." His tone was dismissive, final, or at least he wanted it to be.

"Um-m. So was I thinking of Knossos tomorrow. It's only thirty or forty minutes from here by bus, according to the hotel. I asked about it a few minutes ago. We could go out there around ten, spend an hour or so—" Chester looked at his wife. "Does that appeal to you, honey?"

"What's Knossos? I've forgotten."

"Where the Labyrinth is," Rydal said. "It's the Palace of King Minos." He could have gone on. He still knew the rigmarole about the Palace of Knossos his father had made him learn when he was a kid. Rydal drank his ouzo.

"The Labyrinth? I thought that was a myth," Colette said, sitting on the edge of one of the twin beds. She swung her light Scotch highball in circles, making the ice click.

Rydal kept his mouth shut.

"No, this one's not a myth. The myth grew up around this particular palace," Chester told her. "You should read the guide book on it." Chester moved towards the bathroom. "Well, I'll put a shirt on." He went into the bathroom and closed the door.

Colette looked at Rydal, unsmiling now, yet it was an intimate, questioning look. What does she expect me to do, Rydal thought, steal a kiss while Chester's out of the room? He lit a cigarette. Colette walked to him and stood on tiptoe, and before Rydal could step back she caught his shoulder and kissed him, on the side of the mouth. Frowning, Rydal went to the mirror over the low chest of drawers. He bent close, wiping, but he didn't see any lipstick. He turned around.

"Don't do silly things like that," he said, frowning.

Colette opened her arms in a shrug. "I like you," she said in a high, barely audible voice, a voice like a little mouse's.

Chester came back, sliding his tie knot into place. He looked at himself in the mirror. "Sit down, Rydal. Say, you're about ready for another, aren't you?"

They decided to go for dinner to the place where they had spent most of last night, the big nightclub-restaurant by the sea. It was Colette's idea. She probably wanted to dance, Rydal thought.

The waiter recommended the shish-kebab, and they all ordered it. There was wine, more ouzo, and Scotch for Chester. Chester danced with Colette on the small, again remote dance floor, where hefty girls in low-cut peasant blouses danced with undernourished-looking young men in dark suits. Then Rydal danced with Colette, submitted to her close hold on the back of his neck, out of the range of Chester's eyes, and finally enjoyed her closeness, thinking that after tomorrow, by this time tomorrow night, he'd be free and on his own again. In the great city of Athens, he could disappear at once, rejoin his friends in the tavernas, go back to his old room at the Hotel Melchior Condylis, if he wished. The old Condylis suddenly had the attractions of home for Rydal. When the orchestra stopped, Rydal moved to leave the floor, but Colette kept hold of his hand.

"They're starting again. Look."

It was true. The clarinet was tootling a few practice notes, the bass viol tuning up. The orchestra was terrible. They danced through four more numbers, including a slurring, drunk-sounding "Mean to Me". A collision with one of the hefty girls' behinds could be quite jolting, Rydal discovered.

"Will I see you in Athens?" Colette breathed in his ear.

"Well—I expect to go back to the States in a couple of days."

Silence.

Rydal's eyes sought Chester's grey suit in the distance, and then he stopped dancing. "Come on. Let's go back."

"What's the matter?"

"Somebody's talking to Chester." Two men were talking to him, and, even from far away, Rydal had seen Chester's agitation. "Go slow. Take it easy." Rydal slowed his own walk.

One was a shirt-sleeved fellow of about thirty, a little the worse for drink, and the other a bigger, blondish man with a hanging underlip, better dressed and soberer. Chester managed a chuckle as Rydal and Colette came up.

"Don't know what they're trying to tell me," Chester said. "It's all Greek. Maybe you can figure it out."

"What do you want to say to him?" Rydal asked them pleasantly, sitting down as Colette did.

"This man," said the drunker fellow, pointing. "He looks like the guy Mac-Far-land," he said, accenting each syllable equally. "My friend thinks so, too. So we asked him his name."

"This is Bill," Rydal said, smiling, slapping Chester's shoulder, and pretending to be a little high himself. "Bill Chamberlain. His wife—Mary Ellen. How do you do? What's your name?"

The two strangers looked at each other. Then the drunker one stared at Colette, and said to his friend, "A blonde wife, too."

"A redhead," said the man with the hanging underlip.

The drunk fellow shrugged. His big hands were planted on the table.

"So what's your trouble?" asked Rydal.

"How come you speak Greek? You look American," said the fellow with his hands on the table.

Rydal was glad they were shifting the attack. "I've been living here a few months. I'm a student here."

"Here? In Crete?"

"Well, I happen to be in Crete now. At least I think so."

The two strangers murmured together, and Rydal couldn't hear what they said for the din of voices and music around them. Then the big fellow said, "Ask him, ask him."

"You got any identification, mister?" the shirt-sleeved man asked Chester.

"He wants to see identification," Rydal said to Chester, smiling indulgently, as if urging Chester to humor the intruders. "Got your passport? If they're so insistent, let them take a look."

"I've got it." Chester, with a bored glance at the two, pulled his passport from his inside pocket, opened it to his photograph, and held it out for them to see. The blondish fellow started to take it from Chester, and Chester pulled it back out of his reach. "My name," said Chester, pointing to the preceding page, where WILLIAM JAMES CHAMBERLAIN was written plain enough for them to see. Chester chuckled triumphantly.

The shirt-sleeved fellow nodded. "Okay." He gave a half salute, half wave, and withdrew.

His companion also walked off. "Watch out. You look like a killer," he said facetiously.

Chester, who couldn't have understood it, gave an appropriate "Hah!" Then he stared at the table, his shoulders hunched, as if he wanted to shrink to a point of invisibility. Beads of sweat stood on his forehead.

"You did that very well," said Rydal. He had glanced around. Fortunately, the conversation hadn't attracted any attention. It was an informal place with a good deal of circulation among tables.

"I need another drink," Chester said, and his voice shook.

"Sure. You deserve one," Rydal said cheerfully, but he could see Chester was really all gone. He clapped his hands for a waiter.

Colette's face looked worried.

"Everybody had better cheer up," Rydal said. "Those two might still be watching. I don't know where they are, but don't look around for them." Rydal said to the waiter, "Another Scotch. A double Scotch. Dewar's."

"It's all right, darling," Colette said when the waiter was gone. "There's nothing to worry about."

Rydal studied her through his cloud of cigarette smoke. Did she really care? Or was she only bolstering Chester, because she wanted to take care of her meal ticket? He'd probably never understand Colette. There wouldn't be enough time to understand her. She could probably like or love several people at once, he thought. A many-chambered heart. *I am the chambered naughty-lust . . .* Rydal wanted to hum a tune, but he didn't. He felt oddly cheerful. He looked at Chester.

Chester glanced at him, furtively. "Just think what might have happened, if you hadn't been here, been here to speak Greek to them."

"Nonsense," Rydal said. "The same thing would have happened. You knew they were asking your name, didn't you? You'd have shown them your passport."

Chester nodded. "Maybe." His Scotch was arriving. As soon as the waiter set it down, he picked it up and drank. His other hand was clenched on the edge of the table. "I'm inclined to agree with what you said earlier," Chester murmured to Rydal. "We ought to go to a smaller town than this. Just for a couple of days, I think. You know. . . till this beard grows out and I won't be in danger of . . . you know, people on the street like this." He gestured.

Rydal sighed, not knowing where to begin talking. Several things had entered his mind. "You don't happen to have any older clothes than the ones you're wearing, do you?"

"Older? Not with me," Chester said. "You're thinking I should assume a disguise?"

"No. But your clothes stand out in Greece. They look like money," he said bluntly. "That's what you ought to avoid, if you can. You, too." He looked at Colette. "Pack that mink stole up, for instance. Don't shine your shoes," he said to Chester. "Get different cufflinks. Put a couple of spots on your hat." Rydal picked up his ouzo and finished it. He felt like something out of a not very good movie.

"What other towns are there in Crete?" Chester asked. "I've seen the map, but I can't remember the other towns."

"There's Chania farther west. It's a port on the north shore like Iraklion. I don't remember any others. You wouldn't want to go to too small a place. You'd stand out there like a sore thumb."

They stayed in the restaurant past midnight. Chester became drunker, and, in a brooding way, more afraid. He rambled on vaguely about what might happen, and he told Rydal of how much he had "at stake" in his businesses in the United States. He bored Rydal. Colette tried to get him to dance, and Chester said heavily:

"Honey, there are times when a man has more important things on his mind than dancing. Dance with Rydal, if you've got to dance!" And his blue eyes flashed in his pink face.

Rydal danced with Colette, just to get away from Chester.

"What kind of things at stake?" Rydal asked Colette when they were on the dance floor, trapped in a swift waltz whose tempo Rydal wasn't skilful enough to cut in half.

"You know. His stocks," Colette said.

It was difficult to talk over the noise, but Rydal felt less bored talking. "I gather he doesn't use the name MacFarland in the States."

"Oh, no. Gosh, his real name was practically like another alias when we left," Colette said, glancing up at Rydal with a smile. She danced with enthusiasm, but she followed him perfectly.

"How many aliases has he?"

"Oh—Damn, I wish that ox would keep in his own lane!"

"Sorry. I'll try to watch out." A huge man and a small woman were describing erratic circles around them. Rydal had been trying to avoid him, but the man was like something caught in an orbit around him and Colette.

"They aren't exactly aliases. See, Chester doubles for several officials in his company. I should say companies. He signs his checks William S. Haight, for instance, for a couple of companies, as treasurer."

"And draws a salary for Haight, too, of course."

"Oh, two or three salaries." Colette laughed. "Maybe it's sort of illegal, what he does, but all his subscribers get dividends, and what more do they want?"

It was like a gigantic check-kiting system, Rydal supposed. Chester had to keep one jump ahead of himself all the time. Charles Ponzi had managed it for a long time, but not quite till the end of his life. "Doesn't Chester have partners who can carry on for him? Now, in the States, I mean?"

"Well—not partners. I guess you'd call them salesmen. Sure, he has four or five. One of Chester's stocks is quite good."

"What's that?"

"Universal Key. It's a magnetic key that opens a magnetic lock. It has to be exactly magnetized, you see. . . ." She broke off, still going strong, but plainly knowing no more about it.

"It's on the market?"

"The stock? No, not yet."

"I mean the magnetic key."

"No, it's being invented. I mean, it's been invented, natch, but it has to be . . . oh, I don't know, *made,* I guess."

"I see."

She danced closer, fairly dove against him. "I wish we could dance like this all night."

Rydal kissed her forehead. They were dancing so close, it was only a matter of turning his head slightly to kiss her.

"I love you," Colette said. "Do you mind?"

"No," Rydal said, and at that moment, he didn't. Rydal opened his eyes and saw Chester at a table only ten feet away, staring at him, and was so startled he jumped and pulled a little away from Colette.

"What's the matter?" Colette asked, looking up at him.

"Chester . . . Chester's watching us. He's moved to a closer table."

Now Colette saw him too, smiled and gave him a wave with her right hand—whose fingers were still locked in Rydal's. "Looks furious, doesn't he? He's had a rough night."

"All right, let's sit down, and you dance with him for a change." The number was coming to an end. Rydal broke from her, and motioned for her to go ahead of him towards the new table.

Chester had his drink with him, or a fresh one. Their overcoats had been checked. There was no doubt about it, Chester was jealous, and furious. But he forced a smile and said with elaborate casualness, "Thought I'd move. Those two back there were still staring at me."

"Oh," Rydal said, sitting down after Colette did. "Maybe you'd like to take off. Soon. It's getting on to one."

"No. I thought I might have a dance with my wife," said Chester, starting to rise. His face seemed twice as flushed suddenly. He held his hand out for Colette in a way that brooked no refusal. They went off to the dance floor together.

Rydal smiled a little at himself, at his rise of emotion—sudden fear, guilt—on the dance floor when he'd seen Chester looking at him. Colette should be the one to feel some guilt, but she had been cool as a cucumber. But of course he *had* kissed Colette's forehead, and Chester *had* seen it. Rydal lit a cigarette with a casual air and pretended to be looking over the whole crowd, though his eyes moved again and again to Chester and Colette, Chester was talking to her, talking forcefully, and Rydal could imagine what he was saying. It probably wasn't the first time such a thing had happened.

Chester came back with Colette, ordered another drink and asked Rydal what he would like. Rydal did not care for anything more, but he ordered a FIX beer.

"You don't want it, I can tell," Colette said. "Want to divide it with me? I'd like a glass."

Rydal nodded. "Bring two glasses, please," he said to the waiter.

Chester was serious and quiet now, unresponding to Colette's remark on the endurance of certain Greek couples who had not missed a dance since they arrived. At last, at 1:35, they left the place and took a taxi to the hotel. Chester was a bit unsteady on his feet.

"Oh . . . uh . . . Rydal. Mind if I come in and have a word with you?" Chester asked when they were about to say good night in the hall.

"Not at all," said Rydal, but Chester's phrase and even his manner had been so like his own father, that Rydal's blood had run cold for an instant. It was the phrase his father had used when he had spoken to him about Agnes, that fulminating speech which had only been exceeded in its heat by the speech his father had delivered to the judge recommending reform school for him. *I'd like a word with you in my study.* The irony of it, Rydal thought. He was going to be chastised about Agnes for the second time.

They went into Rydal's room and closed the door.

Chester seemed to be having a hard time getting started. He declined to sit down. He stood staring at the floor, frowning, and swaying slightly.

"Hm-m. Well . . . you probably know what I'm going to say," Chester began, still not looking at Rydal.

Rydal had hung up his overcoat. He sat down on a straight chair and looked at Chester attentively.

Then Chester lifted his pinkish eyes from the floor to him. "I'm going to need you . . . when I go to that small town. Oh, no, wait a minute," he interrupted when Rydal started to protest. "You know the language, you know the ropes, it'll be easier. And safer. And I'm also prepared to pay you for it. I want to pay you."

"But I don't need the money. And frankly—I'm not very comfortable in this role."

"Who is? I know you're not. That's why I want to make it worth your while. You'll be helping me and . . ." He paused, lost, as if the image of Colette and his irritation with Rydal's attraction to her had swum into his mind, obliterating what he meant to say. "I'll feel . . . more at ease," Chester went on solemnly. "I speak for myself and I know. If someone's saying something about me, right over my shoulder, I want to know what it is. The news in English here is a day late, and that's dangerous. I'm prepared to give you five thousand dollars, if you stay with us—say, three days. At least till this beard grows out more. What about it? You've been . . . you've been great up to now . . ."

Rydal thought, until tonight? He leaned forward on his knees, squeezing his palms together. "For less than five thousand dollars," Rydal said, "you can get yourself an artificial beard till yours grows out."

"Oh, you know it's not just that. I want you to stay with me," he said, low and passionately. "Name your own price."

His emotion wasn't only from fear, Rydal thought. It was hurting his pride to beg him to stay on, when he'd been furious enough to punch him in the nose tonight. Five thousand dollars. For three days. For risking a police rap himself for collusion, if a police officer picked them up in Chania. Five thousand dollars would be a nice nest egg to have in the bank, when he got back to the United States. Or was he weakening because he wanted to stay on where Colette was?

"Well?"

"Five thousand is plenty," Rydal said. He could see that Chester saw he was weakening. Chester was no doubt good at seeing signs of weakening.

"Then it's a deal? We'll leave tomorrow morning?"

Rydal nodded. "All right. It's a deal." He stood up, avoiding looking at Chester.

Chester walked to the door, turned, and Rydal heard his heavy sigh. "Well, I guess it's time we turned in."

They said good night.

Colette's name hadn't even been mentioned, Rydal realized. Yes, it had been a pleasanter interview than the one in his father's study ten years ago.

8

For all he had drunk, Chester slept badly that night. He had gone to sleep almost as soon as he had hit the pillow, but an hour later—he could see the radium dial of Colette's travelling-clock—he woke up again, his heart pounding, the tingling emptiness of hangover beginning to creep through him. He remembered swearing to himself tonight, as he sat watching Rydal and Colette dance—*dance?*—that he would make love to her when they got back to the hotel, but tonight it hadn't been in him, and he hadn't even begun. Chester cursed his fate. To be tied up with someone like Rydal Keener, just the age and the type Colette liked, to be dependent on him, to have to ask him to stick with him and stick by him!

Still, Chester supposed, it could have been worse. Rydal could have been a crummier type, a type who'd really take advantage of Colette and of him, too, financially. Rydal was a gentleman, really. Yet gentlemen went to bed with women, too, of course. And unfortunately Rydal had just the kind of "good manners" Colette admired, that air of restraint, gentleness, gentility, even if it was a little threadbare. Chester set his teeth. Three days. He supposed tomorrow or the next day Rydal would be wearing something Colette had picked and bought for him, a new shirt, a sweater, a tie. She liked buying things for men she liked. That Hank Meyers in New York who'd tagged around with Jesse for a while. She had bought Hank a wristwatch. Jesse had told Chester about it. Chester had ordered Jesse to get rid of Hank, and he had. Hank was a good-looking kid, about twenty-five, too. But Colette hadn't been to bed with him, Chester was sure. He'd had a real showdown with Colette about Hank, shook her till her teeth rattled and she'd been too scared to tell him anything but the truth, and she said she hadn't slept with him. Colette had cried for a whole day after that talking-to, and she had carried bruises on her arms for two weeks where Chester had held her, but it was all for the good, he thought. A woman liked to feel that a man cared what she did, that a man would beat the hell out of her if she got out of line. Yes, women liked that, and it did them good, and it did a man good, too. That was Chester's philosophy.

The next thing Chester knew, Colette was kissing his forehead, wakening him. She was standing by his bed in her robe. There was sunlight in the room. On Colette's bed was a large tray with two breakfasts on it.

"Ordered a couple of soft-boiled eggs for you this morning," Colette said, smiling. "I thought you could use them. Go brush your teeth and hurry back."

"Great. I sure could." Chester got out of bed and went on bare feet to the bathroom.

After breakfast, Chester called Rydal's room. It was 8:35. Rydal had already inquired about the buses, and there was one leaving at 10:30 bound west. Rydal was brief, and Chester sensed that he was guarding against possible eavesdropping by the hotel switchboard.

"Why don't you come in for a minute," Chester said.

Rydal said he would.

There was a knock on the door a few seconds later.

Colette was dressing in the bathroom.

Rydal had the papers, but he said there was no news at all in them this morning.

Chester smiled. That helped a lot. "No news is good news."

"I think I should leave first," Rydal said. "I'm packed, so I'll take off in a few minutes and meet you at the bus station. It's a square up the street and to the left, not far from that restaurant by the fountain. You can ask the hotel where the buses for Knossos take off from, because it's from the same square, I know. I talked to someone on the street this morning about it."

"Good boy," said Chester.

"I'll be there at ten thirty," Rydal said as he walked to the door.

"Right-o."

"Tell your wife to dress simply—if she can," Rydal said, and went out.

Chester and Colette left the hotel at 10 in a taxi. The square was a grassless area of ground, bordered by a few benches on which people sat with bundles and knapsacks and cardboard suitcases, waiting. The two or three buses that were parked there had no markers on them. Chester saw Rydal standing with a newspaper several yards away, and Rydal pointed to the bus nearest him, then came forward and helped Chester with his luggage. They had already dismissed the taxi-driver. The bus-driver was very nice, and got out and loaded the luggage on the top of the bus for them.

People straggled or ran to board the bus until the last minute—which was a couple of minutes past 11. They lurched off, Chester and Colette sitting midway in the bus, Rydal at the back in a row of five or six men who sat with bundles on their laps and between their feet.

The bus bumped over stretches of bad road, then sped ahead at terrifying speed, and stopped now and then to let people off in the middle of nowhere. The sun came and went, changing the blue of the sky from bright to dark and back again. Tall farmers in boots, with embroidered knapsacks over their shoulders, paused at the roadside to look at the bus and sometimes to wave. Chester held Colette's hand between them on the seat. She was looking out the window, taking a lively interest in the scenery, commenting on a snow-capped mountain on the horizon, or a string of baby goats trotting along behind a farmer. Chester hadn't mentioned to her that he had offered Rydal five thousand dollars to stay another three days with them. It was a little strange, he thought, that Colette hadn't asked him how long Rydal was going to be with them. She was taking it for granted, Chester supposed, that Rydal was going to stay with them, because she liked Rydal, and because she had probably asked him to stay on. Chester intended to tell her of his arrangement with Rydal as soon as they had a moment alone, and he was sorry he hadn't this morning when they were having breakfast. If Colette knew Rydal was being paid for it, she wouldn't toy with the idea that his staying on was entirely due to her. He was of half a mind to tell her now, on the bus, among people who wouldn't understand a word of what he was saying, anyway, but he preferred to do it tonight, when they were in some hotel room. He'd say it in a firm, businesslike way, because it was business. By Sunday, Rydal's services would be over, and on Monday, or even Sunday night, he could disappear. The hum of the bus began to make Chester sleepy, but when he closed his eyes, his drowsy mind drifted back to that kiss he had seen last night when Colette and Rydal were dancing. Rydal's lips against her forehead, and his eyes closed—and the sudden fear on Rydal's face when he had opened his eyes and seen him looking at them. And then later in Rydal's room, when he had said, "You probably know what I'm going to say—" Yes, Rydal had braced himself for some strong words then, maybe a flat "Get the hell out of here!" and then he had offered Rydal money to stay on. Chester recrossed his legs restlessly and lit a cigarette. He wished he had taken the trouble to dash a note, or rather send a cable, to Jesse in New York, asking him to write or rewrite the latest news to William J. Chamberlain care of the American Express in Athens. But he hadn't.

They came to a town called Rethymnon, where there was a fifteen-minute stop. Fruit vendors and soda-pop wagons. Nearly all the passengers who were going on got out to stretch their legs. Rydal had got out before him and Colette, and was buying something from one of the peddlers.

"Like a coffee, my dear?" Chester asked Colette.

She held her topcoat around her. The wind was sharp. She had packed her mink jacket into one of the suitcases, as Chester had suggested this morning, but her high-heeled shoes still made her look very chic. Well, she was chic, Chester thought, and he was glad of it. She'd look chic in a house dress and flat shoes.

"Coffee?" he repeated. Then he realized she was looking at Rydal, not staring at him, but more aware of Rydal than of him.

"Yes, thanks. If it's hot."

Chester went off to buy two cups. Rydal was standing by the vendor, with his cup and a small bun with a sausage in it.

"May as well buy something to eat," Rydal said. "I don't think this bus is going to stop for lunch anywhere."

"No? That's too bad." It was already 1:30. Chester bought two of the more palatable-looking buns from the vendor's basket.

Colette came up to join them. "Six hours this trip takes?" she asked.

Chester had guessed six hours in Iraklion.

"We should be in Chania a little after three," Rydal told her. "It's a hundred and twenty miles from Iraklion or something like that."

Chester had no appetite for his sweet roll. The Greek passengers, he noticed, had brought substantial sandwiches with them. He nodded towards the newspaper under Rydal's arm. "You're sure there's no news this morning," Chester said quietly.

"I looked through it twice in my room," Rydal said.

Rydal was not looking at Colette at all, Chester noticed. He was acting as if she didn't exist. Chester didn't care for that, either.

"Well, look at our driver," Colette said. "I suppose he's had himself a meal."

The bus-driver was coming out of a small restaurant near-by, lighting a cigarette.

"You can't ever tell," Rydal said, still not looking at Colette. "They tell you it's a fifteen-minute stop, and it's liable to be thirty-five."

But the bus-driver got back in his seat immediately, and the passengers followed suit. They were off again.

Chania, at 3:30, presented a town square sprinkled with idle men, centered with a cement memorial statue of some sort, and ringed around with various shops and restaurants. It had a backwater, fifty-years-behind-the-times look of certain towns Chester had seen in the United States, an atmosphere that inspired him to wonder how the inhabitants could possibly make a living. Consequently Chania appeared a little sad. It was not nearly as big as Chester had expected. A couple of bellboys in shabbier uniforms than those of Iraklion came up at the sight of their luggage, and hawked their hotels. Rydal said something to them. Both the boys began shouting, evidently each claiming the hotel with the hottest water or the most heat.

"Warter—*'ot,*" said one boy to Chester, poking himself.

Chester left it to Rydal. Rydal chose the other boy. But both boys began picking up their luggage.

"I offered the other boy twenty drachs if he helps us with the suitcases," Rydal said to Chester. "He says the hotel's just around the corner."

It was the Hotel Nikë, on a paper-littered street barely wide enough for two cars to pass in. The street and the buildings were a light tan, a color Chester associated with Athens also, only here one had the feeling the color had been made by dust and sand blown by the wind into the stone of the houses. Rydal spoke to the pleasant, moustached fellow behind the desk, who attempted English at first, then switched to Greek.

"It's certainly cheap," Rydal said when he came back to them. "I asked for a good room with bath for you, so we'll see what happens. You can give them your passports and sign."

Chester gave his and Colette's passports to the clerk, then signed W. J. Chamberlain. He had meant to sign hastily and casually, but he couldn't, not yet, and make it look anything like the passport signature. Colette, he thought, did better with her Mary Ellen Chamberlain, which she had practiced several times in the Hotel Astir. The clerk copied their passport numbers beside their names. Then he handed the passports back, and Chester put them into his breast pocket.

Chester's and Colette's room was so stark it was amusing. A double bed, a table, a chair, and that was it. No waste-paper-basket and only one ashtray the size of a pin tray. It was also cold. The bellboy went over and turned the wheel on a radiator with a triumphant air, said something to them, then waited for his tip. Chester paid him.

"I think this is very exciting," Colette said. "It's like camping or something."

"Um-m. Want to wash up first?"

Colette did.

Chester felt the radiator, which as yet showed no sign of losing its coldness. He had a vision of its being cold tonight also, and Colette staying up all night dancing somewhere with Rydal, instead of trying to sleep. Colette's energy was astounding to Chester—ice-skating all afternoon in Radio City or riding in Central Park, then dancing till dawn at a party, for instance. The energy of youth, of course. He simply couldn't keep up with it. His legs wouldn't hold out. Well, it hadn't come to that yet, and if the room didn't get warm in a couple of hours, he'd change the room or change the hotel.

"I'll be in Rydal's room," Colette said as she came out of the bathroom, rubbing lotion on her hands.

They were all going out to have a late lunch in a few minutes. Chester only nodded to her. He washed up, had a Scotch, hung up a suit from his suitcase, then went down the hall to number 18, which Rydal said he had been given. The door was slightly ajar, but he meticulously knocked, holding the knob so the door wouldn't swing open. He heard Colette's and Rydal's voice, and heard Colette laugh.

"Come in," Rydal called. "We're comparing notes on our rooms. How do you like that tub?" He nodded towards the bathroom.

Chester went to take a look. The hot-water tank projected over the front half of the tub, leaving hardly any room to sit in it. Chester came back smiling. "And how's your heat?"

"Coming along, I think," Rydal said. He put on his jacket.

Chester wandered over and put a hand down on Rydal's radiator. Definitely on the way to being warm. Rydal's suitcase was open on a chair. Its lining was worn and coming unglued at an upper corner. Chester saw a sweater, a shirt, a rolled pair of pajamas with a pair of shoes inside them.

"I'm starving," Colette said.

"Well," Rydal said, "let's go out on the town."

They lunched in a tile-floored restaurant on the square. Bunches of bananas hung down from the ceiling on black chains, with big black hooks stuck through their stems. The portions of their lamb and rice orders were small but adequate, the red wine was drinkable, and Chester felt much better after the meal.

"What's there to do in this town?" Colette asked.

"I really don't know," Rydal said. "But it is a port. We might take a look at the water."

"I've got to buy stockings," Colette said. "I left two pairs drying on the back of the john door in Iraklion, damn it. I'd like to get some before the shops close this afternoon."

"Oh, that should be easy," Rydal said. "I imagine these shops stay open till seven."

They strolled in the direction of the sea, which was visible down the street from the main square. The town seemed to offer nothing in the way of beauty. The shops were tiny and poor-looking, there was nothing like a museum or a government building in view. The port was a long curve with a wide wharf going out into the water. The only boats in the harbor were two old tankers.

"Must be a slack season here," Chester remarked. Colette was holding his arm. He put his hand over hers.

After ten minutes or so, they turned back in the direction of the main part of town to look for a shop that sold stockings. There were shoe shops, women's lingerie shops of a simple sort with cotton stockings, but no nylons. Rydal pointed out to Colette a cellar tavern with a billboard in front of it showing a buxom woman in a peasant blouse, her mouth open, singing.

"I suppose this is the town hotspot," Rydal said. "Dancing nightly, it says."

Colette bent to look down the narrow stairs which ended at a red door. "How exciting. Why don't we give it a whirl tonight?" She looked at Chester.

Chester saw, or imagined he saw, a taunting in the look: come or not, I'm going. But Colette looked away, and he wasn't sure. The place looked miserable to Chester, and semi-peasant dancing wasn't the kind of folklore he was interested in. The gaudy, baubled woman in the photograph looked Turkish or Romany or worse. But he'd go, of course. He foresaw it.

It was Rydal who spotted a stocking shop across a street, Rydal who negotiated for Colette and got the right size.

"What's the word for stockings?" Chester asked him, and Rydal told him. But a minute later the word had gone out of Chester's head.

Then back to the hotel for a rest before the evening began. Rydal was to give them a ring around seven, by which time he said he would have bought what evening papers he could find. Chester lay down beside Colette, who was reading on the bed in her dressing-gown. She was reading one of the pocketbook novels they had bought in Athens. Chester put his arm across her waist, but she soon extricated herself and got up.

"I'm sorry you don't like beards, honey," Chester said, "but just now I don't know what I can do about it. It won't be for long."

"It's not the beard," Colette said with her back to him. "I was just about to do my nails." She turned around with her box of nail polish in her hands.

She came back and sat on the bed, propped up against a pillow, and Chester fell asleep while she was putting on the polish. When he woke up, it was ten minutes to seven by Colette's clock on the bed table, and he thought at once of Rydal's promised call. If Rydal had found anything important in the paper, Chester thought—such as that Chester MacFarland was believed to have left Iraklion this morning—he would have called by now. Then a thought, or rather a disturbing question, occurred to Chester: what kind of a young man would aid and abet a man he knew to be wanted by the police, a man he knew had killed someone, even if it was by accident? The answer was a crook, of course, a young man who expected to play the blackmail game slowly and carefully and for a long time. Chester had thought of it before, but somehow now, after the nap, it hit him with a new freshness. The worst was yet to come. Chester shivered. He was cold. The room was cold.

"Chilly, darling?" Colette was reading beside him.

"Yes. It's cold, isn't it?"

"The radiator's doing better. I just felt it."

Chester got up and poured himself a Scotch. He saw Colette glance at him for drinking it, but she didn't say anything. Well, he was stuck with Rydal Keener for the next few days. He thought he would ask Rydal a little more about himself, his schooling, his ambitions, if any, and he could tell a lot about what he was in for by what Rydal told him.

The telephone rang.

Rydal reported no news in the local Chania paper. "I thought you and your wife might like to have dinner by yourselves tonight," Rydal said.

But Chester's mind was on questioning Rydal a bit. "Not particularly, unless you'd like to be alone," Chester said.

"He's not coming with us?" Colette asked, reaching a hand up for the telephone. "Let me speak to him."

Grimly, without a word to Rydal, Chester passed the telephone to her.

"Hello, Rydal. What's this about being alone? . . . Of course not, don't be silly. . . . Nonsense, knock on the door around eight and come in for a Scotch. . . . Oh, that sounds interesting. Fine, I'll tell Chester. . . . Okay, see you." She hung up and said, "Rydal found out that nightclub we saw serves dinner, so why don't we eat there?"

As Chester had foreseen, Rydal and Colette were dancing at midnight, he himself was beginning to feel tired, and he had found out very little more about Rydal Keener. He had gone to Yale and taken a law degree, he said, and then he had done his army service. The two years he had spent in Europe were a present from his grandmother, who had left him ten thousand dollars when she died. Chester believed him about the grandmother, but he was not sure about the law degree, or Yale. Chester had only a superficial knowledge of the Yale campus in New Haven, from one visit. He had gone to Harvard for two years. Chester had no questions he could ask Rydal that would prove he had gone to Yale or not. At any rate, Rydal Keener had never worked, and that was a bad sign. Chester looked every few minutes at Rydal and at Colette in her bright-blue dress, dancing on the small floor. The place was dimly lit. Rydal and Colette stood out, because everybody else was dancing faster than they. Chester ordered his fourth Scotch. When Colette and Rydal returned to the table, Chester said:

"What do you say we take off? We've had a long day."

"Oh, darling! At twelve thirty they're having another floor show. A different one. Can't you wait that long?" She sat down.

Chester sat down, knowing he would wait that long.

Rydal continued a conversation he had evidently been having with her on the dance floor, about Greek tavern music and dances, and why men sometimes danced with men. Chester had heard about that. Some shyness between the sexes, perhaps. There were two men couples dancing here, not touching each other, dancing very lively steps. It was not very interesting. But Colette was listening to Rydal as if fascinated.

"That's mentioned in our *Guide Bleu,"* Chester put in.

But it made no stir in their conversation, because Rydal was talking about something else now. Lace blouses, something like that. He was so full of information, Chester wondered if it were not all made up.

"Have a drink?" Chester asked Rydal when his Scotch arrived.

Rydal looked at Colette. "A drink?"

"No. Oh, maybe I'll have a beer," she said.

Both she and Rydal ordered beer.

The floor show at last arrived. It consisted mostly of patter and jokes, judging from the laughter, and Chester understood not a word of it. He was terribly tired of sitting, sitting on the bus all day, and now this. At last the floor show was over, and though he had meant to ask Colette to dance—they had danced only once all evening—he was just tired and stubborn enough not to ask her to dance now, and to show by his sullenness his displeasure with Rydal and his boredom with the whole evening.

"How about it? Shall we take off?" Chester said to his wife.

"One more, darling, and I *promise* you," Colette said, standing up.

She was asking Rydal to dance, Chester saw. Rydal hadn't said a word to her or made a sign. He watched them go off with a deliberately indignant expression on his face, which, however, neither of them looked back to see. Chester brooded over his drink. He thought of the letters waiting for him in Athens. There were bound to be letters. He was expecting reports from his man in Dallas, who was also an accountant, on Unimex's current situation. Was it being investigated? Then there was Jesse in New York, Jesse who knew his real name, Chester MacFarland. Jesse might have seen it in the papers by now, if it was in the papers. Jesse might panic, if he didn't get a reply to some letter he'd sent to Athens. What were the papers in New York saying about him? That was what mattered. In Iraklion, even a Paris *Herald Tribune* was unobtainable.

The music was now soft and slow, nothing but a violin and an accordion, playing as if they played for Colette and Rydal alone, and Chester saw to his annoyance that they really were the only couple on the floor now. Chester set his teeth and reconciled himself to the possibility that the music might go on for another fifteen minutes. The musicians were looking dreamily at Colette and Rydal, or so Chester thought. Chester went to the men's room.

When he came back, Colette and Rydal were sitting at the table talking, and the music had stopped.

"Shall we go, darling?" Colette asked him.

"If you're ready," Chester said with a taut smile.

He and Rydal divided the bill and the tip, which Rydal said should be about a hundred, and Chester casually added another fifty to his share. They walked back to the Hotel Nikë, disturbed a snoozing bellboy to take them up in the elevator, and said good night to Rydal in the hall.

"Good night. Pleasant dreams," said Rydal, waving a hand as he walked away.

Chester thought his smile cocky.

In their room, Chester removed his jacket, and drew a glass of cold water from the tap. He would have preferred a nightcap of his own Scotch, but he thought with a glass of water he would make a soberer impression on Colette when he spoke to her.

"You didn't have much fun, did you, darling?" she asked, hanging up the blue dress she had just pulled over her head.

"I don't think it's very wise of you to get chummy with a blackmailer," Chester said quietly.

"A blackmailer?" She turned her innocent, lavender eyes on him.

"A potential blackmailer." He moved closer to her, and spoke as softly as if Rydal were trying to listen at the door, and it occurred to Chester that he might be. "Last night in Iraklion, I offered him five thousand dollars to stay with us three days." Chester sipped his water, looking hard at Colette. "He accepted it, you can be sure."

"Well—he didn't ask you for it, it seems." She hung up her dress and walked towards the bathroom. "You offered it."

Chester was momentarily distracted by her black panties and her bare back with the black strap of her bra crossing it. "I can't talk to you if you go into the john," he said with annoyance, but still softly.

"I'm only getting my dressing-gown. Goodness, what's all the excitement about?" She came back, tying the belt of her dressing-gown.

"Just this. I don't know what you're saying to him, but . . . he already knows enough. After Sunday night, he's leaving. After Sunday night . . . I'll feel a little more secure. I'll feel quite secure when I see the last of him." He nodded in the direction of Rydal's room.

Colette said nothing, only lifted her eyebrows. She sat down on the edge of the bed, picked up a nail file from the night table and began filing away at a nail, waiting for more from him.

"He's plainly getting chummy with you. I don't like it, and I want you to watch what you say to him. You understand, Colette, don't you?"

"Um-hm," she said coolly. "I don't understand why you're so upset, though." She went on filing, staring at her nail.

"It's quite simple," Chester said, moving closer to her. "I'm not sure I can get rid of him Sunday night. If he chooses to stay on, ask for more money, what in hell could I—"

"He hasn't asked you for *any* yet."

"Why're you defending him? He's already taking advantage of the situation by smooching with you every night!"

"Chester, don't be silly! Smooching!"

Chester snorted, went to his Scotch bottle and poured a little into his glass that had some water in it. "What I'd like to know, so I'll know my own position, is what you've told him already."

"About what?"

"About my affairs. About us. About anything."

"Darling, you're getting red in the face, and I think you've had enough Scotch. I haven't told him anything," she said positively. "I bet not as much as you've told him after a few drinks. Matter of fact, tonight he did most of the talking. He was telling me about a girl he'd been in love with at fifteen."

"At fifteen?" Chester frowned.

"Yes. She was fifteen, too. His cousin. Agnes. She was visiting in his family's house over Easter holidays, and they had an affair together for about ten days, and his mother and father found out about it and had Rydal thrown out."

"Hm-m," said Chester, only mildly interested. "Thrown out? Disowned? And that's how he got through Yale?"

"No, he wasn't thrown out right away. He was severely reproached by his father. He was accused of seducing the girl, though Rydal said it was a mutual thing. The point was, the girl came to his mother, after the family found out, and said Rydal had seduced her and she was trying to get away from him and all that, and she asked Rydal's parents to keep him away from her. Isn't that awful? And Rydal had thought they were both in love and they'd been planning to get married as soon as they got of age. I mean, it's an awful betrayal for a boy of fifteen, don't you think?"

"I don't know." Chester lit a cigarette.

"Well, I think so. It nearly wrecked Rydal. He robbed a grocery store just after that, and then his father really cracked down on him and managed to put him into reform school."

"He must've learned a lot of useful things there."

"Why're you so cynical? No, he hated it. He was there two years. Can you imagine, the son of a Harvard professor?"

"Is that what he says he is?"

"Yes," Colette said firmly. "Then, after the two years, his grandmother helped him to get through college, because she still believed in him, you see, and his father—well, he said his father contributed a little bit, but they never were really reconciled again. Agnes, he said, got married at seventeen. A shotgun wedding in her home town. Great Barrington."

Chester sank into an armchair. "Well. You seem to've heard a real saga tonight. All this on that noisy dance floor?"

"Well, just in snatches. Rydal told it to me in less words than I'm using, probably. But it's the *meaning* of it you don't seem to grasp. How a young man—a boy can have all that happen to him and still come out decent, I think that's something. Still finish law school at Yale, for instance, that's something, isn't it?"

Chester could see that Rydal had totally won her over. It was even worse than he'd thought, though rather amusing, he supposed. "And how do you know every damned thing he says isn't a lie?"

Colette put the nail file back on the night table, and looked directly at Chester. "Because of the way he says it. Said it."

"Hm-m. It doesn't sound like a true story to me. And what brought it on, I'd like to know?"

"He said—Oh, you're not going to understand, and you're just going to get mad." She got up, turned her back to him, and began to unfasten her stockings.

"What brought it on?" Chester asked slowly, braced.

"He said I reminded him of Agnes. Not the way I look, but something about my personality. Build."

"Build? Hm-m. He knows a lot about your build?—Well, I suppose he does. He dances pretty close, doesn't he?" Chester stood up suddenly, wanting to hit something, tear something, anything, but he only flailed a fist through empty air. Colette saw it.

"Calm down, darling, please. And go to bed," she said gently.

"I don't want you to have another dance with him, do you understand? Not one more dance." Chester pointed a finger at her.

She looked back at him, blank and calm. "I think that's absurd."

Chester saw in a flash that they could both blackmail him. Both. Colette trailing along in Rydal's lead, Rydal having his money and his wife, too. "It is not absurd, and I have a moral right not to have to . . . not to have to watch my wife being mauled and fingered and even kissed every night by some gigolo we had the bad luck to pick up."

"*We* picked up?" Her eyes flashed as she lifted her head. "And who're you to talk about moral right? You who killed a man," she said softly, coming towards him. "You can kill a man and think nothing of it, and you're trying to lay down the law to me about *dancing*?"

Chester had never heard her talk back before, and he was so astounded he couldn't say anything for a moment. He realized his hand with the glass was shaking. "So, he's been talking to you—talking to you a lot, hasn't he?"

"What do you mean?" she asked, still aggressive, frowning.

"He's got you on a line of reasoning there that isn't yours. He's trying his best, isn't he?"

"I think you're insanely jealous. Or maybe just insane."

"I know when you're quoting someone else and when you're thinking for yourself," Chester came back.

"I don't want to be challenged on my morals by a murderer," Colette said. "I don't like being married to a murderer, if you want to know the truth."

"Don't use that word, because you know damned well that guy's death was an accident."

"It's still a death, and it's horrible!"

"There're more horrible things!"

"What, for instance?"

This, Chester realized, was Colette being herself, not playing dumb, or innocent, or pliable, nor using any feminine wiles to make him feel more of a man. He might as well be up against another man. No, he thought, that wasn't true. Chester swallowed, with difficulty. "Just what're you getting at?" he asked in a deep voice.

"I'm getting at that I don't like taking orders from you anymore. Orders like this."

"Are you in love with that jerk?" Chester asked.

"I don't know."

"Don't *know*?" Chester felt a silent cannonball explode in him. It left him empty. "What . . . what kind of an answer's that? Because if you are, we're getting out of here right now, you understand? Right now. Tonight!" His voice became a loud growl.

He saw that he had frightened her. It appeased him a little.

"I am not in love with him," she said quietly. "And if you don't tone your voice down, we'll get thrown out of the hotel tonight."

He lit a cigarette and flung the match in the direction of the tray on the night table. "That's better," he said.

She turned as if the words made her angry all over again. "Why? I still haven't promised you anything. I still don't care to take orders from a—" She stopped, tears starting in her voice. Then she controlled herself. "I think he's a nice young man. I don't want to hear him called a this and a that that he's not. I like him. And he likes me." Her look at him was like a challenge.

But Chester was spent. He was suddenly tired enough to have dropped on the floor by the bed. He put on a frown, sat down heavily on the bed, and started removing his shoes. No more tonight, he thought. Tomorrow was another day. He loved Colette, and he was going to hang on to her. He was married to her. Marriage was nine points—Marriage was *ten* points, God damn it!

9

On Saturday morning, Rydal slept until nearly 10, and got out of bed in a hurry when he saw the time, thinking that he should have gone downstairs hours ago for the newspapers, if he meant to be worthy of his five thousand dollars. Then he smiled and rubbed the back of his neck. Chester was probably snoozing in his room down the hall, so why rush out to buy a paper that would probably say the police had not picked up any trail as yet? Rydal indulged himself in a bath and a careful shave before he went downstairs. The paper of Chania, a slim, four-sheet affair, reported what Rydal had expected, absolutely nothing. Rydal asked and was told that the Iraklion and Athens papers would be on sale that evening. Rydal walked into a café and had a cup of coffee. It was a dull town, Chania, but Rydal rather liked dull towns, because they forced one to look at things—for want of anything else to do—that one might not otherwise notice. Like the number of flowerpots on window-sills as compared with the number in Athens or in other small towns he had been in on the main land; the number of cripples on the street; the quality of building materials used in the houses; the variety or lack of variety of the foodstuffs in the market. The public market looked a bit impoverished, like the rest of the town. Perhaps he could interest Colette and Chester in exploring it today.

Rydal went back to his room to make his report on the newspapers. Colette answered the telephone. "Good morning. Nothing in the paper today—I should say this morning."

"Oh. I'll tell him. That's good, isn't it?" She sounded wide awake.

"I suppose that's good," Rydal said.

"Listen, uh—Chester wants to stay in for a while and I felt like taking a walk. Do you?"

She had lowered her voice, and Rydal thought Chester was probably in the bathroom just now. "I have to write a letter," Rydal said. "But it'll take only about twenty minutes. Shall I meet you downstairs—around eleven thirty?"

"I'll knock on your door. Bye-bye," she said, and quickly hung up.

Rydal shook his head, took off his overcoat, and got out the limp tablet of white paper that he carried at the bottom of his suitcase. Since yesterday when they had arrived in Chania, Rydal had had an impulse to write his brother Kennie. He thought he should seize the inspiration while it was still seizable. Tomorrow it might be gone. He had not written to his brother in months, he didn't know how many months, but not since long before his father died. And Kennie, no doubt a bit disapproving because Rydal had not come to their father's funeral, had not written to him.

Chania, Crete
Sat. January 13, 19—

Dear Kennie,

How goes it? I am in the oddest of places—places to be in Greece, that is. A rather uneventful Cretan port. Perhaps it does more business in the summer. I won't be here long, however, and my address remains American Express, Athens. I have written to Martha, as she may have told you. How are you? And Lola and the kids?

I have had a strange experience recently. In fact, it is still going on. Someday I'll tell you all about it, but I can't now. It has to do with a fortyish American I've encountered, who is a dead ringer for Papa at forty (I barely remember him then, but I've seen plenty of pictures). This man is in all other respects Papa's exact opposite, though. Knowing him, being with him for a time, has had the oddest effect on me. (Pardon the many odds and pardon the apparent lightness of the tone of this letter. I feel happy this morning. But it's not the same as feeling flip, which I don't about this.)

You know, I never felt Papa was really a man. Of flesh and blood. To us kids (me at least) he was a nearly godlike figure we saw at dinnertime, when we talked some other language from what we'd been talking, at least outside the house. I never saw him make a gesture of affection to Mother, though I remember you once saying to me that you had. At any rate, knowing this particular American, who must for certain reasons be nameless here, has made me somehow see Papa better, see him more really. It is very hard to explain—especially since, as I've implied, this man is quite far from a pillar of virtue and I've yet to see anything in his character (apart from generosity with money) that might be called commendable. So much the better for my purposes. I use purposes purposely. I am using this man for my own inner purposes. He is helping me to see Papa a little better, maybe to see Papa with less resentment, more humor; I don't know, but God knows I would like to get rid of resentments. I am older now. That's what matters, of course. By an odd coincidence, his wife, much younger and quite attractive and vivacious, reminds me of—that unhappy mistake of my youth. A psychological purge by some sort of re-enactment that I don't even understand yet is going on in me—and I am sure it is all for the good. You were always sympathetic towards me about Agnes, old Ken, so I hope you will be the same about what I have said here in regard to Papa, and not think I am being disrespectful of his memory when I write about him here. I did not mean disrespect when I did not come home for his funeral in December, but at that time I simply could not force myself to go back for it.

Here Rydal stopped and took a breath, sorry he had got launched on the funeral business again. He put a period to the sentence and went on in a new paragraph.

I'll be coming back to the States pretty soon, and intend to get settled in a job somewhere at once, either Boston or New York, I suppose. Meanwhile, dear brother, it's quite obvious from this somewhat ambiguous letter that I very much needed to make contact with you again after so long a time. Take it in that spirit. Greet your family for me. Take care of yourself. God bless you.

Your brother,
Rydal

Colette's knock came as he was sealing the envelope. He opened the door for her.

"Hi!" she said. "How do you like me in sensible shoes?"

Rydal smiled. She was wearing red flats with tassels. "American shoes?"

"Oh, gosh, no. Greek. Can't you tell? They're so much cheaper in Greece, shoes. I bought five pairs." Her high voice cracked on "pair", like the voice of a little girl with a husky throat. "Let's take off, want to?"

"Sure." He picked up his overcoat and his letter.

"Is that airmail? I've got stamps." She put her purse down on his unmade bed, sat down, and extracted Greek stamps from a pocket of her billfold.

Rydal accepted a couple with thanks, and felt surprised again by her efficiency. What had it been last night? Matches for his cigarette. Colette had had a book of matches in her pocketbook, though she didn't smoke. She said she always carried a book of matches. "How is Chester? Feeling all right?"

"Oh, I guess so. Slight hangover. Wait!"

"What's the matter?" He had opened the door for her.

"Aren't you going—" She almost closed the door, then whispered, "Remember what you said last night? You'd kiss me before I went out any door?"

He hadn't said it just like that, he was sure. He had been joking last night. He was joking now. He kissed her on the lips. Then, smiling, they both went out. She made him feel young again, practically like fifteen again. But without the blindness, the awful vulnerability, the kind of innocence that at fifteen has stupidity for a handmaiden.

They walked to the market, drifted down aisles of shoes and boots that smelled of cattle urine, stared with detachment and wonder at hanging meat, cut in a manner that made the pieces unidentifiable. They bought ice-cream cones and wandered on, holding hands to keep from getting separated. Colette found a loose, buttonless vest with fringe at the bottom for Chester, and Rydal helped her bargain for it. They got it for thirty drachmas less than the first price the woman had asked for it.

"I don't think people should pay the first price they ask in places like this, do you?" Colette said. "It's silly tourists who make the prices go up everywhere."

Rydal nodded agreement and smiled. "Do you think Chester'll wear it?"

"Oh, at home he will. Not out. He's very stuffy about what he wears in public."

The ruddy-cheeked peasant woman rolled the vest carefully in a sheet of newspaper, tucked the ends in, and presented it to Colette.

"Efharisto," Colette replied. "Thank you."

The woman said something back to her, smiling.

"What does she say?" Colette asked Rydal.

"Oh—she's happy to serve you, go in health, something like that," Rydal replied.

They walked on, Colette holding on to his arm now.

"You must be awfully good at languages to have picked up Greek so well. It's so difficult sounding. Nothing sounds like what it *is*, you know what I mean? French sounds like what it is, Italian, even German a little bit, but *Greek*!"

Rydal put his head back and laughed. How his father would have enjoyed that comment! He could see his father's face, if he or Martha or Kennie had said that at home. His father would look from side to side, stony-faced, as if he were in acute physical distress, and then he would announce that that was the remark of an imbecile. Chester's face superimposed itself on his father's, and Rydal's smile went away.

"Can you speak Italian and French, too?" she asked.

"Yes. Much better than Greek. But it's no achievement. I had to speak them as a kid."

"Really? Your family travelled so much?"

"Oh, no. Hardly at all. But my father made us learn languages at home. Starting about as soon as we could speak. We had to speak French for a month in the house, then Italian, then Russian, then—"

"Russian?"

"Yes. That's a nice language. Very cozy. My father thought it was easier that way. Well, not easier, he didn't give a hang, but he thought people who learned a language in childhood were going to know it better later on. Or something." Rydal smiled at her attentiveness.

"Golly."

"And if he caught any of us speaking English during a month when we were supposed to be speaking Spanish or something else, we got demerits. We had a demerit chart in the hall upstairs, where everybody could see it. Even my poor mother got on it now and then." He gave a laugh, a sad one.

"Holy cow."

"Or if we mixed up languages we got demerits. First half of sentence in Italian, last half in Spanish, for instance, two demerits. My brother Kennie could never think what the French for lawnmower was, but he knew it in Russian. Kennie and I used to make puns when Papa wasn't around. Kennie'd say at night, 'Don't open the window tonight, Ryd, I'm a fresh-air *Fiend*.'" Rydal laughed.

"I don't get it."

"*Fiend* means enemy in German. If you're a fresh air *Fiend*—"

"Oh, I see, I see." She laughed. "That's rather good."

But she was thinking of something else already, Rydal saw, hanging on his arm and looking down as she walked in long, slow steps, like a child trying not to step on cracks. He said nothing. They were out of the market now, walking down a quiet street of two-storey houses where they had never been before. At the end of the street, not far away, a blue notch of sky opened at the top into space, into a blue dome. The air felt washed and pure, as if it had just rained, though the unpaved street was dry. A black and white cat rolled in the dust, its belly turned up to the sun. Rydal leaned over to see if Colette still had her newspaper package. It was under her other arm.

"I was just thinking," she said, "when we go back to New York, we can't be—Well, we aren't now, of course. I mean we *weren't*." The wind blew her short, reddish hair over her forehead. She still looked down as she walked.

"What do you mean?"

"Well, in New York, Chester was Howard Cheever. That was the name on our mailbox, the name we signed the lease for the apartment under. Then we were Mr. and Mrs. Chester MacFarland because of the passports. Chester's real name." She looked up suddenly, straight ahead of her, and laughed. "Chester told me he got in trouble *years* ago in San Francisco in some used-car deal under the name Chester

MacFarland. That's why he never used it again. I guess he thought it was so long ago, or so unimportant, it wouldn't matter if he used it for his passport."

Rydal frowned, trying to grasp it. "Um-m. Howard Cheever wasn't in that Greek agent's notebook, I don't think. Was it?"

"No-o," Colette said, as if it were all a gay conspiracy, a game. "And was Chester glad about that! That would have meant he'd have a couple of bank accounts seized and God knows what else."

Rydal suddenly felt a disgust for Chester. It was a momentary thing, like a twinge of nausea. He shrugged involuntarily.

"You don't like Chester much, do you?" she asked.

He looked at her, not knowing what to say. "Do you?"

"Me? Well—" She shrugged also.

Their shrugs bound them together, Rydal felt. Then he thought he was wrong: Colette's shrug meant, "I've got to like him. I'm married to him." Rydal didn't like that. If it meant, "I'm not sure if I like him or not," Rydal didn't care for that, either. A nice, intelligent girl shouldn't like a crook. Rydal frowned at her face in profile, at her long lashes, her young nose, her full lips. Maybe she and Chester liked going to bed together. Maybe Chester was just a good meal ticket to her. Who knew?

"I like you better," she said, still not looking at him.

They had stopped. A dirty old man, an unwashed old man, lounged in an open doorway just ten feet in front of Rydal, watching them both with folded arms. "And why?" Rydal asked with a sigh.

Her blue eyes looked up at him, light purple eyes, like all the blue of the sky compressed into the two irises, Rydal thought.

"Because you're honest," she said. "You're very frank and I can talk to you. You can talk to me, too, can't you? You have."

Rydal moistened his lips and nodded. He couldn't think of a word to say. He suddenly wished they were in his room, alone, at the hotel.

"Well, that's why I like you." She looked around her, as if she had abruptly stopped thinking about him. "I'm getting hungry, are you?"

"A little." Rydal looked at his watch and was surprised to see that it was after three.

"Can we eat something in a crummy place?" she asked.

"Crummy?"

"Where the Greeks go."

Smiling, Rydal pulled her by the arm back in the direction of the town. "Does this town have anything else?"

Colette was quite definite about what she wanted. She wanted a hole-in-the-wall, stand-up kind of place, and Rydal found one on a street next to the market. They ate a piece of hot goat meat on a slab of grey bread, and shared a glass of the worst retsina Rydal had ever put in his mouth. Colette sampled one of the sweet rolls the proprietor had under a soiled cloth in a basket, and found it too hard even for her teeth, which she said had been "strong enough to chew blubber the right way in Alaska".

Rydal supposed she had been to Alaska with Chester. He did not ask her about it.

When they got back to the hotel around 4, Chester was not in. Colette knocked on Rydal's door to tell him so.

"Well—the clerk downstairs would certainly have told us, if anything had happened to him," Rydal said. He meant, if the police had come and picked him up, but after saying what he had, he wasn't sure if the clerk would have told them.

"Oh, I don't think anything's happened to him," Colette said, coming into his room, closing the door. "He's just gone out for a walk." She leaned against the door.

Rydal suddenly put his arms around her, inside her open coat, and kissed her on the mouth. The effect was like a mule kick, a blackout, or falling off an edge, and then he heard himself protesting, and he was trying to get her tight arms from around his neck, and Colette wouldn't let go, and she was saying she could tell Chester she had just been out for a while looking for him, and Rydal was saying, "No." And finally he got her arms away and held her wrists together. She was open-mouthed with surprise, or she was dazed or shocked, he didn't know.

"Just go," he said. "Please. Go now."

"Why? What's the matter?"

"Just go. Go." He pushed her out of the door and closed it.

Then he sat for several minutes in a chair, his face down in one hand, thinking of nothing. He realized he was avoiding thinking, avoiding trying to feel anything, avoiding trying to figure out what he had felt. And all because it reminded him of Agnes. *Damn Agnes!* He stood up. Maybe this was the last of it, maybe it wouldn't happen again with any other woman, that terrible, stupid bolt of pleasure-pain. Colette wasn't like Agnes, really. It didn't make any sense.

"She's not like Agnes," he said softly. "She's not like Agnes."

That evening, he had too much to drink, but Chester had even more. That evening, he allowed himself to believe he was in love with Colette. It was just a physical sensation, after all, he told himself. It was a pleasure to dance with her. Chester saw that it was a pleasure for him, and Chester was furious about it. Colette also had a bit too much to drink. But they all said good night earlyish, before midnight, Chester sullen, he and Colette very merry and cheerful. Chester, while Colette had been to the ladies' to powder her nose, had told Rydal that they would part company tomorrow night or Monday morning. Chester had said it like a heavy pronouncement, and Rydal had solemnly nodded his accord. After all, those were the terms.

And five thousand was the price.

Rydal focused his blurry vision until the numbers on the bills in his hand became very clear. 500. Five zero zero. They looked unreal. Ten of them. Ten clean new bills. Chester had passed them over as casually as if he were handing Rydal a menu, while Colette had been in the ladies' room. "Thank you," Rydal had said. Just that and nothing more.

He pushed the bills in a small, sharp-edged stack through the slit in his suitcase lining, where his other dirtier but more honest money was.

10

Chester had never detested any town as much as he detested Chania. The pattern of the buildings on the street of the hotel had taken on a meaning to him: they were a symbol of hell, a trademark of hell, the very face of hell. Chania was where he had lost Colette. Chania was where he had existed for three days like a hunted dog and watched a seedy young bum seduce his wife. Chester was sure they'd been to bed together. Colette denied it, but naturally she would, and it was the first time she'd ever lied to him, Chester thought. And Chania was where he'd hit his wife for the first time. He'd hit her hard on the shoulder Saturday night, after they got home. On Sunday morning, she had a darkening bruise. On Sunday, she was very angry with him. Chania was the town where Colette had turned against him. Now she was determined to keep the seedy young bum with them, just because she knew he wanted to get rid of him. Chester would have liked to leave Chania Sunday afternoon, but there wasn't any bus back to Iraklion on Sunday afternoon. A boat had come and gone in the port overnight. Chester had longed to be on it, with Colette, alone. It didn't matter where it was going. Well, they were leaving tomorrow morning on a 9 o'clock bus bound east, for Iraklion. Chester supposed Rydal would take the same bus, which would be annoying, but certainly in Iraklion they could lose him, and if Rydal said anything about taking the same plane with them back to Athens, Chester was going to ask him to find another.

Chania reminded him of his second year at Harvard, when the news of his father's bankruptcy had come, and when Annette, the girl he had been engaged to, had broken the engagement—instantly, on hearing of the bankruptcy—so that the shock of his father's situation and the loss of Annette had seemed a single, world-shattering catastrophe. Chester had left school and tried to apply what he had learned of business administration to the saving of an artificial-leather factory up in New Hampshire. He hadn't saved it. Flat broke, he had sworn to himself he would get rich, and fast. So he had started to operate, more and more shadily, he could see it now, though when he had started out, he hadn't intended to get rich by being crooked. It had been a gradual thing. A gradual bad thing, Chester knew. But now he was stuck with it, really deep in it, hooked on it like an addict on dope.

Chania reminded him of all that. Chania reminded him of failure.

At half-past two on Sunday afternoon, Chester lay in bed with a headache. He would have liked a couple of cold beers, but Chania was the town where a man couldn't get a cold beer if he needed it. Chester had called down for some beer hours ago, and been told something in faulty English about a store not being open until 4 p.m. Chester alternately read Colette's pocketbook novels and dozed. Every doze made him feel a bit better, but each one brought ugly half-dreams of Rydal and Colette together—they *were* together this minute, "taking a walk" somewhere, unless—He grabbed the telephone, and asked for room 18.

No one answered him. He had spoken into silence. At last a man's voice came on the wire.

"Would you connect me with room eighteen, please . . . *Eighteen*. . . . One eight. Yes. . . . No, no, the *room*. On the second floor."

"Yes, sir. I ring."

Chester couldn't hear anything like a ring. Several seconds went by, then the man's voice said:

"I ring," like a repeating record.

Chester sighed, not knowing if he had already rung or was going to. There was still no sound of ringing. Chester lost his patience. "Never mind, before you can ring them I can knock on the door!" He hung up.

In two minutes, he was dressed, except for a tie. He went down the hall to room eighteen, listened for only a couple of seconds at the door, heard nothing, and knocked firmly.

After a moment, Rydal's voice said, "Yes?"

"It's Chester."

Rydal opened the door. He was in shirt-sleeves, but his tie was tied. He looked worried. "Are you all right?"

"Oh, sure. Can I come in?" Chester went in as Rydal stepped aside, expecting to see Colette there, but the room was empty. On the bed—it was rumpled, but it had the counterpane on it—lay a scattering of sheets of paper, written on in longhand, and a black-and-white-marbled notebook. Chester cleared his throat.

"Just wondered if you've seen Colette. I thought you were taking a walk with her."

"We did take a walk. She . . . went out again for something, I don't know what."

"Went out again? Was she here?"

"We got back to the hotel, and she went out again." Rydal folded his arms and looked at Chester levelly.

Chester nodded, took a step towards the bed and said, "What's all this?"

"Poems," Rydal said flatly. "I write poems sometimes."

"Oh." Chester turned around, glanced again around the room, then his eyes stopped at Colette's pocketbook, peeking from under a newspaper in the armchair, and he smiled. "Where is she? Hiding under the bed?" Chester asked Rydal.

Rydal let his arms drop. He frowned. "She happens to be in the—"

The bathroom door behind Rydal opened, and Colette came out, her face tight with anxiety. She was carrying her coat. "Ches, don't make a scene. For gosh sake, I've been reading some of Rydal's poetry."

"Then why do you have to hide in the bathroom?" Chester thundered out.

"I wasn't hiding," Colette said.

"Yes, you were, or Rydal wouldn't have said you were out!" Chester retorted. "Why were you hiding?"

Rydal hurled a pencil he had had in his hand down onto the bed. "I'll tell you why she was hiding, because she knew the stink you'd make if you found her here. All right, now you're making it. Go ahead."

Chester moved closer to him, his hands closing in fists. You've got a fine nerve talking to me like that. You with your nasty, scheming—"

"Yes, I have, I have." Rydal stood his ground. His own hands were fists, too. "I've got the nerve to stand up to you. You're used to pushing people around, aren't you? Having them cringing around you. Like your wife here, hiding in the bathroom."

"You admit she's my wife, eh?" Chester said, feeling his face grow hotter. "I'll thank you to keep her out of your bed!"

"*Chester ple-ease!*" Colette rushed to him but stopped before she touched him, her hands also raised in fists, fists that pled.

"This is my room, and you can get out," Rydal said, and lit a cigarette.

"I don't let anybody talk to me like that," Chester told him.

"I have news for you. I don't let anybody talk to me the way you have. Insult . . . insult Colette the way you have." Rydal was shaking. He could hardly get the cigarette into his mouth.

Chester noticed the shaking, and interpreted it as guilt. He felt in a sense triumphant. He had fairly caught them both in adultery, caught them red-handed. They really had nothing to say for themselves. "I think you're both a couple of animals. Animals!"

"You call me that?" Rydal said, moving towards him.

Colette grabbed Rydal's arm. "Don't, Rydal." She held his right wrist.

Chester stared wide-eyed for an instant at her hands on his wrist, then looked at Rydal. "Do you know what I'm going to do to you?"

Rydal broke Colette's hold with a sharp movement of his arm. "I'm going to do something to you, too. I'm going to inform on you. Try doing the same thing to me. I'll match you. All right?"

"I'll kill you first," Chester said, and felt his mouth curve in a smile. His heart pounded. Triumph again! He'd never said those words before. Plain strong words.

"I'm sure you would. Try it. I'm not afraid." Rydal folded his arms.

"Nobody's going to kill anybody," Colette said. "Please. Can't you both apologize—" Her voice trembled.

"I see no reason to apologize," Rydal said.

"Nor do I," Chester said automatically. "But I think—I think he'd better take back what he said about informing on me, or else."

"No." Rydal walked to the night table and flicked his ash into the tray. "I've decided to give you what you deserve, and that's it."

Chester gave a laugh. "What do you think's going to happen to Colette, if you do that?"

"She's not guilty of your crimes," said Rydal.

"You've 'decided', you've 'decided'," Chester said, and walked in a circle. His armpits were cool with sweat. "You don't know the consequences even for yourself! Don't you know—" Chester stopped. Rydal was staring at him coolly, his eyes hard and steady.

"Get out of my room," Rydal said. "Oh! One thing more. Would you like your five thousand back? You'll get it back." He went quickly to his suitcase.

"I'm not interested. What's five thousand to me?" said Chester. "Come on, Colette." He moved towards the door. "No, no, no," he said when he saw Rydal coming towards him with the money. "Keep it for the informing—sneaking—" He blinked as the money hit his face.

The banknotes fluttered and spun and settled to the floor.

"Now isn't that silly," Colette said chidingly, and began to pick them up.

Rydal laughed, a little hysterically, Chester thought.

"Honey, don't bother," Rydal said. "Let the maid pick them up. Or Chester."

"Calling her 'honey' now?" said Chester. "I think that'll be the last time."

"And you know," Colette said, still gathering the bills, "I think that's the first time he's called me 'honey'. I know it is."

Rydal laughed again, and Colette glanced at him.

"Come on, he's nuts," Chester said, pulling at Colette's arm.

"Here, Rydal. It's yours." She handed him the money.

"No, thanks," Rydal said, and turned his back on them.

"Come on," Chester said to her, "and don't forget your pocketbook." He snatched the bills from her hand and plopped them down on the back of the armchair. Rydal still had his back to them. Chester thought his back would make a fine target for a pistol shot.

"I'll talk to you later, Rydal," Colette said as she went out.

Rydal did not answer.

Chester poured himself a Scotch as soon as they got to their room. He watched Colette as she moved about, hanging her coat, getting a comb from her pocketbook, combing her hair. After a couple of minutes, Chester felt calm enough to sit down in the armchair.

"An empty threat, that," Chester said, gesturing with his glass towards Rydal's room. "That bastard. He's a sad case." He gave a short laugh. "Throwing my money back at me. My, my, I'll bet he'll remember that. I bet it'll be the last time he'll ever have five thousand to throw at anybody. I only wish I'd accepted it." And Chester chuckled, stretching his legs out, leaning his head back.

"I think you were both acting like a couple of children." Colette lifted the lid of a small box of candy on the night table, took a piece, then pushed off her shoes. She sat on the bed, put her feet up and pulled a pillow behind her. "You know, he writes quite good poetry,

I think. Better than that what's-his-name—You know, that book of love poems you gave me? What's his name?"

"Dunno," Chester mumbled.

"Chester."

"What?"

"That was the honest truth. I went into Rydal's room to see his poetry. He's never made any pass at me and I certainly never got into his bed. You shouldn't say things like that."

"All right, all right, I don't want to hear any more about it!" Chester said loudly, and stood up. He felt he had a right to be loud after what he'd just been through. He also had a right to another Scotch.

"Darling, haven't you had enough? Why don't you go for a little walk? It'd do you good."

"Why? So you can go back to him again?" Chester poured another drink. His headache was returning. It had left him for a while.

"Chester, darling, come here." She held up her arms to him.

Chester put the glass down, sat down by her on the bed, and buried his face in her neck. He gave a long sigh. Her fingers were delicious on the back of his neck, soothing, reassuring. Like her body, small and round and soft under his arm.

"You know I love you, Chester. Don't you know that?"

"Yes, honey, yes." It was true. What else mattered, Chester thought. Rydal Keener's stupid threat seemed far away now, far and small and petty. "Why don't you take off your clothes?" Chester said.

Colette did.

Chester was asleep when Colette came into the room at a little after 5. The closing of the door woke him up. He hadn't known she had gone out.

"Hi," she said, and he heard at once something strained in her voice.

"Hi." She'd been back to see Rydal, he thought groggily, and hauled himself up a little in bed. "Where've you been?"

"Mind if I turn a lamp on?"

"No."

"It's more cheerful, no?" She turned on the night lamp.

"Where'd you go?"

She looked at him. Her eyes were tense. "I think I might have a cigarette."

"Sure. Mine are—There they are by the Scotch." He watched her. She took a cigarette about twice a year, usually at a big, late party.

"I went in to see Rydal. Now don't get excited." She sat down on the edge of the bed with the cigarette. "I went in—you know, to see how he was. I mean, what he was thinking. Well—"

"Well?"

"He's angry, Chester." She looked at Chester in an intense, bewildered way. "I don't know why. I don't know what's the matter with him. He's very bitter. He says he's going to report you to the police."

"Um-m," said Chester contemptuously, but a very cold chill had gone over him. "When? If he's going to do it, what's he waiting for?"

"Athens," Colette said. "He says he's going to tell the police in Athens."

Chester frowned. "Light me one, will you, honey?"

"I tried to reason with him. I couldn't. He was quite calm, but—" She lit the cigarette and handed it to him. "What do you think we should do, Chester?"

Chester chewed his underlip. "I don't think he intends to do it. If he did, he wouldn't wait till he got to Athens. If he did, he wouldn't tell us, either. He's in this as much as we are."

"I don't think he cares about that."

"Don't be silly."

"No, Chester. Talk to him yourself, if you want to. You'll see what I mean."

"Wouldn't dream of talking to him. Asking him—Oh, yes, now I get it. I'm slow today. He wants more money. A big hunk this time, I suppose."

"No, he doesn't. He didn't mention money. Not a hint."

"He wants me to mention it." Chester got out of bed, reached for his shirt, which was on a chair, and went into the bathroom, where he put on his robe. He felt on familiar ground now. The bum wanted money. "Wait and see. I'll see what his attitude is tomorrow—or tonight. He's going with us on the bus to Iraklion tomorrow, I'll bet."

"Yes. He says he doesn't want you to get out of his sight."

Chester smiled. "Well, either tonight or tomorrow morning, he's going to mention money. Or you. The only thing else I can think of that he'd want is you." Chester bent and pinched her cheek gently. "Now, don't worry about it, will you? I've got enough to pay him off. Not that I'd want to make a second payment," he added, looking musingly at the rumpled bed. "They always lead to more."

"You won't have to worry about that. That's not what you have to worry about."

"We'll see. I don't want you upset about it. What did you arrange with him about this evening? Anything?"

"He doesn't want to eat with us."

"Good. Let him eat alone. Pay for his own dinner for a change."

"He pays his way enough, doesn't he? He's not going to eat tonight." She drew lightly on her cigarette and let the smoke out in a thick, uninhaled puff.

Something in her voice, a sympathy, made Chester look at her. "How sad. He announced that to you?"

"No. I know him, that's all. I know the mood he's in."

"And you're feeling sorry for him because he's not eating dinner?" Chester came towards her. "That bum in there?"

"Chester, if you hit me again, I'll scream! I forgave you once, but I won't do it again!" She had jumped up from the bed and moved towards the door.

Chester pushed his fingers through his thin hair. "All right, honey, for Christ's sake. My God, I wasn't going to hit you. Listen, honey . . ." Scowling, treading heavily on his bare feet, he came towards her and only stopped when she drew back from him again. "Honey, you'll drive me nuts if you keep on like this. We're going to drop that guy in there. In Iraklion. Wait and see. And when we get rid of him our troubles'll be over. We mustn't—we absolutely mustn't quarrel like this."

"All right, Chester."

11

Rydal's anger had gone through several stages by Monday morning. Beginning with the moment Chester had roared at him that Colette was hiding in the bathroom, his anger had been "blind", as the classicists said, and Rydal knew why. The whole scene had been just too much like the one with his father over Agnes. His father had accused him of a seduction—even worse, practically a rape, according to Agnes—and there had been Chester, accusing him of adultery with his wife. It had been like being hurled back to some traumatic instant in time, like the instant of birth, which some psychiatrists said was so awful that nature made people forget it. Rydal hadn't stood up to his father, but he had stood up to Chester. He had hit back at Chester in the only way he could, by saying he would turn him in. And an hour later, when he had cooled down a little, he had seen the absurdity of his anger, but he had not turned loose of his idea of informing on Chester. Yet there were a couple of strikes against it: Rydal loathed the role of stool pigeon; and, second, Colette was going to be hurt by it as well as Chester. Rydal could turn himself in, as an accessory, as well as Chester, but he didn't want to, which meant that he hadn't the moral courage to.

He had pondered the problem all Sunday night in bed, and had not slept at all. He was really sure of only one small thing, and that was that he didn't want the filthy five thousand dollars. Colette would take them back for him, he was sure. Chester, however, probably wouldn't accept them, because he knew they caused him shame.

During the night, Rydal's anger had flared again, a dozen times, as he thought over the scene in which Colette came out of the bathroom. Fatigue doped his brain until he had no control over it, and he could not stop the scene once it began unfolding again. And so had the scenes in his parents' house unfolded again, his mother coming to him and saying in her careful, gentle, embarrassed, word-choosing way that Agnes had said he had been annoying her, that Agnes had said he "used force on her". And, irrationally, Rydal's anger against Chester had been more and more whipped up in the night. "I thought it best to tell your father about this," said his mother, "and he would like a word with you in his study, Rydal." (Yes, Rydal realized last night that it had been his mother who told him his father wanted to see him, his mother who had used the phrase "a word with you".)

The night had been a chaos, but there was a thought that had remained steady, with him, since before he went to bed. That was that he should keep Chester thinking that he would inform on him, keep Chester in fear of it, whether he really did it or not. That was why he had been so firm about it when Colette had come in to talk to him. Rydal wanted to see Chester panicky. Chester making an attempt on his life was ludicrous. Would Chester want another corpse on his hands? Chester was already on the brink of panic. Yesterday, or the day before, he had been murmuring something to the effect that he had better not try to get the film that was in his camera developed. Pictures of him and Colette in Athens or somewhere else in Europe, Rydal supposed. No, he had better not. And he had asked Rydal about the strings of amber beads that so many men carried in their hands, jiggling and fondling them as they stood idly on street corners. Rydal had explained that people bought them to twiddle, just to relieve nervousness. Chester had looked at one jiggler almost enviously. The beads were on sale at every newsstand. Rydal had been amused.

As early as possible, Rydal had checked on the bus to Iraklion. It was leaving at 9 this morning. Rydal telephoned Chester's room at a quarter to 8, spoke to Colette, and told her about the bus. Colette sounded as stiff and formal as he. Rydal paid his bill, walked with his suitcase to the bus terminal—the bleak square—and boarded it at twenty to 9. He had bought a newspaper, not because of Chester, but because he wanted to see the news. The five thousand dollars were a resilient lump in his left-hand trousers pocket. Colette and Chester arrived in a taxi at ten to 9, and got on the bus.

"Morning," Rydal said to Colette from his seat.

"Good morning," her clear, high voice replied.

She and Chester sat down side by side two or three seats in front of Rydal and across the aisle. Chester's beard was quite visible from a distance now. Rydal noticed that a few people looked at him as if he were a man of importance, a scientist, perhaps—or a college professor.

Rydal was soon asleep, once the bus began moving. It was a shallow sleep, full of tension and sprinkled with incomplete dreams that startled him half awake and made him stir in his seat. They were not dreams, he thought, but daydreams of a tired and anxious mind. He saw Chester shooting him, in one. He imagined Chester grabbing him from behind with an arm across his throat, in some dark street of Iraklion or Athens, where there was no one around to see, when Rydal didn't have a chance against Chester's surprise attack. But between these violent imaginings, he embraced and kissed Colette, a relaxing and pleasant thing to imagine. It made even the hardness of the window-sill bearable to his elbow, the throbbing metal back of the seat in front of him pleasant to his knee-cap. He looked through half-closed eyes at Colette's reddish blond head next to Chester, who had kept his hat on. Now and again, Colette turned her head to talk to Chester, and he saw her face, but mostly she rested her head back against the seat.

By Rethymnon, the mid-point more or less of the journey, he had determined to stand fifteen minutes with Colette, to bring her coffee or a Coca-Cola, a sandwich fetched with effort from the best restaurant. At Rethymnon, he found himself behaving stiffly, nodding a greeting to her, lighting himself a cigarette, turning his back on them. He drank a cup of sweet coffee, rushed to a W.C. in a near-by café, rushed back, still clinging to the newspaper of Chania, and got into his seat again.

It clouded over, then began to rain in a fine, drizzling way. As they neared Iraklion, Rydal looked for Mount Ida, which he had seen leaving the town, but it was too misty for it to be visible. The road worsened, grew smoother again, and then they were back in

Iraklion, the bus unloading in the unpaved square. There was time to make the 3:30 plane for Athens, Rydal saw. He assumed Chester was going to do this, and he also felt sure Chester would ask him not to take the plane, if he appeared to be going to. That was just too bad, Rydal thought. Chester was going to have a very hard time shaking him off. They might even return to the States all together. Rydal stood in the Iraklion square, his suitcase between his feet, watching Chester and Colette gathering their luggage from the bus.

Chester hailed a cab.

Then Rydal walked over to them. "You're going to the airport?" Rydal asked Colette.

"No. He wants to see the Palace of Knossos," she answered, dropping the K in her pronunciation of Knossos. "Not such a hot day for it, is it?" She looked chilly and unhappy. Her hands were in the pockets of her topcoat.

"So you're staying over tonight," Rydal said. "In Iraklion."

"I guess so. We'll miss that afternoon plane, if we go to Knossos."

Rydal saw that Chester was having difficulty explaining something to the driver. Chester was pointing to his luggage. Rydal was not going to go to his assistance.

"Chester wants to check the luggage somewhere while we visit the palace," Colette said. "I suppose he's asking the driver to go to some other hotel besides the Astir. Chester doesn't want to go back there."

But Chester was asking the driver for a place to check the luggage, Rydal could tell, because the driver was yelling back in Greek, "There *isn't* any baggage depository!"

Rydal let them fight it out. He heard them talking about the Hotel Corona, agreeing to that. It was only three blocks away, Rydal remembered, over by the Iraklion Museum. Chester beckoned for Colette to join him.

Colette looked from Chester to Rydal in a confused way, then said, "Bye-bye" to Rydal, as if it were a temporary parting.

Which it was, Rydal thought. He picked up his own suitcase and walked to the Corona. By the time he got there, Colette and Chester were just coming down its front steps. It was an old-new building, vaguely yellow and vaguely dirty, its design in the bad taste of an American movie house of the 1930s. Chester's taxi was waiting at the curb. Chester looked at Rydal coldly, and for the first time that day.

"Mind if I join you in Knossos?" Rydal said. "I'd like to see it, too."

"I do mind. I'd rather be alone," Chester said. He turned around, after starting towards the taxi. "And if you don't leave us alone, I'll ask a policeman to remove you."

"You'll ask a policeman?" Rydal asked in an incredulous tone.

Chester turned away and got into the taxi in which Colette was already installed.

Rydal looked around hastily for a taxi, saw none, and decided to try the square, or little park, by the Iraklion Museum, one street away. Here there were two taxis standing at a curb, one with a driver in it. The driver was very happy to make the trip to Knossos.

They left the city on the same road the bus had come in on, but soon made a slight turn to the left. Chester's taxi was not in sight. Rydal sat up and looked at the scenery. He remembered the picture of Knossos in his father's study, an old photograph showing some of the remains of the old palace in the background—not enough, Rydal remembered, to satisfy him as a child. "But where is the *labyrinth*?" he had used to ask his father, and, with a sigh, his father would explain that most of the palace was out of sight in the photograph, that the palace was four storys high and most of it behind the hill in the photograph. Rydal remembered the hill best: a dark grassy hill on which a few cypresses stood like black exclamation points, a hill bisected by a pale, undulant path that crossed the whole picture, and in the foreground, two grazing sheep and a black donkey. He looked now for such a hill on the approach to Knossos. *Was there really a labyrinth?* He had used to ask his father that, too, his child's mind unable to grasp the subtle blending of fact and legend. Rydal had later understood that the bewildering and interconnecting rooms of the palace itself had given rise to the legend of a labyrinth, or maze, and the bull-dancing of the young men to the legend of the monster bull, the Minotaur, who breathed fire at the depths of the labyrinth.

The fine rain still came down.

"Knossou," said the driver, pointing to a wire fence they were driving along beside. There were no buildings or houses in sight.

"Where's the palace?" Rydal asked.

"Behind the hill."

They drove into a graveled semi-circle where there was a ticket booth. Rydal saw Chester's and Colette's figures walking up the hill beyond, towards the cypresses, towards the palace columns and roof, which Rydal could see now. This was the hill of the photograph. Rydal paid the driver and tipped him so well that the driver wanted to wait for him. But since Chester had apparently dismissed his own driver, Rydal told the man not to wait.

"There're buses every hour, aren't there?" Rydal asked.

"Every hour, sir."

Rydal waved good-bye to him and went to the booth to buy his ticket of admission. In the booth was a sleepy-looking man in an overcoat and a hat, swathed to the eyes in his muffler.

"Ena, parakalo," said Rydal, presenting his money.

He was given a small white ticket.

"Not many people today, eh?" Rydal said.

The man gave an unintelligible, rather Italian exclamation like "Gwah!" and lifted his hands, as if to say only idiots would come on a day like this.

Rydal turned up his overcoat collar, picked up his suitcase, then, on second thought, asked the man if he could leave the suitcase with him for a few minutes. The man said certainly.

"Oh, it's not heavy. I'll take it along," Rydal said. He didn't trust the man.

Rydal climbed the hill. Slowly the palace came into view, a flat open area on his left, paved with stone, like a court or stage, a drop of ground behind it, and, on the right, the palace itself, which looked like a conglomeration of huge boxes, outside stairways without handrails, open terraces whose roofs were supported by dark red columns—the renowned russet red of Crete.

Rydal walked through a doorway barely higher than his head. Stairs led up and stairs led down. The floor appeared to be hard pounded earth. At least it was dry here. The room had three open doorways. Rydal took the one on his right. It led to another room which also had three doorways. Two long spears leaned against a wall, and after staring at them for a few seconds, Rydal realized what deadly weapons they would make, running through a man, and he shivered a little and set his suitcase down. Then he carried it to a corner of the room, out of the way. There seemed to be no one in the palace, not even a caretaker. But of course it was January, a Monday, and raining.

He walked to a doorway—the doorways were open and doorless—and listened. Now he heard Colette's voice from above. Rydal looked up. He saw only part of an outside stone stairway, and the straight edge of a terrace floor or a roof, with the grey sky behind it. He took some outside stairs going up, careful to keep a bit close to the wall of the building, as there was a two-storey drop on his right. The stairs brought him to a hallway whose mural made him catch his breath. Here were the spindle-waisted bull dancers, leaping over the horns of the graceful bull.

"Chester?" That was Colette's voice, still above him.

Smiling, Rydal took another flight of stairs two at a time, and emerged on the roof, or a roof. There was still another terrace above him, and there stood Chester silhouetted against the sky, his hand on a pillar which rose at the head of some steps. Chester saw him. Rydal waved. Chester turned away with apparent annoyance. Rydal climbed up to Chester's level. Colette was walking under a stone portico ten yards away, where some large vases were lined up. Chester strolled, with his head down, on Rydal's right, on an extension of the terrace roof. Rydal went closer to him. Where Chester walked was a blind alley. There were round pits on the right and left of Chester, four feet deep or so, where, Rydal remembered from his father's description, containers of oil and wine had once been stored. Chester saw him coming, and immediately came back, as if he were afraid Rydal might rush him and push him off. Rydal stepped aside to let him pass, though there was room for two people to pass without touching.

"Fascinating, isn't it?" Rydal asked. "I suppose these were the store-rooms."

"Servants' quarters," said Chester in a corrective way, and Rydal smiled, thinking of his father.

"Hello, Rydal," Colette called. "What do you think of all this?"

Rydal walked directly to her, happy at the sound of her voice, happy to be near her. "Terrific! I can see what they mean by a labyrinth. I can't imagine a systematic tour of this place, can you? Every room goes into three others."

"Let's go down the grand stairway! Chester says the big inside one's the grand stairway." She took his hand, suddenly as excited as he.

They came upon another mural, this one of several women elegantly dressed but with exposed breasts, chattering and laughing as if they sat in the box of a theatre.

"Look at those *bozooms*! I suppose this one's famous. Is it?" she asked, giggling. "It ought to be."

"I suppose. Come on. This is the grand stairway. Look. See those grooves for the rain-water? My father used to tell me about these. The grooves rise up to slow down the water at the curves so it won't slosh over on the steps. Hydraulic engineering—even if it's primitive."

"Colette?" Chester's voice called. It sounded remote.

"I'm down here!" Colette answered. "On the grand stairway."

But a moment later they had left the grand stairway and entered a room labelled THE QUEEN'S BATH CHAMBER. They both went on tiptoe suddenly.

"Gosh, if that's the tub, it's awfully small," said Colette, looking at a stone receptacle that sat in a slight depression in the floor.

"Maybe the people were littler in those days."

Colette giggled at this idea. "I think we're the only people in the whole place. Isn't that marvelous?"

Suddenly, they were kissing. Their bodies strained together for a long moment, then Colette broke away, caught his hand, and pulled him through another doorway.

"Look at that chair!" she said.

It was a straight chair with a high back.

"That's the throne," Rydal said. "That's the throne of King Minos."

"Really?" she asked, breathless. Carefully, she sat in it, and lifted her face, smiling. "It's even comfortable."

Tall shields leaned against the wall. And more of the spears.

"Colette!" Chester was in the next room. He came quickly in through the doorway, his face angry, his guidebook closed in his hand. "For Christ's sake, it's damned easy to get lost in here."

"Why don't you?" Rydal said, in a burst of insolence.

Chester's face reddened.

"Come on, Chester," Colette said soothingly. "At least there're no closed doors. We're not going to get locked in anywhere."

"I think I've seen about enough," Chester said. "If you're ready to go—"

"No, I'm not. I don't think I've seen half of it yet. I keep finding new rooms."

Rydal wanted to stay close to her, but tactfully, prudently, he drifted on, stared for a moment at a vessel labelled LUSTRAL BATH that was only a little smaller than the queen's bathtub. Then suddenly he wanted out, and he walked quickly through a doorway on his left, in the general direction of the grand stairway and the outside stairs, he thought. Two wrong turns, two wrong rooms, and then he made it, out on a terrace at ground level. The rain was in his face again. He walked slowly, getting his bearings. Straight ahead was the direction from which he had approached the palace, the direction he or Chester and Colette would have to leave in. Rydal kept watching in that direction, so they could not leave without his knowing it. Then he remembered his suitcase, circled the palace to the door he had come in through, got his suitcase, and waited outside for them.

"Chester?" Colette's voice sounded very faint. "Chester, where are you?"

"Where are *you*?" asked Chester.

Rydal smiled. Was Chester playing a game with her?

"Chester? Tell me. What room? You sound higher. Are you up? I'm down."

No answer from Chester.

Silence for a few seconds.

"The exit's this way!" Rydal called. "Can you hear me, Colette?"

"Yes, but—Yell again. I'll follow the direction."

Rydal set his suitcase down and trotted around the corner of the palace. He thought there was a more direct route out, at the side terrace, or maybe it was the back terrace, but he knew where the terrace was, at least. He went below an overhang, stopped in a doorway and called:

"Colette! This way! Can you hear me?"

"Yes. Okay!" merrily. "Thanks!"

Rydal looked at the other two doorways in the room, watching for her, then repeated, *"This—way,"* smiling, and turned and walked out on the terrace again. He trotted to the corner, looked for Chester, and didn't see him. He went back to the center of the terrace.

Colette was just coming through the doorway where he had stood, running towards him, smiling.

Then a slight sound, a shadow, a sixth sense—*something,* made him glance up, and with a reflex quick as the blink of an eye, he ducked and flung himself out of its way.

There was a crack and a boom like thunder, a deep rattle of stone on stone.

Rydal, sprawled on the terrace floor, got to his feet, shaking. "Dio, mio," he whispered, "dio mio, dio mio," over and over.

Colette lay bleeding, her head crushed. She lay face down. On either side of her, two gargantuan fragments of a stone urn rocked like ugly cradles with jagged edges. Rydal looked up. Chester gripped the low parapet of the terrace two stories above him.

"Dirty bastard!" Rydal said in a voice so shaky, it was not even loud.

Chester made a yelping sound, like a sob, like the cry of a dog.

Rydal darted for the steps to his left, tripped and went on, up, then suddenly was weak in the knees. He caught the steps in front of him with his hands. He was going to be sick, going to faint. He didn't know. He looked up. Chester was standing at the top of the steps. Then Chester started slowly down.

Rydal pushed himself up a little.

Chester came on, ready to kick his face, Rydal knew.

Rydal lunged for his legs, put both arms around them, and Chester lost his balance. Chester fell first, Rydal still clinging to him and on top of him, the six or eight feet to the terrace. Rydal was not hurt by the fall, and Chester seemed only groggy, sitting up, holding his head. Rydal breathed hard, trying to recover his strength, to shake off the faintness. He looked at Colette.

"She's dead," he said to Chester. Then, three yards away from Chester, he let his legs bend and knelt down. He put his hands over his eyes and yielded to the queasiness in his stomach, or his mind. He wanted to throw up and couldn't, or didn't.

Chester was standing near him now. "It's your fault she's dead," he said. "Your fault!" Chester went, in a strange, plodding gait, towards her, and got down on hands and knees.

Rydal frowned as he saw Chester stretch out a hand to touch her shoulder. He watched, wary, as if Chester could do anything to hurt her now. Rydal had seen her head. He stood up.

Chester turned on one knee to Rydal and said, "You won't get away with this, you bum. You bum!" Chester pulled his overcoat sleeves down, perhaps mechanically, but it looked like the gesture of a well-dressed gentleman adjusting his cuffs before taking his leave.

Rydal felt stronger. He walked towards Chester.

Chester stood up and walked away, to the end of the terrace, and turned left. Rydal went after him.

"You're just going to leave her?" Rydal yelled.

Chester had covered several yards, walking towards the entrance to the grounds.

"Hey!" Rydal called.

Chester went on, a dark, plunging figure in the rain.

Rydal started after him, nearly fell over his suitcase, and automatically picked it up. But after running a few steps with it, he set it down and ran back to the terrace.

"Colette! Colette!" he shouted at her, touching her shoulder, staring at her left hand with its wedding ring and engagement ring, the hand that looked quite undamaged and alive. The rain was thinning and widening the blood in a great red aureole around her head. Rydal licked away the raindrops from his lips. Then he stood up and ran with determination, back to his suitcase, and then in the direction Chester had taken.

Chester was not in view.

"Was there a taxi here?" Rydal asked the sleepy man in the admission booth.

"What?" The man sat in the depths of the booth. Its sides hid his vision like blinders.

"Did anyone go away in a taxi—just now?"

"No. Nobody went away. That I saw. How many up there?" He pointed towards the palace. "We close in twenty minutes."

Rydal hurried on without answering. Dimly, he realized that when they found Colette, the ticket-seller would have only his face in his memory to tell the police about. But that seemed quite unimportant. Rydal trotted down to where the road curved. It was still light enough to see anyone on the road, if there were anyone. The road was empty. Rydal looked behind him again. There was a "tourist pavilion"—one of the government-sponsored combinations of restaurant and inn—across the road from the gates of the palace grounds, but Rydal did not think Chester would have dared go there. The low building's lights glowed yellow through the fine rain. No, Chester was hiding in some ditch nearby, behind some bushes. Or maybe he'd had the good luck to pick up the bus. Or even a taxi. Rydal smiled tensely. There would be time.

12

Chester was hiding, or rather he had collapsed, beside a clump of bushes only thirty yards from the Knossos gate and across the road from it. He was alternately shaking from shock, then going absolutely limp, as though he had no muscles in his body. The rain was a low hum in his ears. His clothes were soaked. He was in a half-seated, half-lying position, propped up on one arm, his palm flat on the rough, wet ground. It was a long while, it was starting to grow dark, before he could think, and then his first thought was simply that it was growing dark. From then on, he progressed.

Rydal must have gone by. Rydal must be waiting for him at that hotel in Irakilon, where he had left his suitcases. And Colette still lay in the rain on the terrace. The thought tore through him like a swift catastrophe, and again he was panting, shaking. It was Rydal's fault. Anger filled the void of pain. Rydal would pay. Chester cautiously got up. He was beginning to be able to plan. He walked along the road towards Iraklion. His hands felt empty, and then he realized he'd left the *Guide Bleu* at the palace, back on the upper terrace of the palace. He smiled, and then he wept a little. Then he pulled out his comb and ran it through his thin wet hair a couple of times. He would have to get on a bus. No chance of a taxi on this country road.

He had walked slowly for about thirty-five minutes before a bus going in the direction of Iraklion came into view. There had been at least three buses going in the other direction. Chester flagged it, and it stopped for him. He got on, looking frantically over its lighted interior for Rydal. Only solemn Greek faces stared back at him, some dark with unshaven beards, none Rydal.

Chester looked again for Rydal in the square where the bus unloaded. Rydal was no doubt at the Hotel Corona. Chester remembered its name now. He hadn't been able to think of it a few minutes ago. He made his way somewhat slowly, in an effort to appear casual, towards a café whose lights he saw from the square. He had the feeling people stared at him. He wished he had his hat, but it had fallen off at Knossos.

The next twenty minutes would have been a nightmare to Chester under ordinary circumstances, but Chester bore them with an inexhaustible patience. First, he had to look up hotels in the telephone directory under *xenodochaion,* a word he knew. Then his problem was to call the Hotel Corona and ask them to send the luggage he had left under the name Chamberlain to the Hotel Hephaestou, whose name Chester had just discovered in the directory. Though he got someone at the Corona who spoke English, he either could not make himself clear, or the man was unwilling to lose a customer.

"I'll pay you for tonight, if you like," said Chester. "Understand? Just write me a bill, and I'll send the money with the bellboy you send with the luggage to the Hotel Hephaestou."

Chester had to repeat this, in different ways, many times. At last, the man said:

"You will be sorry, sir," ominously.

"Why?" Chester asked, perfectly calmly.

Calmly still, he gave it up after a minute or two, sat down at a table in the restaurant and called for a Scotch. They had no Scotch. Chester ordered a double ouzo. For once, he felt as seedy and shapeless as the other customers in the place. That was good. He was not conspicuous, except that he was American.

He tackled the telephone again. This time the restaurant proprietor, a friendly, smiling fellow, came to the telephone to help him. Chester explained what he wanted. The man knew a little English, but he did not know "baggage" or "suitcase". One of the patrons conveyed this to the proprietor, and he got on the telephone again and called the Hotel Corona. There was a small argument of some kind, while Chester made positive gestures and said, "*Do* it. Yes," in the background to the Greek on the telephone, and then, Chester thought, it was accomplished.

"Thank you," Chester said, "thank you very much." He left a good tip, and was about to leave the place, when he realized he did not know where the Hotel Hephaestou was. He turned around, then changed his mind: best to ask somebody else. He'd stayed long enough here.

Chester asked so many people who did not know, that he began to think the Hotel Hephaestou did not exist, that that was why the Hotel Corona had been so stubborn. Then a news-vendor knew it, and told him at least the direction.

It was up a dark, narrow street. It had only a dim light over it. But there was its name, Xenodochaion Hephaestou on a sign at one side of the door. Chester attempted to inquire if his luggage had arrived. In the tiny lobby, he could not imagine where they could have hidden it, if it had arrived.

"No," said the man, shaking his head.

Chester was still not quite sure. It had been perhaps twenty minutes since the Greek had spoken to the Hotel Corona for him. He asked tiredly for a room with bath. The man apparently knew the phrase. He nodded, and said:

"You passport, pliz."

Chester walked restlessly towards the door, reaching in his inside pocket for his passport that was with Colette's. He did not want the man to see that he had two. He turned back with his own, and presented it. He must get rid of her passport, he thought. It was not hers, anyway. And when they identified her—*Could* they identify her? Was there enough left of her face? If they could, she would be Mrs. Chester MacFarland. Had she a photograph of herself, or of him in her billfold, he wondered. Why hadn't he thought of that before, days ago? *Oh, Christ, where is my luggage with my Scotch in it, with my money?* Chester looked towards the empty doorway of the hotel. Then he crossed the little lobby to a chair and dropped into it.

The man said something to him, one word, smiling.

"I'm waiting for my luggage," Chester said, not caring what the man had said.

A taxi drew up. Chester sat up in his chair, too tired to stand up.

Rydal got out. Chester felt a jolt in his chest, a throb as if a hand had caught his heart and made it stop for an instant. He stood up slowly. Rydal seemed to be alone. There was no bellboy. But all his luggage was being lifted out of the taxi. Rydal glanced in, saw him, and looked away. Rydal was paying the taxi-driver. The man behind the desk came out to help with the luggage. Chester stood where he was. Rydal looked at him as he walked in, carrying his own suitcase and the antelope duffel. Rydal nodded. His expression was stiff and strange. His wet black hair hung down over his forehead.

The hotel man was saying something to Rydal that Chester could not understand. Rydal answered him briefly, nodding towards Chester, and he gave Chester a faint smile.

"Evening," Rydal said to him. Then he spoke in Greek to the hotel man, who smiled, nodded, and took Rydal's passport. While the man was writing in the register, Rydal walked towards Chester.

"Are you taking the boat tomorrow or the plane?" Rydal asked.

"I was going to take the boat," Chester said quickly.

"And now?"

Chester did not answer. It was as if his mind had stopped working.

Rydal turned and went back slowly to the desk. He said something, several sentences, very quietly, to the hotel man, who listened and nodded solemnly. Chester watched them through narrowed eyes. Rydal was no doubt telling the man that he wanted to be notified if his friend left the hotel, checked out of the hotel. Rydal perhaps was telling the man he was upset by some bad news, something like that.

Chester—Rydal declining to go first into the small elevator—went up with the desk man and a couple of his suitcases to the third floor, which was the top floor, of the hotel.

"Where is my friend?" Chester asked the man, pointing downward. "What room is he in?"

"Room?" The man showed him a key tag on one of the keys in his hand. It had a 10 on it.

Chester's room was 10 he noticed, as they walked towards it. "The other key. For him," Chester said, reaching for the other key in the man's hand.

"Ah! *Pende!* Five," said the man.

The floor below, Chester thought. He was almost too tired to care. Then, as he sat in the ghastly, lumpy armchair, after tossing his damp coat on the bed, waiting for the rest of his luggage, he thought, no need to worry Rydal's going to get away from you, because Rydal's not going to let you get away from him. Chester smiled bitterly. All he needed was Athens, any big city, and he'd telephone a message in to the police about Rydal Keener. He wouldn't have to give his own name to the police—Chamberlain, or anything else. If they suspected he was Chamberlain, or if Rydal told the police he was MacFarland alias Chamberlain, when they picked Rydal up, Chester could be miles away by then, in some other country. He'd arrange, before anything else, to get still another passport from Niko, one Rydal wouldn't know about. He'd pay enough to Niko for him to keep his mouth shut. Which of course might be plenty, but he had it. Yes, he had it.

Here it came, the money, in his big tan suitcase, and here came the duffel with his Scotch bottles. Chester tipped the panting manager, and, as soon as he had gone, poured himself a badly needed drink.

He'd catch the plane tomorrow. They'd both be on the plane tomorrow back to Athens. It was funny.

Then Chester realized that he couldn't afford to wait until 3:30 to catch the plane. Better that he took the boat tomorrow morning at 9, even if the boat took twenty-four hours (which it did) to get to Piraeus. They would certainly find her body tomorrow morning, when it became light, find it as soon as they opened the place to the public. Chester vaguely believed that she wouldn't be found tonight, even if a guard went through the place calling everybody out. A guard wouldn't necessarily or very likely flash a torch around on all the terraces to see if anyone was still there. But by 9 or at latest 10 tomorrow morning, the body would certainly be found. Chester tried now not to think about her *body*, just the fact that it would be found.

Chester drank off his Scotch, and poured another. There was water from a basin in the room. The bath was down the hall somewhere, the proprietor had said, and Chester supposed that he would be able to find it.

He took off his shirt and bathed himself with a face towel at the basin. He stank of sweat. His face in the mirror shocked him—haggard and old, grey and exhausted-looking. Like a man moving in his sleep, Chester dragged on his jacket, for warmth, without putting on a shirt, and lay down on the bed on his back. He did not sleep. Consciousness was like a little whirling knot in the center of his brain, indestructible, useless also, for he was not thinking. The creaking of a floorboard in the hall made him go tense. Then he flew from the bed, saw the key in the lock, and turned it. The door had not been locked. His heart pounded as if he had been in mortal danger.

There were no more creaks in the hall.

He fell into a half sleep. The rain peppered the windows now and then, when the wind blew. Somewhere outside, there was a cat fight. Chester saw two mangy cats fighting on the edge of a roof, clinching in battle, falling over the edge together. He woke up with a start, sat up.

What's the matter with now, he thought. Call the police now, tell them where Rydal Keener is. Tell them Rydal Keener killed his wife, because he couldn't get her away from her husband. Tell them Rydal Keener is off his rocker, Rydal Keener killed the police agent in the King's Palace Hotel, and threatened to kill him, if he told anyone about it. Chester had seen the murder in the hall. Chester was a victim of circumstance. Chester had paid the fellow five thousand dollars to get free of him. The money was on Rydal Keener, the police could find it, if they looked. Yes, go the whole way—No, Chester changed his mind about that. He wouldn't be able to say he was Chamberlain, had always been Chamberlain, when he'd been registered at the Hotel King's Palace as Chester MacFarland. How would he explain the passport with the name Chamberlain on it? Well, he'd acquired it as a last, desperate measure, to keep himself from being caught and blamed for the Greek agent's murder, for a murder that Rydal Keener had done. The motive? Worry about that later. Rydal Keener was a psychopath, that was it. Rydal Keener had murdered his wife to spite him, murdered her because he couldn't get her. Chester had heard of men doing that.

What was the matter with now?

Chester stood up. There was no telephone in the room. He could go downstairs, go to a telephone outside somewhere. Of course. That was better, anyway. Chester could hear himself saying, *You will find the body of Mary Ellen Chamberlain on a terrace of the Knossos palace. . . . Yes. Now. The murderer is Rydal Keener. He is at the Hotel Hephaestou. K-e-e-n-e-r. . . .*

It could be done. It could be done. Just tell them, he thought. Just say, *Rydal Keener is also responsible for the death of George Papanopolos in Athens last week. . . .*

Chester opened his suitcase to get a fresh shirt. Lifting the suitcase to the bed had sent a pain of fatigue through his right arm. With the clean shirt in his hand, he realized he was not going to go out and call tonight. The town was too small. How many Americans in it? It was ridiculous. He'd have to check out of the hotel before the police came for Rydal, Rydal wouldn't let him check out—No, it was impossible. But Athens, that was another matter. Chester decided to go down and speak to the proprietor about the boat tomorrow. He might have to buy his ticket in advance. Chester put on the clean shirt.

There was a knock at the door. Then the knob turned.

Chester knew that it was Rydal. He went to the door. "Who is it?"

"You know who it is. Open the door."

"I don't care to see you."

Rydal's shoulder crashed against the door, made the wood creak, but the lock held.

Chester opened the door.

"Thanks," Rydal said, and came in.

Chester thought for a moment that Rydal was drunk. But his eyes did not look drunk. Rydal swung the door shut carelessly behind him. He stood looking at Chester for several seconds, his thumbs in the waistband of his trousers. Chester looked away from his eyes, then back again.

"Just what do you want?" Chester asked.

"I came in to kill you," Rydal said, his fingers moving a little at his waist. "You know—I'll just say you were a suicide. I've already planted the idea in the hotel-keeper's mind."

Chester had started to sweat, though he was not at all afraid. It was too absurd. He smiled slightly. "And how were you proposing to do it?"

"Hang you. A couple of ties'll do it. That light fixture looks substantial."

Chester glanced up. The light fixture was not at all substantial, he thought, not at all. He shifted his feet to a firmer stance. "Get out of my room."

"Oh, no." Rydal smiled. "Maybe you'd like to turn me in to the police first. You wouldn't want to die before you'd done that, would you? Do it now, what're you waiting for? See how far you get! You disgusting swine, *haven't you a brain in your head*?" Rydal's voice was suddenly loud. He leaned forward. A vein stood out in his neck. *"Swine!"*

"Get out of here. You're hysterical." Now Chester was afraid of him.

Rydal bit his lip. He became visibly calmer, as quickly as he had flared up. "I don't think I'll bother talking to you," he said, and walked to the door. "We'll continue this in Athens, all right? You'd better take the boat tomorrow, not the plane."

Chester did not say anything. He was looking at Rydal, but he had not moved from where he stood.

"Unfortunately I'd better, too. The police might pick me up before three tomorrow, and that'd give you time to get away from me." Rydal went out and closed the door.

Chester did not want to go down and ask about the boat now. Let Rydal take care of it, as long as they both had to catch it. He went to the door and turned the key. Then he undressed slowly, and slipped between the sheets without bothering with pyjamas. But he left the light on. He felt safer with the light on. He realized that he was afraid to turn Rydal in to the police, even turn him in by means of a telephone call in which he would not give his own name, and even in Athens. Rydal had too much against him. Rydal could call Niko in as a witness, as a corroborator of the passport falsification, if he had to. Rydal could tell the police about his Chamberlain alias—and God knew what Colette had told Rydal about him, maybe plenty. There was only one thing to do, and that was to get rid of Rydal by killing him. On his second try, he mustn't fail. The safest, Chester thought, was to get someone else to do it. Maybe someone Niko in Athens would know. Tell Niko he had a dangerous job for someone, an important job he was willing to pay a lot of money for. Niko would know the right person. Don't tell Niko what it's all about. Just talk to the one man who would do it. Chester would be able to tell as soon as he saw the man. If the first man weren't right, he might know someone who would be right. It could be done.

13

Rydal was surprised the next morning at 7:30 not to get any response from his knock on Chester's door. He knocked several times and called Chester's name. No answer. Then he ran downstairs.

The same man was on duty behind the desk, dozing now, tipped back against the wall in a straight chair. He sat upright when Rydal rapped on the counter.

"Excuse me. The gentleman in number ten. Has he checked out?"

"Who?"

"Number ten. Mr. Chamberlain."

"Ah, no, he went out at . . . oh, four or five o'clock."

"This morning? With his luggage?"

"No, no," the man said, smiling. "Not with his luggage. I don't know, maybe he was going for an early morning walk."

"Thanks." Rydal walked to the front door and looked up and down the little street. Well, relax, he thought. Chester would be back. Unless of course he'd taken all his money from his suitcase and gone off with it, left his luggage behind. Rydal couldn't believe that. Just as he was about to turn and go back into the hotel, Chester came around the corner. Rydal walked back into the lobby. "He's coming," he said to the man.

"Ah, good. He sleeps badly, your friend, maybe."

"I suppose. We'll be leaving in half an hour, so could you make up our bills?"

"Yes, sir."

Rydal walked slowly towards the stairway, not wanting the proprietor to see any hostility between him and Chester. As Chester approached the stairway, Rydal, on the fourth step, turned and said, "Good morning. I've just asked the man to make up our bills. We ought to leave as soon as possible. The boat leaves at nine."

Chester looked puffy-eyed and pale. "Okay," he said.

Rydal went to his room on the second floor, and Chester went on to the third. "See you downstairs at eight," Rydal said.

Around 8, they paid their bills in silence, loaded their baggage into the same taxi, and set off for the port. There was a newsboy on the dock near the ship. Rydal bought an Iraklion paper. One glance at the front page and he saw there was no mention of a body having been found at Knossos. Rydal spoke to a ship's steward on the dock, and was told that tickets could be bought in the main saloon on the main deck. Rydal asked a porter to take their luggage on board.

Fortunately, there were still state-rooms available in first class. Rydal did not care to go even second class on such a ship. There was a third class probably relegated to the ship's bowels, and the open stern of the main deck was already jammed with people who had no shelter at all for the twenty-four hour trip, people who were eating oranges and bananas and sandwiches and throwing the remains over the side or simply dropping them at their feet. A glimpse of them as he had gone up the gangway had depressed Rydal. They looked like cattle in a pen, except that these were already pushing and squabbling over sleeping room for the night, some providently holding positions by lying down on the deck and refusing to budge: man was capable of thinking ahead.

"I can give you a state-room together," said the purser.

"No, no, that's quite all right," Rydal said, almost too vehemently. He was speaking in English to the purser, who sat behind a desk in the main saloon, and Chester was standing four feet away. "Separate ones are fine." The prospect of sharing a state-room with Chester had brought a reaction that he felt was visible.

Chester got a number 27, Rydal a number 12. They were on opposite sides of the ship.

To Rydal's great joy, his state-room, a room for two, was empty, and more than likely it would stay empty. He hadn't seen anyone else buying tickets from the purser. As soon as his suitcase was inside, he took off his jacket, pushed the curtain of his porthole aside and glanced out—getting a glimpse of Iraklion that looked like yellow-white stones tumbled down a hill, and a close-up of a blue-capped porter hurrying by just outside on the deck—then he sat down on a bunk and put his hands over his face. Now, he thought, surely just about now, they were finding Colette's body. That was what this morning's sunlight would bring, Colette's body. Rydal lay on the bed with his hands behind his head and his eyes closed, listening to the ordinary, workaday shouts, bumps, clanks and footfalls all around him and above him. The news would come in on the ship's radio before noon, he thought. The news would get around the ship, among the passengers. It was bizarre enough. Rydal thought of Colette's pocketbook—it had been under her right arm, under the elbow—and wondered what was in it. Not her passport, Rydal thought, but maybe a driver's license, for Mrs. Howard Cheever, maybe a photo of herself and Chester, maybe a photograph of Chester, or had Chester thought to make her take all such things out of her billfold? He imagined the ticket-seller at the Knossos palace, chattering away now, telling the police about the young man with the American accent who had asked him if anyone had driven away in a taxi. Yes, the young man had behaved more suspiciously than the older man. In fact, he hadn't seen the older man leave at all, perhaps. Rydal imagined the police speculating as to whether Chester might also have been murdered by the young man, his body still somewhere on the grounds, down in one of the oil-vat pits, or in a corner of one of the labyrinthine rooms, or lying in some drainage depression in a floor, perhaps behind the queen's bathtub.

Rydal realized he could be out of it, if he chose. Chester was under his heel, not the other way around. Rydal quite expected that Chester would try to kill him, probably try to hire someone to do it, because he wouldn't have the cleverness or the courage to do it himself. Yes, Chester was in a very, very bad position, his morale worsened by the death of his wife. Rydal enjoyed seeing Chester in a bad position, enjoyed seeing terror in his face. It was not at all that he was playing policeman, avenger of Colette, Rydal told himself. He was simply amusing himself, and he was going to grow tired of it in about four days, he thought, even if they got to Italy or France in that time, and then he would quit it. He would leave

Chester, after giving him some worse scare than he had yet known. After perhaps preparing a way for Chester to run right into the police. That was his idea, in principle. Rydal slid the chain bolt in the door, so that the door could open only about three inches, if anyone tried to open it, and then he shaved at the basin. To the right of the basin was a narrow door which gave on to a shower. The boat was getting under way.

Around 10:30 he went on deck to look at the sea. But he did not look behind, at Crete. He did not want to see Crete disappearing. Ahead and on either side, there was no island in view, nothing but blue, rolling, and slightly choppy water. The sky seemed unusually bright and clear, as if yesterday's rain had swept the world of clouds. Rydal explored the boat, went through the little main saloon again, where the purser's desk had been, and down some central stairs covered with worn linoleum that was held down by fixtures of brass-plated tin, stairs with a heavy wooden balustrade that might have had a certain elegance in the days of Queen Victoria. The ship was fairly clean, but everything on it had been allowed to wear out. The first-class lounge had a dreary atmosphere. It was a round room at the stern, above the open deck where the cabinless passengers were crammed. There were not enough chairs, and only one sofa, fully occupied. There was not a piano or a card table. A few men—two looked Italian, one might have been French—leaned against the partitions between the wide windows, smoking quietly, gazing out at the water. A Greek radio program of dance music was on. The ship had begun to roll. Rydal heard a plump woman on the sofa say in French that, if this kept up, there wouldn't be many for lunch. The rolling of the ship made the floor alternately push and fall away from his feet. There was a tiny bar to the left of the door, Rydal saw now, only a short counter, with no seats provided, and no barman, either.

And here, standing at a window smoking, Rydal heard it on the 11 o'clock news. It was the first item:

> . . . the body of a young woman found on the south terrace of the Palace of Knossos . . . killed by a large vase which came from an upper terrace . . . not yet been identified (static obliterated a phrase here and there) . . . believed to be American. . . . are certain she was the victim of a deliberate attack, as there had been no vase directly above her on the parapet . . . Police are withholding other information until . . .

"Knossou?" One of the men Rydal had thought were Italian was taking it up in Greek. "What a place for a murder, eh?" And the two laughed a little.

Rydal turned his eyes drearily away from them.

"What's the news?" asked the Frenchwoman. She was knitting away briskly at something beige.

"A murder in the Palace of Knossos," answered her companion in Greek-accented French.

"Tiens! A murder! And we were just there Sunday! A murder of whom?" The knitter sat up.

"Une jeune américaine! Mon Dieu, ces américains!" Head shaking.

Rydal watched it spread slowly, like a small fire as yet undangerous, through the lounge, watched the smiles, the shrugs, the eyebrows lifted with interest, and dropped again. Many had no doubt just been to the palace. It was a tourist must. The interest in the lounge was only mild, but enough to make people ignore the rest of the news.

The news report came from Athens, Rydal heard at the conclusion. It had gone from Crete to Athens and bounced nearly all the way back again. Rydal carried his cigarette to a standing ashtray, put it out, and went back to his state-room. The long metal key was in his pocket. Chester, he supposed, was drinking Scotch in his own state-room. Rydal took out his black-and-white covered notebook, and wrote:

January 16, 19—
11:10 a.m.

No entry for the 15th, Monday. This is the Tuesday after the Monday. Monday will not be forgotten, and I know I could not do it justice. Now I am on a boat with C. between Iraklion and Piraeus, and have just heard the news report, which mentions no names. I am on a boat full of hogs and idiots, attached to one hog-idiot as if he were a particular magnet for me, as if he had some important relationship to me (like a father's), and as if we have some important destiny to fulfil together. I know the destiny, it's all quite clear, simple, sordid, nothing mysterious about it, and there'll be no surprises. I detest him. I think I am fascinated by that. I have no desire to kill him, have never wanted to kill anyone. But I will say I would like to see him fall. Just fall, in every sense of the word. He has certainly begun already.

On the contrary, it's my own life that I have to protect. Chester has every reason to get me out of the way, not only because of what I know about him, but because he thinks I have had his wife, and he hates me for that. And she's gone, and all that. That's why I am ready to weep for the nonsense and the idiocy of all this, she's gone.

And Chester hates himself for that. Like all stupid people who hate themselves, he'll strike out against anybody else.

Rydal waited until very late to enter the dining-room for lunch. But there was Chester in a corner, a bottle of yellow wine beside his plate, eating away. Rydal turned in the doorway, and went back to his state-room. Chester had not seen him. Around 4 Rydal ordered a small but elegant lunch, as elegant as the ship afforded, which was—Rydal consulted with the steward—a mushroom omelet, salad of endives, Brie cheese. There were meat dishes, but Rydal did not want meat. With this he had a cold white Montrachet, the most expensive white wine on the list.

Then he added to his notebook-journal (the front part was for poems, the back part for his irregularly kept diary):

What bores me is the mundaneness of all this—wrong word, I mean prosaicness (prosaism?), its dreariness and drabness and its predictability. I am expecting something to hit me like a flash, a bright light in my face. I want a moment of truth—that may also kill me. I want illumination. I am sure it comes in a flash of comprehension, and that it's not something one sits down and works out on paper or in one's thoughts. Colette was beginning to give me it. *Beginning*, yes, but with her it would have been a flash finally also. It was beginning when she made me break out in a smile, or laugh as I haven't laughed since I was a kid. She would have lifted me to a certain plane that would have lasted for days and then—wham! The truth. It might have happened if we had ever made love. Yes, the flash, the flash. She would have given it to me and I let her die! If I'd only rushed forward instead of sideways or back or whatever I did, I could have caught her by the shoulders, pushed her back—with *me.* And then, my God! Would she have stayed with Chester then?

No. She would have said, with the simple logic that any child is capable of "Chester, you were trying to kill him. You're evil and I hate you." And maybe, "I love Rydal." All simple, all so simple. Now idiots smirk in the sleazy first-class lounge, listening to the news of her death. I am bound to say, to be honest, that I would take great pleasure in avenging her. My Pallas Athenae, Vestal intacta. Back to Latin, more than Greek a language for warriors. The wine is in my blood. I'll sleep a while.

At ten to 6, Rydal was in the lounge again with a glass of metaxa in his hand, awaiting the news. A man came up to him and asked in Italian-accented English if he would like to make a fourth at bridge. Rydal glanced, and saw that a bridge table had mushroomed at one side of the room.

"Thank you, I . . . not feel so well." Rydal lifted his glass of reddish-brown aperitif to imply that he was taking it for medicinal purposes.

"You are Italian!" said the man in Italian, smiling.

"Si, Signor," Rydal nodded. At least his suit was Italian. His shoes happened to be French.

"I thought you were American."

"In these clothes?" Rydal smiled. "No, thank you, I am honored by your invitation, but I think I'll go to bed after a simple dinner."

The news was coming on.

"Seasickness?"

"No, a bug I picked up in Crete," Rydal continued in Italian.

"Hope you feel better tomorrow!" said the man, going off.

Rydal waved in reply to him.

Now the news of Knossos was the third item. The ticket-seller had been queried, and, as Rydal had supposed, he had described him and not Chester. Dark hair, dark eyes, about twenty-five. A man's grey felt hat of American manufacture and also a guidebook of Greece had been found on the palace grounds, but there was no name or initial on them. Rydal had to force himself to stay where he was, leaning with crossed legs against a windowsill of the lounge, gazing dreamily at his metaxa. He must not speak a word of Greek to anyone on the ship, not even to a steward. He had spoken a mixture of English and Italian to the steward today in regard to his lunch. The ticket-seller had stated that the young man spoke fluent Greek with an "English" accent, which could mean either American or English, Rydal supposed. When the news report was over, Rydal stared sideways out the window on to the darkening sea for a minute or two. There was more noise in the lounge than there had been this morning. He did not hear any of the passengers discussing the Knossos news. Then Rydal strolled to the doorway and went to his state-room. He would do without dinner tonight.

It was quite likely, he thought, that the police would be on hand in Piraeus to look over the ship's passengers for a young man of about twenty-five, et cetera, who spoke Greek. Rydal felt sudden panic. Chester might see him being questioned, on deck, by the gangway, before any of the passengers were allowed off. Chester might decide it was the perfect moment to come forth and say Rydal Keener killed his wife, that it was not true that Rydal Keener didn't speak Greek, because he did, that he had been going to turn Rydal Keener over to the police as soon as he could free himself long enough to get to a telephone. Chester could say that Rydal Keener had threatened to kill him if he reported to the police what had happened at Knossos. Rydal's panic did not last more than a few seconds. It just wouldn't happen like that. Chester had too much to lose himself.

In an effort to arrive at a sense of mental orderliness, however brief and flashing it might be, he read poetry that evening. He had two slim books with him, one from America and one from London. The one from America was *The End* by Robert Mitchell, and Rydal opened it to the poem called "Innocence", which was his favorite, next to the longest first poem, which concerned a young man's consciousness of being alone—or merely existing—in a large city. The one called "Innocence" said, in part:

I have never sung. Never sung a song.
I have been happy and opened my mouth and only
shouts would follow.
Great bellows.
I was trying to make the world see me.
. . . But I did not sing when I was young although I have
always been all song
My lips have burst with the songs I have never sung
and never even known—
all disconnected and bursting to be said.

The final verse was a sad one, maturity had set in, there were no more songs to be sung, said the poet, and Rydal did not read the last stanza.

The poem to him spoke of the incompleteness of his love during the time of Agnes. This had crossed his mind on the first reading of the poem more than a year ago, and until now he had avoided the poem, though he liked it. Now he read it with savor, looking at the spelling even of every word. Rydal remembered an early poem of his own, written at fifteen, not in the notebooks he now had with him:

What was purple last week
Has become red.
The sky is wider.
The brook out the window
(something something)
With the waterfall—
Does its water change,
Or is it the same water
Arrested, forever tumbling its pretty length downward?
I wish the landscape out the window,
The barren, beautiful trees,
The swifts that flew by
When you and I stood watching,
Would arrest themselves forever.
Your hand, your eye have captured—
I want no spring.
I want for nothing.

In later years, Rydal had read so many poems that spoke of waterfalls being arrested, that the image had become a cliché to him. The most imaginative element of his poem, probably, was that he had written it in spring, when the trees were not barren, and he had set the poem in winter. It evoked Agnes to him more strongly than better poems he had written since, to her or about her.

Around 10 he put on his overcoat, swathed the lower part of his face in his muffler—it was now windy and rainy—and went out on deck. It was not possible to walk around the deck, but only for a stretch on either side amidships. Rydal walked steadily and tensely, up and down the port side. A man with a pipe stood hunched at the rail, looking out at the sea. Rydal crossed the ship through a corridor and went out on the starboard deck. It was empty. Spray bounced from the broad rail and hit his face. The stars were hidden, the sky black. The ship drove straight against the wind, and Rydal stood leaning against it, the tails of his overcoat flapping. He was glad the voyage would be over tomorrow morning at 9, glad it wouldn't last for another two or three days. The ship cast a small glow of light in a circle around it, and beyond the glow was darkness, and no star or light showed where the sky or sea might end or begin. He stepped inside the corridor to light a cigarette, and went out again to the rail. The door opened again, and was whammed shut by the wind. Rydal glanced over his shoulder.

Chester had come out. He was wearing a cap. He seemed to hesitate, balanced on the balls of his feet, and Rydal could not tell if he were drunk or swayed by the wind against his back. He came towards Rydal.

"Evening," Chester said, his voice deep and steady.

Rydal straightened a little, on guard. "Just as well we're not seen talking together."

"What?" Chester leaned closer.

Rydal repeated it more loudly, and glanced above him to see if anyone were in sight, able to listen, on the deck above. He saw nothing but an empty white rail, the glassy face of the pilot-house above the bridge.

Chester said nothing, but came a few inches closer and leaned on the rail.

Rydal wanted only to get away from him, but not so quickly that it would seem a retreat, that he were running. An unexpected roll of the ship lifted them both a little, on to their toes. Another like that, Rydal thought, and he could fairly lift Chester like a doll and toss him over. Chester could probably more easily toss him over.

"Good night," Rydal said, turning away.

Chester's blow caught him in the pit of the stomach, an unbelievably fast blow, and even through the overcoat, it hurt. Chester gave him another, right on the hand that covered his stomach. This one hurt the fingers of his right hand. A blow to the jaw knocked him down. Rydal lay partly in the trough below the rail, motionless, clutching his stomach and trying desperately to start breathing again. Then he grabbed Chester's ankle with two hands and pulled. Chester kicked him with his other foot and caught him in the neck. The pain made him almost pass out. He went limp, and for a few seconds could not move. He felt Chester lifting him by the front of his coat, by an arm between his legs. He was half-way up the rail, and then he began to struggle, and Chester dropped him.

There was a long moment of stillness. Rydal lay with his cheek against the deck, drawing his hands up slowly in a position to push himself up.

He heard Chester's footsteps walking away. He heard the slam of the door. Then someone's whistling, a tune. On hands and knees,

Rydal crawled forward, into shadow. The whistling stopped. A hand touched his back.

"Hey! What's the matter? You're sick?" The words were Greek.

Rydal could barely see a seaman's rough shoes, uncreased blue trousers. He struggled upright. "Thank you. I lost something. On the deck here," Rydal said in English.

"What do you say? You are all right?"

Rydal took a deep breath and smiled, though they stood now in the patch of darkness just aft of the deck's roof, out of the flow of lights from the covered part of the deck. He managed to throw off the sailor's hand on his arm, to give the sailor a slap in return. "I'm okay. Just looking for something on the deck."

The sailor nodded, not understanding a word. "Take care. Rough sea. Good night, sir," he said, and turned away and climbed a white ladder to the bridge.

Rydal clung to the rail for a few minutes, until his breathing became normal. His stomach still hurt. His jaw stung. Rydal smiled bitterly. For a middle-aged man, Chester fought very well. Of course it had been a surprise attack. It wouldn't happen again. He passed his hands over his face, then looked at his hands for blood. There seemed to be no blood. Then he went in to his state-room.

14

The Greek police officer, scarcely looking at Rydal's face, laid a hand on his shoulder, and said in English, "Would you step aside, please?"

There was another police officer on the other side of the gang-plank, watching the trickle of debarking passengers. About thirty of the first and second class had already debarked. The third and steerage classes were getting off from a lower deck.

Rydal had without remonstrance stepped to one side of the officer and slightly behind him. The officer, like his colleague, was still closely watching the slowly moving line of passengers. Rydal was alone. Then he saw, beside the other officer, a sturdy young man with tightly waving light-brown hair, a frown between his eyes as he tried to find someone down on the dock. Then his hand shot up, he grinned, and a voice yelled something from below.

"Non *so!*" shouted the young man with brown hair. "Non *so!*" Then, also in Italian, as he broke out in a laugh, "Maybe they think

I'm a dope smuggler! Do I look like a dope smuggler?—Wait for me! Wait there!"

Chester appeared in the saloon doorway, stepped onto the deck, taller than the people in front of him. He was wearing his cap. Then he saw Rydal standing behind the tall, slender police officer. Rydal saw in his face that he understood. There was a slight smile, one of nervous satisfaction, on Chester's lips. Chester loitered, letting several people get in front of him. He carried the duffel in which he kept his Scotch. Now was the time, Rydal thought, for Chester to tell the policeman *his* story, confirm their suspicion that Rydal was the young man the ticket-seller at Knossos had seen on Monday afternoon. And Chester seemed to be turning this over in his mind, but his wary eyes avoided those of the tall police officer, and Chester drifted on with the other passengers, down the gang plank. Chester was afraid to stick his nose in too far. Rydal kept his eye on him, down on the dock. He was waiting for his porter with his luggage. Eager taxi-drivers were pouncing on people's luggage, dragging it towards their taxis before it was completely assembled, and distraught tourists shouted at them in half a dozen languages to keep their hands off.

A young man with dark, curly hair joined Rydal, glanced at him with wide, alarmed eyes, then stood by Rydal at the rail.

The police questioned the young man with light-brown hair first. He spoke Italian and a little French, but no Greek. One officer tried him out in Greek: "Are you stupid? Can't learn Greek?" with an apologetic chuckle. The young man's face was blank, and he looked helplessly at the other officer, who asked him in Greek if he had visited Knossos. This brought no response, and the question was put in primitive French.

"Si. Domenica. Dimanche, je visite," said the young man, looking at them with a square, open face.

"Combien de temps est-ce que vous êtes dans Crète?" asked one of the officers.

He said he had spent three days in Iraklion, staying at the Hotel Astir with his aunt and uncle, who were down on the pier. He was asked for his passport. Both policemen looked at it, and then the young man was asked in French where he was going from here.

"Nous allons à la Turquie demain," said the young man.

"Bien." The officer closed the dark-green passport and handed it back to the young man, who rushed happily down the gangplank.

They turned to Rydal.

"You are American?" one asked him.

Rydal nodded. "Yes." He pulled his passport case from his overcoat pocket, a brown cowhide case, opened it, and handed them his passport.

The officers compared the picture with him. In answer to their question, he said he had been in Iraklion four days.

"You have been in Greece more than two months. You speak Greek?" asked one of the officers in Greek.

Rydal was attentive, but gave no sign of understanding. "What are you asking me?"

"If you've learned any Greek," said the other officer, still in Greek.

"Eef you know some Grick," obliged the young man on Rydal's right, with a smile.

"If you please," the officer said sternly in Greek to the young man.

"Just a few words," Rydal said. "Kalispera. Efarhista," with an apologetic shrug.

"When did you visit Knossos?" This question was also in Greek.

Rydal said, with annoyance, "Can't you talk to me in English? What're you asking me?"

"Quand—" He began again, "Vous avez visité Knossou, sans doute."

Rydal smiled. "Vous—avez—visité—Knossos. Yeah. Saturday. Or maybe Sunday. Yeah, Sunday. Why?—Pourquoi?"

"*Why?* Is he stupid?" the officer said, nudging his companion.

They were hipped on the stupid bit.

"Di—manche?" Then, in Greek, "Any witnesses for that? Anyone with you?"

Rydal continued to lean against the rail. "I don't know what you're asking me."

"Who are you travelling with?" the officer asked in French.

Rydal frowned, and asked him to repeat it.

"Je . . . moi . . . seul," he said, frowning now. "Nobody." Rydal spread his hands, palms down.

His passport was handed back to him, and the officer shrugged, and moved sideways towards the young man beside Rydal.

"Partir," said the other officer to Rydal, with a faint gesture in the direction of a salute.

"Thanks," Rydal said, put the passport into his pocket, and went down the gangplank with his suitcase.

Chester was not in sight. Rydal looked for him in every direction. Then he got into a taxi and told the driver to go to Athens. Chester was not going to stop anywhere near the King's Palace again, Rydal was quite sure. He'd go to a hotel around Omonia Square, most likely, like the Acropole Palace or the El Greco, both first-class hotels, because Chester liked his comforts. Chester would also probably try to talk to Niko the first thing, but not before he dropped all that luggage off somewhere. Rydal couldn't imagine Chester getting out in front of the American Express and having a crucial talk with Niko on the pavement with the taxi waiting at the curb with the luggage in it.

"Where do you want to go?" asked the driver as they were entering the city.

"To . . . to the American Express," Rydal said. He wanted to talk to Niko immediately.

Constitution Square with its face of white, expectant buildings gazing on the jumbled area of short trees, of criss-crossing cement walks, gave Rydal a wrench at the heart, and he thought of Colette. The Square had the atmosphere of an empty room, a room that waited for someone, not knowing that the person would never come. It had become suddenly a sad place. He sat up and watched for Niko as they rolled along Othonos Street towards Niko's sidewalk. Then Rydal caught sight of his sponges.

"Hundred drachs, okay?" Rydal asked. He could have got the ride for eighty, but he was in no mood for bargaining. He gave the driver a hundred note, and got out with his suitcase.

Niko saw him when he was three yards away, and his face lit with a surprised smile. "Mister *Keener*! I just saw your friend! Sa-ay—we got to talk!" in a whisper.

"What did he want?" Rydal nervously touched and inspected one of the larger sponges hanging at the height of Niko's elbow.

"He wants to see me today at one o'clock. I should meet him on Stadiou and Omirou on the corner. Say, what kind of trouble is he in?"

"He killed his wife in Knossos," Rydal said.

Niko looked utterly surprised, but he said, in English, "Yeah. Yeah. Seen the paper yesterday. So that was the woman! His wife!"

"Yes."

"You just come from Piraeus? The boat, too?"

"Yes. Listen, Niko, do you know what he's going to say to you when you see him at one o'clock?"

"What?"

"He'll ask you to find a man who will kill me." Rydal said it in the simplest Greek.

"Kill *you*? What in hell!" said Niko, as if this were the most outrageous proposition he had ever heard.

"Oh, he'll ask you to find him a tough guy. He may not tell you what it's for, he knows you're a friend of mine, but that's what it'll be for. Now Niko, what I really need from you is a place to stay in. To hide in, understand? Your place or at one of your friend's, if you know somebody you can trust. Naturally, I'll pay my expenses to whoever—"

"*My* place. Sure, you stay at *my* place," Niko said hospitably. "Just walk in. I don't even have to speak to Anna first. Anna likes you."

Rydal nodded. "You see, Chester was trying to kill me when he killed his wife. She walked under that big vase by mistake. You see, Niko? You read the papers, didn't you?"

"Sure, and I heard it on the radio. Why does he want to kill you? You helped him." Niko peered harder at Rydal. "You ask him for too much money?"

"I haven't asked him for any money," Rydal said patiently, though he was nervous enough to have thrown a curse into his answer. "Oh, his wife took a fancy to me and I liked her, too, and that didn't help." Rydal calmly waited, sadly waited, while this important fragment of the story percolated through Niko's brain. "Mr. Chamberlain, alias MacFarland, is a crook, you know, Niko. Crooks don't trust anybody else. He's afraid because I know too much. Do you see?" It was most important that Niko see, that Niko understand, because, though Niko would do anything for money, and Rydal couldn't begin to compete with Chester in the money department, Niko was still something of a friend of his. Niko wouldn't help to get him killed, Rydal thought. Niko had to know the story, know the real whys of his own behavior, and then—let him make as much money as he could off Chester, Rydal didn't care. "He tried to kill me last night on the boat," Rydal added.

"He did? How?"

"Slugged me and tried to throw me overboard." Rydal saw that Niko didn't quite believe that. No matter. Niko probably thought it was a contributory anecdote, backing up the main theme of his story, which he did believe. "You see, it's just a matter of hours. Certainly by today, they'll identify—" Rydal shut up as a small man with a cigar in his mouth approached Niko.

"A sponge, sir?" Niko said in Greek. "Thirty, fifty and eighty drachs."

"Nyah," mused the man, not looking at Niko, only fingering various sponges that hung from Niko as if they lay on a counter in front of him. "Had a sponge for only a month and it fell to pieces."

"What?" Niko giggled. "Not one of my genuine sponges. Must have been a phony sponge. Maybe sold by a Piraeus man." He laughed, and his lead-framed front tooth showed.

"Which ones are thirty?"

Rydal lingered on, standing some six feet away. The man had not even glanced at him. The transaction was completed, and the man walked away with his sponge, the unlighted cigar stub still in his mouth. Rydal came back. "Okay, I'll go to Anna's now," he said. "But I wanted you to know why, Niko. The police are already looking for a fellow of my age with dark hair. They'll get my name, because I was with Chamberlain at a couple of hotels, you see? In Iraklion and Chania. Registered at the same time with him and his wife. So I won't be able to stay at any hotel where I have to show my passport."

"You want a new passport?" Niko asked, leaning closer to him.

Rydal had to laugh. "Are you coming home for lunch today?"

"Naw. I bring a sandwish today," he said, switching to English again. One hand emerged, holding a lump of paper tied with dirty white string.

"Come home for lunch," Rydal said. "I want to talk to you."

"I got that appointment at one."

"I want you to keep the appointment. Come home for lunch at twelve. Okay?"

Niko pretended to hesitate, then said, "Okay."

Rydal bought a newspaper at a little store between Constitution Square and Niko's place. The paper said the police were inquiring at hotels in Iraklion to see if a young American woman with red-blond hair had been registered, with a husband or alone, the day of or the day before the murder, which was Monday. Since today was Wednesday, the news was Tuesday's or Tuesday night's news. The body had been found only yesterday morning. They would next inquire of the airlines and of the shipping line, Rydal supposed, thinking that the woman might have gone to visit Knossos the day she arrived in Crete, and without registering in a hotel. Then—but then would be no doubt today—they would make inquiries in other towns on Crete, and soon find that a woman answering this description had been registered at the Hotel Nikë in Chania with her husband William Chamberlain, and that they had been accompanied by a young American with dark hair by the name of Rydal Keener, who seemed to be a friend, no doubt the young man whom the ticket-seller at Knossos remembered seeing with them.

Rydal smiled as he walked on. Chester must have seen to it that Colette had removed every identifying paper from her pocketbook. Or maybe Colette, with her practicality, had done it herself. Rydal wondered if Chester would be clever enough to know that it was only a matter of hours before the police would come knocking on his hotel room door, if he registered in a hotel as William Chamberlain? Chester should know that, without any news or any newspaper, if he had any brains at all. Athens had a morning newspaper in English, the *Daily Post.* He supposed Chester had bought it.

Niko's street was a one-way, that the authorities, after digging it up for sewer installation, had never got around to paving. There was invariably a peddler with a pushcart full of cheap shoes on his corner. There was a portable vegetable and fruit shop made of stacked crates two doors away from Niko's semi-basement apartment. Niko's number, 51, was barely legible in worn-out paint beside the door. Rydal knocked loudly and waited. Behind the door was a long cement corridor that led to Niko's and Anna's real door. Rydal had to knock twice before he heard Anna's quick, scurrying footsteps in the corridor.

"Who is it?"

"Greetings, Anna! Rydal," he said.

"Ah-h!" The bolt slid. Anna beamed at him, bright-eyed, apple-cheeked. She was broad and low-slung, her center of gravity down near the earth. Her golden-grey hair was done in a braid around her head, reminding Rydal of classic Greek statues, but her face beneath had been molded by no genius. Her nose was pink and shapeless, she was nearly chinless, but her eyes were lively and kind. Anna was simple, though not stupid.

She led him down the dank cement corridor into the wood-heated room that served as their living-room and kitchen combined. Behind a hanging cloth curtain was a room no bigger than an alcove which was her and Niko's bedroom. Rydal remembered suddenly that Niko had said they had never had any children, because something was wrong with Anna, and she never could have any. Niko used this as an excuse to see other women sometimes—claiming that if any became pregnant, he would be happy to support and care for the child. It was not a pleasant memory to Rydal, because he felt it was a lie. Rydal accepted a cup of tea and a shot of Niko's inferior brandy that was always on the kitchen shelf over the stove. The room smelled of onion and chicken. A big black pot was simmering on the stove.

After two or three minutes of pleasantries, Anna's face grew suddenly solemn, and she said in almost a whisper, "Did you see anything of the trouble in Crete? Holy God, an American woman killed in the Palace of *Knossou!*"

"Did I see anything of it? Yes," Rydal said. He told her all about it, making it as brief and clear as he could, pausing after every sentence for her to gasp, whisper an exclamation, cross herself or send her hands flying out from her breast and back again. When he came to the incident of being questioned by the police in Piraeus just a little more than an hour ago, she rushed to him and clutched his shoulders in her small, strong hands, as if to reassure herself, or him, that he was still among the living.

"I think I escaped by about three hours," Rydal said.

"What do you mean?"

"I think within a couple of hours, they'll have my name. They could have had it this morning, if they'd been a bit faster. I was lucky, that's all."

"Who would tell them your name? Chamberlain?"

It was still a little difficult for her to grasp. "No, as I said, he's afraid to turn me in—I think. He's been too afraid up to now. No, the police could get it from the hotels where I registered with Mr. and Mrs. Chamberlain."

She nodded. Basically, she understood, he thought. She certainly understood that Mr. Chamberlain hated him because his wife had liked him. That was simple and really sufficed as as a motive for Chester. She knew about the Greek agent George Papanopolos's death, of course, but that had been days ago, and he was only an unknown policeman, after all. What she remembered best about that, Rydal supposed, was that it had netted Niko one thousand dollars American. Rydal glanced around the room for signs of prosperity, and saw that the rug was new—a ghastly imitation Oriental with very bright colors that looked as if it had been made, or rather printed, only yesterday, and he saw a new, much larger radio, which was in fact playing softly in the middle of the table on which Niko and Anna ate.

"What a beautiful radio!" Rydal said. It was a sizeable square box of beige wood with lacquered brass knobs, and the sound came from a round aperture backed by dark-red tapestry-like material.

Without a word, Anna turned it up to ear-splitting volume, folded her arms, and waited for Rydal's compliments.

"It's great! Magnificent! Turn it down!"

Anna turned it down. "We can get England! *England!* That is England." She pointed to the radio, which was again playing softly.

"Oh, really?" Rydal said respectfully. He thought of B.B.C. programs coming over, Anna hovering over English plays and poetry recitals, and understanding only a word here and there. Anna was an Anglophile, worshipped everything English, though she had never been to England, and her efforts to learn the language had gained her a vocabulary of only ten or twelve words, as far as Rydal could tell. He wished he had remembered to pick up a couple of packages of Player's for her. He would get them when he next went out. Anna didn't really smoke but she liked English cigarettes because they were English, and she liked to smoke one after a meal.

She was pouring him more brandy. Rydal looked at his watch. It was 11:37. He cleared his throat and said, "Anna, as I said to Niko, I think I'd better stay with you people for a couple of days. At least tonight, I'm sure. I don't know what tomorrow's going to bring."

"Stay with us? Why, of course. You know, Rydal, you're always welcome here. Always. Look at the couch!" She pointed to the sagging three-quarter-sized couch next to the kitchen section.

Rydal had never stayed with them overnight, though they had often invited him "to come and stay a week" with them, mainly because they thought he paid too much at the Hotel Melchior Condylis.

"Are you going to call up Geneviève?" Anna asked with a mischievous twinkle in her eyes.

Geneviève. Rydal's heart seemed to turn over, tiredly. Geneviève was the twenty-year-old daughter of an archaeologist in the French School of Archaeology in the city, and she herself had a Ph.D. in anthropology. Once Rydal had brought her in to meet Anna and Niko, once after a dinner when he and Geneviève had been feeling rather gay. Anna liked to imagine a hot romance between them, a romance that would lead to marriage. Geneviève was very fond of him, but Rydal did not know if she was in love with him or not, probably not. She was the prettiest girl he had met in Athens. He had kissed Geneviève several times, and once they had necked for about fifteen minutes on a sofa in her house while her parents were out. Rydal had thought of asking her to marry him, to go back to the States with him (or maybe he could have found a position in Paris as a lawyer for an American concern there), but he hadn't been absolutely sure, something had said to him that Geneviève wasn't *it,* that he should wait. And now, after Colette, he was quite sure Geneviève wasn't it. Geneviève had paled to nothing, yet not completely nothing, because now she was an episode, an unfinished episode that he felt vaguely ashamed of and responsible for. He couldn't quit Athens, for instance, without saying a thing to Geneviève, without saying a goodbye. He wondered how much he had promised her, how much he had led her to believe? It was strangely all vague to him now.

"Well?" Anna waited. "Or did you meet someone else?"

Anna seemed already to have forgotten about Colette. He'd made the story weak, perhaps, or he had implied that Colette had been fonder of him than he of her. Rydal felt suddenly very much alone.

He stood up. "I'll talk to Geneviève, I suppose." He drank off the brandy. "You see, tonight, Anna, my name may be in the newspapers. I'm suspected of murder—murder of Mrs. Chamberlain."

Anna looked appropriately solemn.

Rydal had the bored, hopeless feeling that comes of trying to explain to a child something that is too complex for it.

Anna saw his discomfort. She took the brandy bottle and hospitably poured him some more, poured his little glass full. "I know. But it will blow over. You'll see."

"The point is, I *am* guilty of . . ." He sought for the right phrase in Greek. "I'm guilty of helping a man who I knew had killed someone. In that hotel. The Greek agent. Aiding and abetting a felon, we'd call it in English," he said, translating the words literally into Greek. "I should never have helped him. I don't know why I did it. Now Chester will say that I killed his wife, and I have no proof that I didn't. It'll just be his word against mine."

"Chester?"

"That's his first name. Chester."

15

Chester had taken a room at the Hotel El Greco at Athinas and Lycourgou Streets, just off Omonia Square. This was a dusty, proletarian sort of square compared to Constitution, and Chester had the feeling of being at the wrong end of town. But at least it was a good distance away from the King's Palace Hotel. The taxi-driver had driven a long way up Stadiou Street, it seemed to Chester, to get to Omonia. Here at the El Greco, in a room that looked brand-new, like a model bedroom in the furniture section of Macy's, Chester had looked for the second time at the *Daily Post* he had bought when he stopped to talk to Niko—Colette had not been identified as yet—and he had gone through her three suitcases to see if there was anything in them he should keep with him. He took her Kleenex box and her toothpaste. His hands were shaking, and he had looked through her suitcases quickly, afraid he would do something odd, if he slowed up, such as scream, fall on the suitcases and tear his hair, or even start cramming some of her things, like his favorite scarf or her perfume, into his own suitcase. He locked the two suitcases of Colette that locked with the keys that hung from their handles. The third he supposed he would have to fasten some way, but let the American Express worry about that. He was going to send them to Jesse Doty in New York to hold for him. Chester could not think what else to do with them.

At twenty to 11, well fortified by Scotches that he had drunk in his room, Chester went out to keep his appointment with Niko at Stadiou and Omirou. Chester had written the street names down on the edge of his *Daily Post.* He was not sure Niko would keep the appointment, if Rydal had spoken to him, and of course Rydal would have by now. Chester had seen from inside his taxi on the Piraeus dock that Rydal had got free from the police there. He had made the taxi-driver wait while he watched what was going on at the head of the ship's gangplank. Chester had hoped, had believed, Rydal had been arrested, they had taken so long with him. And then Rydal had come walking down the gangplank with his suitcase, and Chester had experienced a strange kind of relief which he couldn't understand, until he realized that if Rydal had been detained, he would have told the police all about Chester MacFarland, alias William Chamberlain. Chester would have had to leave the country at once, or try to, try to cross some border illegally, without showing a passport. Yes, it would have been hell. But now he had a chance at Rydal. He supposed Rydal was staying at some friend's place instead of a hotel. It pleased Chester to make Rydal feel uneasy. He intended to make him feel far worse than that.

Chester almost did not recognize Niko at first. He wore a new dark-blue overcoat, a new and spotless grey hat. In fact, Chester recognized him only by the dirty gym shoes, his incongruous footgear. Niko smiled, and Chester saw the horrible framed tooth and the gap next to it.

"Hello, Niko," said Chester.

"Hello, *sir,*" he said, as if "sir" were a name.

"Well—" Chester looked around, saw a café across the street, and proposed that they go over there to talk.

They crossed Stadiou, a difficult operation that stranded them for a few moments in the middle of the street while traffic whizzed by, front and back. It was a very nice overcoat indeed that Niko was wearing, and Chester supposed that his own money had paid for it. They entered the café, which happened to be a pretty fancy one, and Chester felt conspicuous in the company of the gym shoes until they were seated.

"I suppose you've seen Rydal," Chester said at once.

"Oh, yes. Seen him this morning, just after you." Niko accepted an American cigarette from Chester.

The waiter came.

Chester ordered a Scotch. Niko asked for coffee and something else that Chester couldn't understand.

"And I suppose he's staying with you?" Chester said casually. He hated such blunt prying, but on the other hand, he couldn't imagine anything surprising or offending Niko.

"No," Niko said.

"Where is he staying?"

"He stay with a friend." Niko jerked a thumb vaguely.

"Do you know where?"

"Sure, I know where."

Chester nodded. "Where?"

"Ah—near Acropoli." Another jerk of the thumb. "I don't know the name of the street."

"But you know the friend he's with?"

"Oh, sure."

"Who is the friend?" Chester asked.

Niko leaned closer across the table, smiling. "Why you want to know?"

Chester sat up also. He smiled also, man to man, crook to crook. Niko had made a tidy sum from him. "You know, Niko, Rydal and I are connected—somewhat. We have to keep in touch. He did me a good turn here in Athens about the passports. So did you. In Piraeus this morning, Rydal and I got separated, and it was best for us not to stay together this morning. Understand?" He was speaking softly but distinctly. "But Rydal and I may be able to help each other, and very soon. If you don't tell me where he is, I'll find out somehow. Or Rydal will communicate with me. I'm easy to find. I'm at a hotel."

"Where?"

Chester smiled. "I'll tell you, if you tell me who Rydal is with. Plus the address."

Niko smiled broadly, and he looked a little embarrassed. "Oh, okay, if you at a hotel, that's easy. Rydal will find *you*."

Chester chuckled tensely, automatically. "That's right. I'm sure he will."

A silence fell. Seconds passed.

Did he talk to you about Crete? Chester started to ask, but he had decided in his hotel room not to get into that. Niko might not believe him, if he said Rydal killed his wife. There was no reason for him to waste his energy in convincing Niko that he was justified in what he wanted to do. Niko didn't care about justice. Chester was breathing a little harder. He picked up his Scotch and sipped it.

The waiter had set down a cup of thick-looking, dark black coffee and a white pastry of some kind in front of Niko.

"I need two things from you, Niko, and I promise to pay you well," said Chester.

"Yes?" Niko's front tooth showed.

"I'm in the market for another passport. I brought a photograph with me." Chester was speaking softly, so softly Niko had to lean forward, but Chester looked on either side of him to see if anyone were within hearing. Their nearest neighbor was a man buried in a newspaper, ten feet away. "How soon can you get another passport?"

"Hm-m. Maybe day after tomorrow."

"I want you to get it. Here's the photo." Chester handed it across the table to him, the photograph concealed in his palm, held there by his thumb.

Niko's soiled paw came out, whisked it away into his overcoat pocket. He nodded.

"I'll pay you the usual—advance today," Chester said.

"Half," said Niko flatly. "Five thousand. A new passport—ten thousand."

Chester stared at him. "Ten? Why not five?"

"Ten," Niko said.

Chester grimaced. "Very well. And no moustache on this one. The moustache has got to be taken off the photo. Got that?"

"Sure."

"The other thing is—I need a reliable person to do a very important job for me. Someone who isn't afraid."

Niko pushed the pastry into his mouth, and bit off a large piece. "What kind of a job?" he asked, barely intelligibly.

"A dangerous job," Chester said. "Just get me the right man, and I'll explain to him what it is. But I'd like somebody right away. Tonight, if possible."

Niko chewed and reflected.

"Do you think you know such a person? A brave man. Or maybe you know someone who would know such a person. I'd pay well. Five thousand dollars." Chester smiled slightly, letting the figure sink in. Money would make it work, he was sure.

"Yes," Niko said suddenly, positively.

Chester listened to its echo, trying to tell if it were real. "Good," he said. "The next question is, can you arrange a meeting tonight? For him and me. Even late this afternoon. Is the man you have in mind in Athens?"

"Oh, yes. I telephone him." Niko seemed serious about it.

"And—what meeting place would you suggest? You can tell me now. I'll get there."

"He work on—Leoharos Street. You know Klafthmonos Square?"

"No, I don't."

"Ugh. Write it down. Leoharos."

Chester let Niko write it for him. There was a restaurant off Leoharos which had a name like "trapezium", the word for bank. Chester said he was sure he could find it. Niko said he would tell his friend, whose name was Andreou, to be there at 5 o'clock, as soon as he stopped work.

"What does he look like?" Chester asked.

"Oh, he find you. He recognize American," said Niko.

"Yes, but—What does he look like, anyway?"

"Big fellow." Niko spread his hands. "Strong. Black hair." A circular movement with his finger, perhaps to indicate curly hair, perhaps a sign that the fellow was a bit odd.

"You can tell him I will pay him half—tonight—if we come to an agreement. Twenty-five hundred. Understand, Niko?"

"Yeah," Niko said.

"Now about the passport," Chester said softly, and reached for his wallet.

Five minutes later, he parted from Niko on the pavement in front of the café. He had given Niko five thousand. Niko would expect a thousand for himself when the deal was concluded, he had said. Chester had agreed. He walked up Stadiou automatically in the direction of his hotel. He felt better, much better. But he didn't want to go back to that hotel room. *Anywhere* but that. Chester turned around. He walked down Stadiou, thinking of the mail that was surely there for him at the American Express post office. Well, with a new passport—day after tomorrow—he could start over, write his friends in New York, and get them to re-write and send their letters to his new name. And to the American Express in Paris. Yes, by God, the minute he got that passport, he was flying to Paris. Just as well he hadn't asked them as yet to write to William Chamberlain in Athens. He must have known, must have had a sixth sense about that. He wished he had a sixth sense about what was happening in America. It was not at all reassuring to him that the New York *Times* and the Paris *Herald Tribune* were not talking about the investigation of Chester MacFarland or Howard Cheever. He knew he was being investigated now, and the silence of the newspapers gave him the feeling that the investigators were building up a mountain of evidence that would really smash him when it fell.

Chester found himself reaching for his money in front of a movie-cashier's booth. He hadn't the faintest idea what he was going in to see. It didn't matter. It turned out to be a Japanese film with a Japanese sound track and Greek sub-titles.

The Restaurant Trapeziou or Trapezium—Chester couldn't make out the letters—was on a corner, a middle-category restaurant with not very clean white tablecloths and waiters in long dirty white aprons. It was as cold in the place as outdoors, and the handful of patrons, mostly men, were eating in their hats and overcoats. Chester was early. He sat down at a table, and, when a waiter came over and said, "Kalispera," and handed him a menu, Chester mumbled in English that he was waiting for someone. The man came in a minute later. Chester was positive that he was the man, a big, thick fellow with curly black hair, hatless, in a half-wornout grey overcoat. His lips were slightly parted and there was a frown between his eyebrows as he looked over the restaurant. Chester stared down at the tablecloth and smoked his cigarette, confident that the man would come over to him. But what if he spoke no English? They'd have to get hold of Niko. No, someone else, a friend of this man.

"Chamberlain?" asked a voice quietly.

Chester nodded. "Good evening."

The man pulled a chair out for himself. He ordered something from the waiter. Chester asked for an ouzo. Obviously, it was not the kind of place that had Scotch. Scotch was always displayed on a shelf somewhere, if a restaurant had it.

"I . . . hope you speak English well enough to understand me," Chester said, irked by the language barrier which was there, at best. In America, he would have known instantly how to handle a man like this: it was all in the choice of words, all in the way one said them.

"Sure," said the man.

"I am willing to pay five thousand dollars American for what I want done."

The man nodded, as if he heard this kind of figure every day. "What ees eet?"

"Are you a brave man?"

"Brave?" He looked confused.

Chester took a breath. If it wasn't going to work, he didn't want to prolong the conversation.

A tall pink drink arrived for the man, and Chester's ouzo.

"You're a friend of Niko's?" Chester asked.

"Sure. Yes."

"A good friend?"

"Good friend," the man said, nodding. His frown was back.

"I want a certain person killed. Shot, perhaps. Understand?"

The man seemed to hesitate, or balk, one of his thick hands lifted a fraction of an inch from the table, but he nodded. "Sure, I understand."

"But there is one thing I demand in exchange for the money I'm offering you," Chester added hastily, "and that is that you don't tell Niko what you're going to do. Don't talk to Niko at all, in fact. Understand? This has to be a promise."

The man nodded. "Who ees the man?"

"You must first promise not to speak to Niko about this."

"Okay."

It was an unsatisfactory promise. Chester slowly reached for his wallet, looked at it slightly below the level of the table, as casually as if he were about to draw out a hundred-drachma note, and pulled out three five-hundred dollar bills. It was time for the money to show, he thought. "I'll give you fifteen hundred now, on account," Chester said.

The big man stared at the green bills which were nearly concealed in Chester's large hand. He moistened his lips and said, "I want all of eet before the work ees done, because . . . eet would not be safe eef I seen you . . . afterward. Unnerstand? Not safe—me or you." He gestured.

Chester saw his point, but didn't trust him. He wiped his damp forehead with his fingers. "Well, perhaps first you should tell me if you think you can do it at all."

"Who ees the man?" He shook his head at Chester's offer of a cigarette.

Chester lit his, then said, "The man is Rydal Keener." He saw no sign of recognition in the man's face. That was good. Unless the man had been so prepared for the statement that he hadn't had to show surprise. "You know him?"

"No," said the man.

"He's an American, dark-haired, about twenty-five—" Chester spoke distinctly. "Medium height, rather slim. But you've got to find out where he's staying. Niko knows. Do you know where Niko lives?"

"No," said the man in his rather blank tone, shaking his head.

Chester didn't know whether to believe him. A good friend of Niko and he didn't know where Niko lived? "Well—Niko knows where Rydal Keener is. He's either with Niko or with a friend. You'll have to find out from Niko. It'll be up to you to find him, and I would like the job done as soon as possible. Tonight, if possible."

"Tonight?" He considered this. Then shrugged.

"Niko may still be in front of the American Express. It's up to you to talk to him and find out where Rydal Keener is. Niko will tell you. Won't he?"

"Sure. He *tell* me," said the man, as if this weren't all his difficulties, he had others.

"Okay. But I think—" Chester glanced around him, then leaned closer. "I think in all fairness, you had better give me some details as to how you're going to go about it—before I pay you five thousand dollars. That's fair enough, isn't it?"

The man looked as if he had never heard the phrase "fair enough".

"How do you think you will do it?" Chester asked.

The man, still frowning, put out his thick right arm, then jerked his fist towards himself, the gesture of mugging someone, breaking a neck, from behind.

The gesture somehow reassured Chester. The man's anxious expression became the expression of a natural and even healthy tension before a dangerous task. "You're free tonight for the job?"

"For five thousand dollars?" The man smiled for the first time. Two of his front teeth were gold-rimmed. "Yes," he said.

That "Yes" had conviction to Chester. Chester asked a few more questions. No, the man had no gun. Guns were not safe, they made too much noise. He was a strong fellow who could do things with his two hands. Chester felt sure of that.

When Chester left the restaurant at 5:25, Andreou had his five thousand dollars. Andreou had said he was staying on for a couple of minutes to finish his drink, and then he would go to the American Express to see Niko. Chester took a taxi to his hotel. He thought he would take a hot bath, get into pyjamas, and have his dinner sent up from the hotel restaurant.

The police were in the lobby when he arrived. A uniformed policeman and a plain-clothes man sat on a couple of the upholstered straight chairs between the desk and the elevator. Chester saw the man behind the desk give a nod to the policemen. The man stood up and came towards Chester. Chester stood where he was. He saw a man who was depositing his key at the desk look curiously at him and the policemen before he went out.

"Mr. Chamberlain?" asked the plain-clothes man. He was dark-haired, with a long nose. There was something humorous, or sly, in the way he tilted his head as he looked at Chester.

"Yes," said Chester.

"Platon Stapos of the police," the man said, making a pass with his open billfold, too quickly for Chester to see anything, but Chester was sure he was a genuine policeman. He looked around the lobby, at the quiet area with tables and chairs behind him, but the man behind the desk was obviously all ears, even leaning forward over the desk now so not a word would escape him. "May we go up to your room? It would be more private."

"Yes, of course. I'd be very glad to talk to you." Chester looked in a frightened way over his shoulder, through the two pairs of glass doors of the hotel. It was part of his act. Then he went with the men to the elevator. "Oh, my key. Just a minute." Chester walked to the desk. The fascinated clerk turned quickly and got his key, then handed it to him.

They rode up in the self-service elevator, walked down the corridor, and Chester used his key. The room was full of suitcases, opened and closed.

"I am very glad to see you. Very," Chester said. "Won't you sit down? Here. I'll get rid of this suitcase."

The plain-clothes man sat down on the chair Chester had cleared, the uniformed man preferred to stand.

"You are William Chamberlain whose wife Mary Ellen Chamberlain was killed Monday?" asked the plain-clothes man.

"Yes," Chester said. He was standing by the bureau, the Scotch bottle behind him, and he would have liked a drink, but he thought he should wait a few minutes before he proposed one.

"Why did you not speak to the police?" asked the man.

"I was afraid to," Chester said promptly. "Until now, until today—" He broke off. "The young man who did it, Rydal Keener, has been with me every minute. Until today. Even today he trailed me in the streets, watching everything I did. I've been in a—I'm afraid I've been in no state to cope with the police. I mean try to get their help. The loss of my wife was such a terrible shock, I've been nearly out of my mind."

"Tell us what happened," said the plain-clothes man, and pulled out a pad and a fountain pen.

Chester told them. He began with Rydal Keener striking up an acquaintance in Iraklion, then told of Rydal's flirting with his wife.

It went on for three days or so, while they went to Chania. Rydal spoke Greek, so he made himself quite useful to them, and he hadn't much money and Chester had paid him a little for his services, but Rydal Keener kept making advances to his wife, which his wife consistently rejected. On Monday in Iraklion, Chester asked Rydal to leave them, but he insisted on going with them to visit the Palace of Knossos. Rydal Keener was in a furious mood, because he hadn't got anywhere with his wife, and because Chester had asked him to leave. He retaliated in a brutal way, by pushing a vase or dropping a vase from the top terrace on to his wife.

"Of course, he was trying to hit me," Chester said as he finished his story. "That's the only thing that makes any sense. I had just moved away from where she was when she was hit. She'd come forward to talk to me—something like that. It's hard to remember the details." Chester passed his hand over his thin hair. "Excuse me, but may I offer you gentlemen a drink? A Scotch?"

"Not just now, thank you," said the plain-clothes man, his head lowered as he wrote in his notebook.

The policeman shook his head.

Chester poured himself a drink in the empty glass that was on the night table, added a little water in the bathroom. He came back and took the same position by the bureau. "To continue . . . Where was I? Yes. I stayed by my wife a few moments. I was so stunned by what had happened, I didn't know what to do. I then heard—later, from the newspapers—that Keener had asked the ticket-seller if I had gone out, if I'd taken a taxi away. Already he was planning, you see, to make it appear that I'd done the . . . the killing and had run away from the scene." Chester's throat choked up with a genuine emotion—of some kind. He paused, and looked at each of the men, looked for signs of belief in their faces. They looked merely interested.

"Go on," said the plain-clothes man. "What happened next?"

"After a few minutes, I don't know how many minutes, I started looking for Keener. I was in a rage. I wanted to throttle him with my bare hands. I couldn't find him in the palace, so I ran out. I looked on the road. By this time it was getting dark, and I couldn't see very well. I went to Iraklion, thinking—"

"How did you go to Iraklion?"

"I stopped the bus. On the road."

"I see. Go on."

"And sure enough I found him in Iraklion. He was . . ." Chester hesitated, then decided to go ahead. "He was actually waiting for *me* at the hotel where I had left my luggage. He spoke to me and said if I called the police, he would kill me. He said he had a gun in his pocket. I was sure he meant it. He made me go to another hotel with him—I don't know why, it was a worse hotel, and maybe he'd tipped the owner to keep his mouth shut if he saw any strange behavior between him and me, I don't know." Chester took a couple of swallows of his drink. "Then the next morning—"

"You stayed in the same *room* at the hotel?" asked the plain-clothes man, again with his smile that was touched with humor.

"Not ostensibly," Chester replied with a grim smile. "We had two rooms. But he stayed in mine all night, keeping guard on me." Chester suddenly remembered the little walk he had taken early in the morning. The hotel-keeper might remember it, if he were questioned. Maybe they wouldn't question him that closely, Chester thought. Or if they did, and he mentioned it, Chester could say that he had sneaked out and hadn't been able to find a policeman at that hour, or that he was still simply too shocked and too afraid to try to get police help.

"And then?"

"The next morning, we took the boat back to Athens. Even . . . even on the boat, he made an attempt on my life. He knocked me down on the deck and tried to throw me overboard. Luckily, I put up a good fight, and someone came along so Keener had to stop the fight. I was glad to get to Athens, because I thought from here I could certainly get help for myself."

"And did you try? Today?" The plain-clothes man had fairly interrupted him.

"I spent today trying to locate Keener. He disappeared from me as soon as . . . well, as soon as the boat docked. I lost him at Piraeus. I got off the boat first. I was going to report him in Athens, you see." Chester covered his eyes. Then he walked with his drink to the bed and sat down.

"Take eet easy," said the plain-clothes man. "What happened after you got to Athens?"

"I'm sorry," Chester said. "These last days have been such a strain. I'm sure what I'm saying to you doesn't make sense, because it doesn't sound logical. I kept thinking, in Athens there are enough police. I'll just walk up to one, even if Keener's with me and even if he tries to shoot me, and say to the policeman, 'Here's the man you want for the murder of my wife.'" His voice broke on the last word.

There was a silence of several seconds. The plain-clothes man looked at the police officer. So did Chester. The uniformed officer did not so much as twitch a muscle in his face. He might not even have understood English.

"People whose wives are murdered," said the plain-clothes man slowly, "are not always logical."

"No," Chester agreed. "I suppose not."

The plain-clothes man looked at his colleague, and half closed his eyes in a way that might have meant anything—the same as a wink, or that he didn't believe Chester, or that his eyes hurt. Then he looked at Chester. "Where were you trying to find thees Keener?"

"I was looking around Constitution Square," Chester answered. "He made a couple of remarks about spending a lot of time there. Around the American Express."

"Hm. Thees fellow ees an American, ees he not? Not using a stolen American passport?"

"Oh, no. No, no, he's an American, all right. But he speaks Greek quite well, as far as I can tell, and my wife told me he said he spoke several other languages, too."

"Hm." The plain-clothes man looked at his colleague and nodded and said something in Greek.

The other nodded also, and shrugged.

"He was questioned on the boat this morning and got through us. Sleeped by us," said the plain-clothes man.

"Oh?—What do you mean?"

"All the young men passengers looking like him were detained by the police. Questioned. He must have been detained also. But—they were Piraeus police," he said with a chuckle. "Well—we have been checking all the Athens hotels for Rydal Keener since noon today. He ees not registered at any hotel in Athens."

"No. I didn't think he would be. I'm sure he knew you'd get his name sooner or later—in connection with us."

"Yes. Eet was not too easy. Do you know your wife had not one identifying object on her person? Not even anything with an initial?"

Chester shook his head sadly. "I didn't know that. I usually carry her passport for her." He regretted saying the word passport.

Now the plain-clothes man was looking musingly at him. "No, for her identification, we are indebted to a man in Chania, the manager of the Hotel Nikë who spoke to the police in Crete only this morning. He had your names on his register." He stood up. "Please to use your telephone?"

"Go ahead," said Chester.

The plain-clothes man spoke in Greek to the hotel operator. After a moment, he began a conversation in Greek, a conversation in which he did most of the talking. The name "Chamberlain", pronounced suddenly slowly, almost disdainfully, made Chester feel uneasy.

The other man stood like a soldier, hands behind him, occasionally letting his eyes drift to Chester and away.

The plain-clothes man put his hand over the telephone and said to Chester, "Can you tell us—Do you happen to know any other place thees Keener might be? Any other town he spoke of?"

"No," Chester said. "I'm sorry."

"Any people in Athens he spoke of? Anyone he knows?"

Chester shook his head. "I don't remember anybody. I don't think he ever mentioned anybody. But I'm sure he knows several people here, people who would hide him."

The plain-clothes man spoke into the telephone again, and then hung up. He turned to Chester. "We are not going to put into the newspapers that we have identified your wife. We do not want Keener to run farther, you see? We do not want him to think that we have spoken to you and that you have told your story against him. You see?"

Chester saw. But he wondered if Rydal would see through it? "Until you catch him—" Chester began, and abandoned it. "I'm very nervous—with him after me. I'd like to leave for Paris right away. If necessary, of course, I'd be glad to come back to talk to you when you've found him."

"Well, as a matter of fact that would *not* be advisable, because we intend to keep watch on *you.* To guard you and maybe in that way we find Keener. Keener may be unwise enough to try to kill you before you talk to the police—he thinks. Or he may be so impulsive—what ees the word? Wanting revenge that he will try to kill you anyway, thinking you have talked to the police by now. You see?" The man's smile, his easy gesture with one hand was curiously bland. And his eyes were amused.

"You mean I'm to be a sort of decoy," Chester said.

The man thought about this, then nodded vaguely. "I doubt very much really if he will try to find you and kill you. He must know it ees too late. Logically, he would try to sneak out of the country, maybe change his passport." The man was buttoning his overcoat. He beckoned to the officer, and they walked to the door.

Chester wanted to ask them to keep in touch with him, to telephone him tonight and tell him if anything had happened. But he said nothing.

"We shall keep a man downstairs in the lobby. If you go out, the man will follow you," said the plain-clothes man. "Don't let eet disturb you. Eet's for your protection." He smiled. "Thank you, Mr. Cham-ber-lain."

"Thank *you,*" Chester said. "Thank you very much." He closed the door after them.

Then he took a deep breath and lay down at full length on the bed, on his back. With luck, Rydal Keener's body would be found on some dark pavement tonight, or early tomorrow morning. He shouldn't have paid that guy first, however. Chester knew that, just as a matter of business principle. But on the other hand, how could he have paid him off after he did the job, if a police guard were shadowing him? And not getting his money, Andreou might have decided to mug him, police guard or no. Yes, things were best the way they were.

When Rydal Keener was dead, that would be the end of the story, the police guard would be removed, and he would leave for France on his new passport. William Chamberlain would vanish from the earth. Off would come his beard and moustache, and he would be Mr.—something yet unknown in France and in the States.

But if Andreou didn't succeed in killing Rydal—if he was a double-crosser, a friend of Niko, and of Rydal, possibly, too—then a little maneuver involving precise co-ordination would be necessary. It hinged on whether the police found Rydal. If they found Rydal, and he told them his story, Chester would have to have his new passport in hand, give the police guard the slip, even if it meant leaving the hotel with all his luggage in his room, and vanish in the direction of Paris. Chester really didn't think it would come to that. He had a high regard for Rydal's cleverness, and Rydal didn't want to get caught. Rydal might want to hit back at him, but not through the police. In a way, Chester thought, their motives were very much alike—and if anything, Chester considered himself the less vindictive of the two. It was going to come down to a private duel.

Chester was full of hope and confidence. It was something that sang in his veins, an old, familiar sensation to him. Optimism had always won the day for him. A man was no good without optimism, no good at all. Dreamily, Chester put out his right arm on the bed, unconsciously expecting to find Colette beside him. It was a double bed. The bed was empty, flat.

16

Rydal had taken a nap in mid-afternoon, after Niko had returned from his I o'clock meeting with Chester and reported what Chester wanted from him—a passport and an assassin. Rydal knew Andreou slightly. He had come to Niko's apartment one evening in December. Andreou was a florist. He had greenhouses at his home on the western fringe of the city, and he brought in fresh flowers every morning to his shop on Leoharos Street. His wife tended the shop. Rydal was glad that Andreou and his wife, honest and hardworking people, were going to get Chester's five thousand dollars. So after Niko had come and gone a little after 2, Rydal had slept on the three-quarter-sized couch near the simmering iron pot. He had slept for about an hour, and awakened, wonderfully refreshed, to find Anna seated across the room stringing green beans into a pot on her lap, a band of sunlight stretching from the narrow horizontal window behind her and striking her shoulders and her neck. She was like a Vermeer.

"You sleep well? That is good for you," Anna said.

She had turned off the radio, he noticed, no doubt out of courtesy to him. She fixed him a cup of tea. He lay drowsily on the couch, sipping it, slowly coming awake. He thought of Andreou and his meeting Chester at 5 o'clock. Niko said he had told Andreou to look very tough and to say the minimum. Andreou had worked for a while in the Greek Merchant Marine, and had picked up some English in his travels. Rydal thought Andreou would do all right. And besides, Chester had not much choice. It was this that reassured Rydal, that Chester's field of possibilities was so circumscribed. Who else but Niko could he ask for an assassin? Chester would know very well that he was either staying with Niko or that Niko knew where he was. But Chester would not tell the police to question Niko, or to follow him to see where he lived. Chester would not even mention Niko, because Chester didn't really want him, Rydal, to be spoken to by the police. Rydal felt quite safe at Niko and Anna Kalfros's. But he did not think it safe to go outdoors, so when Anna said she had to go out for butter at 4 o'clock, Rydal did not offer to get it for her, and he told her why. Anna understood. She approved greatly of Andreou collecting money for a crime he would not commit. It appealed both to her sense of justice and her sense of humor.

Niko came in just before 7. He said that he had spoken to Andreou around 3, and that he had agreed to meet Chester at 5 p.m. in a restaurant near his florist shop. "Andreou said he would come by tonight to say hello to you," Niko said, smiling.

"Oh? Around what time?" Rydal was wondering if Andreou would be followed, if Chester had been spoken to by the police—say, at some time that afternoon—and if Chester had been followed to the restaurant.

"After work," said Niko vaguely. He was dropping his strings of sponges carefully and methodically on to the floor in a corner of the room. "He work till about eight tonight."

"You talked to him after he saw Chester?" Rydal asked.

"Naw. Don't talk to him since three o'clock." Niko kept on practicing his English—it was a small way of showing off in front of his wife, who didn't understand much or any of it—though Rydal was speaking to him in Greek, mainly because he wanted to be sure that Niko understood what he was saying.

"I hope the police weren't following Chester," Rydal said.

"The police?"

"If they were following Chester, they'll question Andreou. He might not be able to explain why he had an appointment with Chester." Rydal picked up the newspaper Niko had brought in. The Knossos story was on the second page now, a three-inch-long item: the police were still pursuing clues to the identity of "the young woman with red hair", but they had made no progress to date. The police were looking for Rydal Keener, the young man with dark hair described by Perikles Goulandris, the ticket-seller. Keener was believed to be hiding in Athens.

And if they had his name, Rydal thought, they had the Chamberlains', because they came from the same place, a hotel register, and whom did they think they were fooling? The public, perhaps, but not him. Rydal put the paper down.

"Um-m. I read it, too," said Niko. He was pouring three glasses of retsina.

"I don't believe that," Rydal said, half to himself.

"What?" asked Niko.

"That they haven't identified Colette. Anna, what's the best station for Greek news?"

Anna happily went over to her radio and tuned in on an Athens station.

The news came in almost at once. It was 7. Midway in the newscast was a short sentence: "The police of Iraklion are continuing their efforts to determine the identity of the young woman found dead in the Palace of Knossos, but thus far without success."

"They are withholding it," Rydal said.

"Why?" from Anna.

Rydal explained. He said that the police were bound to know by now that the woman found dead was Mrs. William Chamberlain. It was very simple for the police to look for a William Chamberlain registered at one of the hotels in Athens. Chester would not mind being found and questioned by the police, because it would give him a chance to tell them that Rydal Keener killed his wife. "The police are probably keeping it out of the papers," Rydal said, "because they—if they believe Chester—they'll think I might make an attempt to kill Chester before he talks to the police." It seemed quite simple to him, and the likeliest thing also.

"Ah, how horrible," Anna said with a sigh. "That they would think you would kill a man, Rydal."

Rydal smiled. "After all, that's what Chester's trying to do to me. Why, if I had any red blood in my veins, certainly I'd try to kill Chester." He flexed his arms. He felt nervous, not like himself at all, as if he were playing some part on a stage that he was not at all comfortable in.

But Niko laughed appreciatively, like someone watching a play that he was enjoying.

"But—" Rydal went on, sipping his retsina now, "I'm not even interested in knowing what hotel Chester's staying at. I'll wager it's either the Acropole or the El Greco. He'll stay until he gets his passport day after tomorrow. That's when he'll get it, isn't that right, Niko?"

"Is correct. I gave Frank the photo this afternoon."

"And then he'll try to get out of the country," Rydal said.

Anna and Niko looked at him quietly for a moment. Then Anna pushed closer towards Rydal the plate of radishes and little onions and chunks of white cheese that they were nibbling with their retsina.

"And then what will you do, Rydal?" she asked. "I hope let him go. He is an evil man."

Rydal knew she was right. That he should let him go. His common sense told him that, too. But Rydal did not think it would work out that way. He smiled at Anna. "I'll know his new name on his new passport. If he escapes the police, Anna? Gets to another country?" Rydal frowned. "He may well, you know, with a new passport. An evil man shouldn't be allowed to go free, do you think?"

On her face came a slow but unstruggling comprehension. To possess a false passport, she had heard so much about them, was no great misdemeanour. It was as if she had never realized that a false passport invariably concealed a crook of some kind. "You mean, you'll tell the police his new name," she said.

That was not in Rydal's mind at all, but he nodded. "I'll think about it. I may."

Niko's laugh bubbled up in his throat, and he rubbed his hands. "Good! Then he'll send to me for another passport. More business for Frank and me."

Anna looked at him sideways. "Hm-m. No. Let someone else do it. If this man is caught, he'll tell the police where he got the false passports from, eh? What about that?" She pushed her husband affectionately in the shoulder as she got up to stir the pot.

Andreou arrived as they were finishing their Greek style *pot-au-feu.* Andreou was quietly, cautiously radiant. One look at his repressed smile and his glowing black eyes, and they knew his transaction with Chester had been successful. He said that he had got the five thousand dollars. He reached in his pocket.

"My wife is alone in the shop. There might be a hold-up," he said jokingly. "I didn't want to leave the money with her, so I brought it along."

And he brought it along also to show it, Rydal thought. Rydal looked at the new five-hundred-dollar bills on the wooden table beside the soiled soup plates. For a few seconds they all stared at the money, Niko and Andreou grinning, Anna and Rydal smiling. And each of them, looking at the same thing, had quite different thoughts in his head. For Niko and Anna, such a sum might be a house in the country. For Andreou, perhaps a trip to America with his wife. His own thoughts were, there lies my life, my death, my life and death combined, in a handful of green-colored paper.

Then Andreou laughed aloud.

"What're you going to do with it, Andreou?" asked Rydal.

"Oh, I think Helen and I will go to America in the summer." He pointed a finger at Rydal gaily. "Maybe we'll see you there!"

Rydal had a funny sense of *déjà vu,* or perhaps it was a feeling of foreknowledge. It depressed him.

Niko was touching the money lovingly, vaguely stroking it, as one might stroke a small animal. He had washed his hands at the sink, but his nails were still dirty.

Anna poured coffee for Andreou. He said he was going to eat later with Helen.

"You're sure you were not followed, Andreou?" Rydal said.

"Sure," Andreou said seriously. "I looked."

"In the restaurant you didn't see anyone watching you?"

"No. I was just on time. Mr. Chamberlain was already there."

Rydal asked how long they were there, who left first, whether Chester had appeared very nervous. Andreou thought not.

"He wanted to give me only half," Andreou said, smiling, "but I asked for the whole thing."

"So you have no more meetings with him? No date?" Rydal asked.

"No."

"Good." Rydal sat back in his chair, relieved. But a bumping sound just then in the cement corridor made him start.

"The kids," Anna said, gesturing. "They kick the door sometimes."

Rydal had been touching the roll of bills in his left-hand trousers pocket. He pulled them out impulsively, smiling at Andreou, and said, "I'll trade you."

"What's that?"

"Five thousand dollars."

"Five thousand?" Andreou's eyes widened.

Niko and Anna had fairly gasped also, and were leaning forward to look at it.

"Same as yours. Count it. I'll trade you," Rydal said, handing his money to Andreou.

Patiently, smiling with pleasure at what he was doing, Andreou counted Rydal's bills one by one, laying them down on the table. "Ten!" he announced. He looked from one stack to the other, two or three times, as if he were trying to find a difference between them, then said to Rydal, "Why do you want to trade?"

"Because I don't like this money. I'd rather have the money that was paid for my death."

"Where you get that?" Niko asked in English.

"From the same place. For keeping my mouth shut. Mr. Chamberlain insisted."

"Okay, we trade," said Andreou, and put Rydal's money into his pocket.

Rydal picked up Andreou's money. He put it into the same pocket the other money had been in. Niko was watching him with fascination. "Mr. Chamberlain insisted," Rydal repeated.

Andreou looked at him fondly, his eyes glazed with his dreams.

"Andreou, I have another request," Rydal said. "For a favor for which I'll pay—say, a thousand."

"Dollars?" asked Andreou.

"Yes. I have to cross the border. Into Yugoslavia. I thought you might know someone who is going by truck."

"What is this? Why Yugoslavia?" Niko asked.

And Rydal suddenly knew he was going to be defeated on it, that his idea was dangerous, uncomfortable, slow, and carried several strikes against its success. "I want to follow Mr. Chamberlain," Rydal said.

Andreou and Niko looked at him blankly for a moment.

"You need a passport," said Niko.

"Passports are your panacea!" said Rydal, but he laughed.

"Mr. Chamberlain will fly on his passport, no?" asked Niko.

"Probably," Rydal said.

Niko exchanged a slow look with Andreou. "I'll speak to Frank about a passport. What kind do you want?"

Rydal sat down in the straight chair he had been sitting on before. "Italian, perhaps. I can't afford an American."

"I will speak to Frank tonight." Niko looked seriously at his wristwatch, an enormous thing of false gold. "By eleven I will try to call him. You have a photograph? I will see that he gets it tonight."

Rydal had a photograph.

When Andreou left, Rydal went with him to the front door at the end of the corridor. Rydal felt a compulsion to see for himself if there were anyone loitering on the street, waiting for Andreou, watching the house. He saw a young man walking away on the opposite pavement, but no one loitering. He said good-bye to Andreou with a firm handshake. A real, bona-fide handshake, Rydal felt.

"My regard to your wife," Rydal said to him.

Andreou laughed. "Thank you. And eternal blessings to you!"

Niko asked Rydal some more questions about the five thousand dollars that he had received from Chester. Was it just for keeping his mouth shut? Had Rydal had to threaten Chester in order to get it? Rydal tried to explain that Chester was the sort of man who felt more comfortable after binding people, or trying to, with money.

"At one point, I threw it back at him," Rydal said. "The money fell on the floor. His wife picked it up and handed it back to me." Rydal shrugged. He had the feeling Niko didn't believe this story, either, that he thought it merely an added dramatic touch. Rydal smiled.

Niko's absolute bluntness in discussing money was rather refreshing. Rydal could see the wheels turning in Niko's brain. Perhaps he was wondering, for instance, if he could keep the five thousand for Chester's new passport without giving him the passport, and without involving Frank? But it was rather late now. Niko had given the photograph to Frank, he said. "Oh, if you continue to know Chester, he'll probably need a little service here and there from you," Rydal said.

"He's got a lot of mazuma, eh?" Niko asked dreamily.

"Lots," said Rydal. "Keeps it in a suitcase lining."

"You ever see it?"

"No. Just the suitcase."

"You think—fifty thousand maybe?"

"I don't know. Maybe."

The childlike conversation continued. Anna was washing up the dishes.

"Too bad, if the police catch him with all that," Niko said, shaking his head. "They'll just take it, won't they?"

"Yes. If they find out he's the embezzler named Chester MacFarland."

Niko's eyes began slowly to glow with his new idea.

Rydal smiled at him. "You don't know what hotel he is at, do you?"

"I can find out."

"You would have to have someone else do it for you. You can't threaten Chester, because he can threaten to tell about you and Frank and the passport business."

"Um-m. Yes. But there are ways."

"Oh, yes. Ways—Don't ask Andreou to do it."

"Why not?"

"He's done enough. He's happy. You wouldn't want to see him get caught, after gaining five thousand dollars, would you?"

"No. No." Niko shook his head, agreeing emphatically.

"Think of some other needy countryman."

Niko grinned. "I think of plenty," he said in English.

At 10:30, Niko went out with Rydal's photograph and fifteen hundred dollars of Rydal's money as an advance payment against a possible price of two thousand for an Italian passport. Before twelve he returned, saying Frank could do it.

The next morning the newspapers did not even mention the Knossos affair. Rydal had sent Anna out for the *Daily Post* as well as the Greek language papers.

If the police had spoken to Chester, Rydal thought, and he was sure they had, they would probably speak to him a second time, maybe a third time, trying to get more details from him, or find a hole in his story, perhaps. He thought of the moustached, beardless photograph in Chester's passport. Chester had been going to get it retouched in Athens, have a beard put on it. He surely wouldn't now. Rydal wondered if the police would see a resemblance between the photograph and the one of Chester MacFarland, alias whatever it was, as a young man, in the Greek agent's assignment book? And why didn't America come through with Chester's passport photograph which was on record as that of Chester MacFarland? Was there some reason for the delay? Rydal could only suppose that it was a result of America's slow gathering of evidence on Chester's frauds and embezzlements. They were probably collecting all they could from everywhere, and not saying anything about it until they had everything. And MacFarland was still not connected with Chamberlain of the Knossos tragedy. Rydal was tempted to go outside to a telephone—Niko and Anna had none—and see if Chester was at the Acropole or the El Greco. But he restrained himself and stayed indoors.

He wanted to call up Geneviève Schumann. He was very bored and restless that day. He had nothing with him to read, and Niko and Anna had nothing in the house but a few popular magazines and a Greek Bible.

"Why don't you call up Geneviève?" Anna asked him.

Rydal smiled. "Because I'm afraid to stick my head out the door."

"Would you like me to call her for you?"

It was a quarter past two.

He shrugged, not knowing where to begin. "And then you explain to her—her Greek's not so good. You explain to her for ten minutes that I didn't kill the woman found at Knossos? Meanwhile a servant's listening on a telephone in the house? You say I'm at your house and would she possibly come and visit me? Something like that?"

Anna giggled. That was probably exactly what she had been thinking of.

"No, Anna, it can't be done."

"You could write her a letter. I would deliver it."

Like the nurse in *Romeo and Juliet,* Rydal thought. "I don't want her or anybody else to know that you know where I am." He sat down on the limp couch.

Anna went back to the sink. She was washing some shirts for Niko.

Rydal considered writing Geneviève a letter. He imagined writing the whole story out for her. But why? She was an intelligent girl, imaginative, too, but also very practical. She would say, "But why did you get yourself into such a mess in the first place? Why did you help this man hide the body in the King's Palace Hotel? What possessed you, Rydal?" Her opinion of him would go down. He could try to explain it, but it wouldn't satisfy her, he knew. He felt a depressing distance between himself and Geneviève. What the distance said to him was that Geneviève didn't matter. That was the simple truth.

He stood up and went over to Anna. "Anna, I don't want you trying to take any message to Geneviève. Understand? It's too dangerous. My name was in the paper yesterday morning." Rydal gave a laugh. "Which is proof the police are talking to Chester. I can just hear his story. Unfortunately, he's a good liar." He thrust his hands into his pockets and walked away. His fingers closed over the roll of money. Three thousand five hundred dollars.

At a little after 5, there was a knock on the front door. Rydal stood up. Anna was not expecting anyone, he knew. She had said that she had told one of her neighbors, who often came in the afternoon for a cup of tea, that she was going to visit her old aunt on the north side of town this afternoon.

"Don't worry," Anna whispered as she slipped out of the door into the corridor. "It's maybe Mouriades."

"Who?"

"Mouriades. An old man. Father of Dina."

A neighbor, Rydal supposed. He looked around the room. The place was a cul-de-sac. Outside the narrow windows was a slit of a space between this house and the next, with no exit to it without a grappling iron and a rope to climb a twenty-foot high brick wall.

Rydal had looked. Anna was talking to someone. Rydal put his ear at the partly opened door and listened.

It was Pan.

Rydal relaxed, and gave a tense sigh of regret. Anna was putting him off. No, Rydal was not here, no indeed. Anna was doing a good job of it. Pan was a friend. Pan would understand and wouldn't talk. Rydal was tempted to run down the corridor and say hello and ask him to come in. But better he didn't.

Anna came back. She closed the apartment door. "Pan."

"I know. Thanks, Anna. You were very good."

"I don't like that Pan," Anna said with a troubled frown, shaking her head. "I don't trust him."

"Oh, he—" Rydal stopped. He had started to say she was wrong, that Pan could be trusted. But it was better left the way it was. Pan just might have remarked to a friend of his that he knew where Rydal was, the friend might blab it still more.

"You trust Pan?" asked Anna.

She didn't know him well. He had brought Pan here perhaps twice for a glass of wine. "Oh, I think he's all right," Rydal said.

At just the time they were expecting Niko home, there was another knock at the door. Anna went down the corridor again.

"But he is not here," Anna's voice said in a protesting tone. "Ah!" in an exasperated tone. "All right, all right, but it's useless. . . . All right. . . . Well, do you think I know any better than you?"

The front door slammed.

Anna came in with a mischievous, delighted smile on her face. She had a pale blue envelope in her hand. "From Geneviève! That was a messenger!" She pushed the envelope into his hand.

Rydal opened it, with a small pain at his heart, a fear of the worst, a sense of embarrassment—the mingled emotions he nearly always felt when he opened a letter from one of his family. The letter was in French.

Thursday 5 p.m.

My dear Rydal,

I am thinking you *might* be at Niko's. Or is it Pan's? I am sure you didn't kill the woman at Knossos. Is it really you they are talking about? Why did you not tell me you were going to Crete? It is as if you were kidnapped and a crime pinned on you. At least you seem to be alive, as the papers say you were on the boat from Iraklion to Piraeus yesterday morning. Why are you hiding? I feel you may not get this. I miss you so and I am so worried. [The last word—*souci-euse*—underlined three times.] If you do get this, come to us for help. Papa has said he will help you. You know how much he likes you. Don't be [an untranslatable phrase, one of her and Rydal's private phrases meaning a meaninglessly rebellious and stubborn person]. I love you and I pray for you. Are you all right? Wounded? Sick? Please answer if you get this. Get somebody to deliver a note from you.

Bébises,

Geneviève

"What does she say?" Anna had not taken her eyes from his face.

"She wishes me well."

"Ah, and what else?"

"It's a very short note," Rydal said evasively.

"But what else? Doesn't she want to see you?"

"Now, Anna!—She says her father has offered to help me, if I need it."

"Her father? The professor of archaeology?"

"Yes."

"Well—let him help you. Can he help you?"

"No," Rydal said.

"But you—you need somebody to speak for you. You can't go on hiding all your life."

"No, Anna. Just till tomorrow, I think. I'll be off tomorrow."

"Oh, not that you're not welcome to stay here as long as you like, Rydal. You are our friend."

The conversation irked him. He lit a cigarette, and stood looking at the dusty rectangular window. One could hardly see the red-brick wall three feet beyond it.

"Doesn't she want you to answer her?" asked Anna.

"Yes."

"Good, then, answer her! Do you want a pen and paper?"

"No, I have them, thanks." Rydal looked at her. "Can you get someone to deliver it?"

"Certainly. I myself can—"

"Not you, Anna. Do you know a boy in the neighborhood you can ask? Tell him it's about some laundry or something?" Rydal remembered that Anna sometimes took in laundry.

"Ah, trust me."

Rydal wrote in French:

My dear Geneviève,

Your note received a moment ago. I wonder did you send one to Pan also? So you know where I am from that question. Please do not tell your father. I am grateful indeed for his offer of help, but I don't need it, I should say better, I cannot use it just now. You are right I am not guilty of the mess on Crete. It is difficult if not impossible to explain why I am in the predicament I am in, but it is in the nature of an experiment, one which I must see through, one which isn't finished yet. How I wish, a month from now, we could sit at a table at the Alexandre in Paris and have dinner and I should tell you all about it. Shall we make a date for February 18th, a month from today, at the Alexandre? At 7 p.m.?

I am grateful for your belief in me. You are in a distinct minority at the moment. But "public opinion does not concern me at all", I say, remembering the words, more or less, of the trouserless man in the National Gardens in December! In answer to your question, I am not wounded. Not trouserless either.

My love to you and with a loud *à bientôt!*

He left it unsigned.

Anna went out to find a messenger for it, as soon as Niko came in. Niko had no news. No one, and no policeman, had asked him any questions. Frank was going to have Chester's new passport ready for him by tomorrow, perhaps tomorrow morning.

"I want to know the name on it as soon as possible," Rydal said.

"Oh, I told Frank that," Niko said.

"Can't you reach him now? I thought you would know it by now." Rydal frowned, anxious.

Niko looked thoughtful for a moment. "Frank has no telephone where he is. But I have an idea. There is a taverna near Frank."

When Anna came back, Niko went out to make a telephone call. Rydal had pressed a pencil and a piece of paper on him. He wanted the name down accurately.

Niko came back after thirty-five minutes. Chester's new name was to be Philip Jeffries Wedekind. Frank was having the passport delivered in a shoe box to Chester's hotel, the El Greco, tomorrow morning at 9:30. The messenger was going to ask a bellboy to put the shoe box in Mr. Chamberlain's room, in case he wasn't there, by Mr. Chamberlain's request. Rydal's Italian passport was to be ready at the same time tomorrow morning, and would be delivered to Niko on the street.

"Bring it home right away!" Rydal said, clapping his hands. "Before lunch."

"Before lunch. Okay." Niko rubbed his nose and looked at Rydal, smiling.

"Two thousand dollars. Very reasonable. You deserve some thanks also, Niko."

Niko put up his broad, dirty palms. "Ah, no. We are friend, you and I. When I am in America . . ."

17

January 19, 19—

To the Attention of the Greek Police:

As you well know, Rydal Keener is still at large and his objective is nothing less than my death. Having murdered my wife, he now means to murder me. It is reasonable to think that he is in this city. I am grateful for the protection you have given me up to now, but I have premonitions that your efforts will not succeed forever, perhaps not even the few more days needed to track him down. I am still willing, as an honest man who prefers to cooperate with the law, to remain in the city, no doubt under the very eyes of Keener, in order to provoke another attack by him on my person. But he is a very clever young man, and he may defeat us both—that is, manage to kill me without being apprehended himself. These, I repeat, may be only the premonitions of an anxious and grief-stricken man. But I wished to state officially my fears, my dreads. If I should disappear, it will not be because of panic, cowardice or discouragement. It will be because Keener will have broken through your guard.

Wm J. Chamberlain

For this statement, Chester had borrowed a typewriter from the hotel. He signed it with the signature he was now rather good at, from his passport. It was a quarter to 9. Chester ordered breakfast, a substantial one of orange juice, two soft-boiled eggs, ham, toast and coffee. Then he took the remainder of his American cash from the lining of his tan suitcase, put as much as he could into his left hip-pocket, which buttoned, put some into his black morocco wallet, and the rest into his overcoat's inside breast pocket, which had a flap with a button.

He had just finished his breakfast when there was a knock at the door. Chester glanced at his watch. Twenty to 10. "Yes?" he said to the closed door.

"Package for you, sir."

Chester opened the door. "Oh, yes, my shoes. Thank you very much."

The bellboy handed him a box wrapped in dark-grey paper, and Chester gave him a ten-drachma note.

The package was heavy, just about as heavy as a pair of shoes would make it. Chester opened the box, smiled at the authentic, rather worn, yellow-orange shoes it contained, looked under the tissue they lay in and found the passport. He opened it nervously. PHILIP JEFFRIES WEDEKIND. His own eyes stared blankly, innocently out at him from the photograph above the signature. Wedekind? What kind of name was that? German? Jewish? The handwriting was thin and tall and slanted strongly to the right. The W was a tall, leaning zigzag, without ornament. Chester took his pen and practiced it a few times on a scrap torn from the paper doily on his breakfast tray. He stopped at a knock on his door, put the passport into the drawer of the night table, and wadded the paper in his hand.

It was a waiter who had come to remove the tray.

When he had gone, Chester took the passport from the drawer and looked at it again. Occupation: salesman, and that was fine, as he could be a salesman of anything. Height: five feet ten. Age: forty-five, from the birth-date, not bad. Birthplace: Milwaukee, Wisconsin. The wife and minors boxes bore three Xs each. Fine, too. Home address 4556 Roosevelt Drive, Indianapolis, Indiana. Chester put the passport into the breast pocket of his suit jacket. Then he went into the bathroom and shaved his face clean. He was careful to wash all the whiskers down the drain, and he also cleaned his battery razor of whiskers. He started to burn the paper on which he had practiced the signature, then thought better of it. He'd take the paper away with him, wadded in his pocket. His statement to the police lay beside the typewriter on the writing-table, and Chester read it over. He hoped Rydal was dead, that he had been dead for twelve hours, but in case he wasn't—

Chester put on his jacket and overcoat and left the room. All he took with him was the pair of shoes wrapped up in yesterday's *Daily Post.* He was on the fourth floor. He took the service stairs down, was glanced at by a cleaning man in a white jacket on the second floor, but the man did not speak to him, only went on with his sweeping.

Chester emerged in an alley behind the hotel, and walked towards the street that he saw some twenty yards away. He turned down Stadiou Street in the direction of Constitution Square, and dropped the shoes into a metal rubbish bin at the next corner. Then he entered a café, and made a telephone call from the booth in the rear. There were two planes westbound that day, one at 11 a.m., one at 1:30. The man he was talking to spoke English, and Chester tried to make a reservation for Wedekind on the 11 a.m. plane, but he was told that no reservations were made over the telephone.

Chester took a taxi down to Constitution Square, got out at Stadiou and Voukourestiou, and found a luggage shop within half a block. He bought a sizeable black suitcase of rippled cowhide, and paid for it with his remaining drachmas. The next step was a bank. Chester changed three hundred dollars into drachmas. In the next twenty-five minutes, he managed to buy three shirts, a pair of slacks and a tweed jacket, pajamas and socks and underwear in two shops and without giving the appearance of being in a hurry. He removed the price tags from the items that had them. Then he bought a toothbrush—one made in America—and toothpaste at a chemist's. At twenty to 11, he was rolling in a taxi towards the airport. He might not be missed by his police guard, he thought, until after noon, perhaps even after 2. He had not gone out yesterday until 11 o'clock. It was conceivable he would stay in all morning and have his lunch sent up by the hotel.

He made the plane nicely. It was only three-quarters full. The first stop was to be Corfu, then Brindisi, then Rome, where he would have to change for a plane to Paris. Chester's companions on the plane were mostly Greek, he thought, and mostly men, a solemn, reserved lot who looked as if they were travelling on business. The passport examination had gone quickly and smoothly at the air terminal. Chester was not worried about false passports now. They were a kind of armour, he felt, an impenetrable disguise. He had signed his name hastily and casually at the bottom of his declaration.

Chester relaxed and even dozed as the plane hummed over the Ionian Sea. When lunchtime came, he ate well. At 10 p.m., he was in France, taxi-ing with his luggage from Orly towards Paris. He felt almost home again, comfortable, happy. In France, he could practically understand the language. From here he could send the telegrams, the simple, short but vital telegrams that had been going through his head during the flight from Athens. One to Jesse Doty. *Hi, Jessebelle!* Maybe not quite that. It was a silly name that he sometimes put on presents to Jesse, that the fellows sometimes called him when they were kidding him. But it would be one way of making sure Jesse knew the telegram from Wedekind was from him.

Chester had the driver stop at Les Invalides. It was the only place Chester was sure he could send a telegram from at this hour. He fired a message off to Jesse Doty:

ADDRESS FUTURE CORRESPONDENCE PHILIP WEDEKIND, AMERICAN EXPRESS, PARIS. ALSO REPEAT MESSAGES OF PAST TEN DAYS. CABLE IF NECESSARY. PHIL.

And at the bottom, PHILIP JEFFRIES WEDEKIND, as the name had to be there in full. Chester added a final sentence to his carefully printed message: INFORM VIC AND BOB.

Then he went out to his waiting taxi and told the driver to go to the Hotel Montalembert. Chester and Colette had had cocktails a couple of times at the Pont-Royal bar in the Hôtel Pont-Royal next door to the Montalembert, but he had never stayed at the Montalembert. He thought it looked like a substantial place that would have good heat and service. He would have preferred the Georges V, but alas, they knew him there. That was the penalty, he supposed, of feeling that Paris was home. He had just a twinge of fear as he walked through the doors of the Montalembert that the hotel might know Philip Wedekind personally, too. But all went quite well. He was given a room with bath on the fifth floor. Chester stayed in his room just long enough to hang his slacks and jacket from his suitcase and to lay out his pajamas on the bed. The French inspector at Orly had said:

"Not much in your suitcase, m'sieur."

Chester had chuckled and said, "I was robbed a couple of days ago. Had to buy everything over again."

The conversation had been in English. The customs inspector hadn't asked him where he was robbed, just said, "Oh? Bad luck."

The inspector hadn't looked at him, Chester thought, not more than to give him a very brief glance. The man's head had been bent over his suitcase the few seconds the inspection had taken.

Chester's snack of superb beluns and a croque-monsieur at the corner of rue du Bac and Université made him see things more realistically, he felt. He had been over his potential dangers in Athens, but now they seemed imminent and new. The main thing was that, if Rydal Keener were still alive, he would know his new name. Chester had asked for Frank's secrecy, had even bought it, because it was part of the deal, and Niko had said he would ask Frank not to tell Rydal—but how much could he count on that? Very little, Chester thought. About as much as he could count on Andreou performing the task for which he had been paid five thousand dollars. Chester felt he could only hope. And his only hope really was that Rydal would be afraid of bucking a charge of having killed Colette, should he try to get the police on his trail. Chester couldn't imagine Rydal wanting that. Then Rydal, if he mentioned the Greek police agent, had also helped Chester hide the body. That wouldn't look so good on Rydal's record, either, as a character recommendation. So far, so good. But all Rydal had to do was pick up a telephone and tell the Greek police his new alias was Philip Wedekind. Rydal wouldn't have to say who he was, where he was, or where he got the information. That was the real danger, the present danger. And what he was doing now was a gamble, a forced gamble, Chester thought. He had to try it, because there was no alternative. He had to get news from the States and had to get back to the States some day.

His confidence or his physical strength returned as he walked back the short distance to his hotel. If it came to a showdown, he'd give Rydal Keener a run for his money. He had plenty against Rydal Keener, plenty. Chester gave himself credit for having guts. Well, he would show them, if it came to that. He wasn't going to be a pushover for Rydal Keener, that spineless vagabond, that half-assed soldier of fortune.

Chester thought of his cable reaching Jesse in the early morning, New York time. He slept quite well that night.

At 12 the next day, he called at the American Express to see if he had any mail. He knew it was impossible that Jesse could have replied so quickly, but still he had a compulsion to see. It was probably the worst possible time to come by for mail. The basement of the building was noisy and jammed with tourists and young Americans in sneakers and blue jeans, girls in tapered slacks and ballet slippers, waiting on the alphabetized lines. It was also a dreadful way to display oneself to fellow Americans, one of whom might know Howard Cheever.

"Wedekind," said Chester, when he reached the busy girl behind the counter. He had his passport open.

She went to look, and came back shaking her head.

Chester thanked her, and made his way up the stairs and out of the building. He wanted very much to write to Bob Gambardella in Milwaukee. Good old Bob. A long, decent letter in longhand. Bob would understand. All Bob said when things went wrong was, "Oh, *Jee-ee* sus," in a tired but resigned way, and then Bob would smile at fate and run his fingers through his hair. Bob never lost his head. Chester had known him now four years. Chester would tell Bob about Rydal Keener, make Keener out a blackmailer from the time he walked in on him when he was talking to the Greek agent. Chester's latest arrangement of that story was that Rydal Keener had been tailing him for a couple of days—as he probably tailed any rich-looking American he might see—with an idea of taking him for a little money. Rydal Keener had followed the Greek agent into the hotel, and after sizing up the situation had slugged the agent with a blackjack and killed him, then threatened to pin it on Chester, unless Chester paid him off. Somehow Chester felt that telling this story to an American friend would count for more in a law court than all the talking he had done to the Greek police in Athens. Chester would also tell Bob about the passes Keener had made at Colette, about Colette's tragic death when Keener was trying to kill him, about the threats, the dangers that had followed, resulting in Chester's having to assume another identity in order to escape from the vicious Keener who was still hiding out, free, in Athens. So, after a leisurely lunch on the Champs-Élysées, Chester tipped the waiter to get him some writing-paper, and sat on at his table over the remainder of a bottle of white wine, writing it. He sat on with a Scotch or two until nearly five, then went back to l'Opéra and the American Express.

Now there was a cable for him.

Chester carried it to a corner of the room and opened it eagerly.

NEWS NOT GOOD HERE. STAY THERE. INFORMING BOB NOT VIC. LETTER FOLLOWS. REGARDS COLETTE. JESSE.

The phrase STAY THERE told Chester a great deal. It meant Howard Cheever was wiped out. NOT VIC meant that Vic had run out, or talked to the police. It meant the Unimex Company was under investigation, or had been declared illegal, dishonest, or whatever they cared to call it. Chester's jaw set. Not *totally* illegal. It was a sort of gambling company, more or less like everything else in stocks. If companies had the money to run themselves, would they sell stock in the first place? Howard Cheever and Jesse Doty were closely connected with the Canadian Star Company. Canadian Star had no other names to hide behind, not names attached to people, anyway. The news was bad.

Chester bought a newspaper, the first he had bought that day. He had thought of a newspaper that morning, but the mail, communication, had seemed more urgent to him. He bought the Paris *Herald Tribune* and *France Soir,* and looked at the *Tribune* first. There it was, front-page news, but without a picture, fortunately. The story was only a few lines long. It said:

> Athens, Jan. 19—Police were mystified today by the apparent disappearance of William J. Chamberlain, 42, an American hotelier who had been registered at the Hotel El Greco in this city. Authorities were reticent as to what may have happened to him, though they disclosed that Chamberlain had been under "police surveillance", presumably to protect him from possible assault. His hotel room was left with all his possessions, as if he had merely stepped out for a walk. A note beside the typewriter which he had borrowed from the hotel expressed fear for his personal safety. Police are releasing no further information at the moment.

It was curious, Chester thought, very curious. They did not care to link Rydal Keener's name with his. When Keener's name was mentioned in the papers, Chamberlain's wasn't. Chester could not see their motive, could not see their reluctance to make an all-out search for Rydal Keener and in connection with the murder of Colette, Mrs. William Chamberlain. He couldn't believe that the Greek police had doubted his story. If they had doubted him, why hadn't they really grilled him, or at least done some much closer questioning than those two sessions they had had with him in the El Greco on Thursday?

Suddenly, Chester wondered if Rydal had gone to the police on his own, day before yesterday, and told them the story from his point of view? Were they somehow weighing Rydal's story against his own? Could it be possible? Chester had heard of such things, of course. The police got the individual stories, which might vary, and then they confronted the two story-tellers with each other, or they confronted one with the other's story and watched how he reacted to it. But Chester, in the second interview on Thursday, hadn't had the least suspicion that the police had spoken to Rydal. The second interview, at 10 p.m., might have been a repetition of the first. Chester had not been out of the hotel since he had seen the police. He had had nothing new to tell them. No, that simply wasn't it. The police had had time enough to confront them with each other, and they hadn't done it. The very thought of what Rydal could say about him—on top of the bad news from Jesse—made Chester shudder slightly as he walked into the Montalembert.

Rydal Keener was sitting in the lobby.

Now not a shudder but a sudden sense of hollowness, of terrible shock, seized Chester and he caught against his body the newspapers and the bottle of Scotch that he had nearly let slip. He vacillated quickly, on his toes, between turning back to the door and going for his key, went for his key, and had to suffer the embarrassment of not knowing his room number, of having to think—it seemed to him—a whole minute before he could drag up even his name from his memory.

"Wedekind, please," Chester said softly.

His key was pushed over to him. Chester moved slowly. He was supposed to think what to do. He couldn't think what to do. He walked on, without looking at Rydal, towards the elevators. There seemed nothing else to do. Rydal was not getting up. Rydal sat in a heavy armchair backed by a column, so that he had a view of the door by turning his head slightly to the left, and of the elevators by turning it to the right. Though Chester did not look directly at him, he saw Rydal's nod and his slight smile out of the corner of his eye. No, *Rydal* didn't care if the hotel personnel knew that they knew each other, Chester thought. Rydal was still sitting, not looking at him now, his chin propped up casually on his fist, when the elevator doors closed him off from Chester's view.

In his room, Chester solemnly and quickly shed his overcoat and got at his Scotch. He needed it, badly.

The telephone rang. Chester picked it up quickly, before he had time to think, to be afraid.

"Hello," said Rydal's smiling voice. "How are you, Phil? This is Joey. Can I come up and see you?"

"Who?" Chester asked, nervously stalling.

"Joey," Rydal said. "I'd like to see you for a moment."

"Never mind. Thanks. Some other time."

"Listen, Phil—"

Here Chester heard Rydal interrupted by the clerk downstairs.

"Oh, he'll see me, I'm sure," said Rydal. Then, to Chester, "I'll be right up, Phil."

Chester put the telephone down.

As soon as he had hung up, the telephone rang again.

"Hello?" Chester said.

"M'sieur, if you do not wish a visit from this gentleman, we will not permit him to go up."

"Oh, well, he . . . he . . . No, thank you, it's quite all right. He's a friend of mine." The words came out quickly. Chester put the telephone down. He folded his arms and frowned at the door, waiting.

Wrong stance. He dropped his arms. He mustn't look angry or even annoyed. Above all, he mustn't look frightened.

Rydal knocked.

Chester opened the door. He had expected a smirk, but Rydal's face was solemn and calm as he came in.

"Good evening," Rydal said. He glanced around the room, at Chester's new suitcase on the luggage rack, then said, "Well, what's the news from home?" He pulled out a package of Gauloises. "Cigarette?"

"No, thanks. Listen, Rydal, if it's money you're after, maybe we can come to terms."

"Oh-h." Rydal smiled and shook his match out. "I'm not averse to a little money, but I doubt if you and I can ever come to terms."

Chester laughed contemptuously. "I don't give money to people I haven't come to terms with."

"No? Think again."

"A pity you didn't make it clear from the start you were a blackmailer. You might have told me before we went to Crete."

"It wasn't clear to me before I went to Crete. I think it's associating with you that's made me so money-conscious. Anyway, there it is." He sat down in the armchair, glanced around for an ashtray, then coolly flicked his ash on the carpet.

Chester went to his Scotch bottle on the night table, and poured some into the glass that was standing there. "Well, you're not getting a cent," Chester said.

"Oh, don't make me laugh. I'd like ten thousand and right now."

Chester smiled, shaking his head. "I'll tell you right now, I've got only twenty thousand left. Is that worth—"

"I want your ten and I don't want to sit here all night talking about it." Rydal sat forward, frowning. "Only got twenty thousand. I'll bet! I'll bet you've got fifty thousand in each shoe."

Chester advanced a step and stood easily, holding his glass. "I don't pay blackmailers, Keener. I'm in quite a good position to blackmail you—if you had anything." Chester looked at him straight in the face, but it was an effort for him. Rydal's hatred, the anger that showed in his eyes, was very disturbing to Chester. He had never seen it quite like this before. It was anger, contempt, and the kind of hostility that looked as if it could burst forth in some unpremeditated action. Chester set his glass down.

"Don't worry," Rydal said. "I'm not going to sock you in the jaw. I'd like to. But there are better ways. More civilized, more deadly ways." He smiled, as if at himself, and stood up. "I won't detain you any longer, Mr. Wedekind. I'd like the ten—in your usual five-hundred-dollar bills. Twenty of them, please."

Chester said, "I think I'll just call downstairs for a couple of strong bellboys and have you removed."

Rydal came slowly towards Chester, and Chester noticed that he was wearing new shoes—handsome black ones with thick rubber soles.

"You'll have me removed? I'll have you in prison, you ass!" The intensity in Rydal's eyes ebbed, and he smiled slightly.

He was quite right, Chester knew. They were unevenly matched. At least here, now, in this room. Thoughts flashed erratically through Chester's brain: go to some small hotel tomorrow. Paris had hundreds and hundreds of hotels. He'd telephone the police and say that Rydal Keener was in Paris. Ah, but he'd been here before. Couldn't do that.

All he could do was try to get Keener off his neck. That meant get to America as soon as possible, get rid of the Wedekind name, take a brand-new name. Yes, for Christ's sake, that was the only way.

"Move and get the money," Rydal said.

Chester moved, slowly. He went to his overcoat on the bed and reached into its breast pocket. "This'll be the last. I'm—"

"Why?"

Chester counted off the bills, without removing the money completely from the pocket. "I'm going to the States. Tomorrow. Try and keep such good track of me then." With a nasty smile, he handed Rydal the twenty five-hundred-dollar bills.

Rydal counted it calmly, slowly, having trouble separating the new bills. Then he put the money carelessly into his right side trousers pocket. "Do you miss Colette?"

Chester saw Rydal's left eye twitch, the lids flutter. "I don't want you saying her name," Chester said.

"She liked me." Rydal looked at him.

"She did not. She was annoyed, she was disgusted by your . . . your God-damned passes at her." Chester spoke vehemently.

Rydal smiled. "It's curious. You really believe that.—I went to bed with her, you know. She wanted me to. She asked me to."

"Get out of this room."

Rydal turned and went out.

18

Rydal walked to Saint-Germain-des-Près and boarded a 95 bus for Montmartre. He was in both high spirits and low. He felt flung up and then down, from moment to moment. That was easily explained: he didn't really like what he was doing. He hadn't liked it when he planned it, when he had thought about doing it. The pleasure it gave him was strictly emotional and irrational. He wasn't interested in heckling Chester because Chester was a criminal, a guilty man, and he wasn't interested in robbing the rich to give to the poor, and least of all was he interested in turning Chester over to the police. Colette was at the center of it, he felt. Colette was more the motivating cause than even the fact—the obvious fact—that Chester looked so much like his father and that he wanted to hit back at his father. No, indeed. What a childish, petty motivation that would have been! But Chester had killed, stamped out a delightful and harmless, kind, young and pretty woman. A woman Rydal had been more than half in love with when she died. Rydal felt even more in love with her now.

With a throb of regret and pain, Rydal remembered that he had not asked Chester for a photograph of her, as he had meant to do. Damn it! How he would have liked it with him in his hotel room tonight! Well, next time. Tomorrow. Early tomorrow. It might be true that Chester was going back to the States tomorrow. It was certainly the wisest thing for him to do. Hanging to a pole on the crowded bus, Rydal bit his upper lip thoughtfully. How to prevent Chester from going to the States tomorrow? Simple. Just inform him that if he left, he would inform the police that Philip Wedekind was Chamberlain and also MacFarland. Or should he keep that MacFarland name back as an ace in the hole? Rydal smiled to himself, and he found himself staring at a girl sitting two seats away from him and next to the window, a girl who was also looking at him and smiling slightly. She looked away. She had short straight hair combed forward from the crown, no parting in it. A purple scarf at her throat. She looked back at him. She wore lipstick—her lips were neither thin nor full, just nice lips—but no powder, and her nose was shiny and even a little pinkish-blue from the cold, or maybe she had a cold. There was a small mole high on her left cheek. She got out at the next station, and he got out, though the bus had hardly begun to climb the hill to Montmartre. It was the Gare Saint-Lazare stop.

"Bon soir," Rydal said, catching up with her. "Où allez-vous, mademoiselle?"

She looked away, but she was controlling a smile. It would take only one more try.

"If it's far, we'll take a taxi. Whether it's far or not. Please. I have to celebrate this evening."

"Celebrate? Celebrate what?"

"I've just won a lot of money," he said, smiling. "Come on. Taxi!" They were just approaching a *tête de taxis,* and there were three at the curb.

"Do you think I would get in a taxi with you? You must be an idiot!" she said, laughing.

"No, I'm not an idiot." His hand was on the door handle. "Come on, I'll let you speak to the driver. I won't say a word."

"I live only three streets away. With my parents," she said, smiling, undecided.

"Bien. Get in. Or are you walking for your health?"

She got in. She spoke to the driver, gave her address. Then she sat back, waiting for him to say something. He was silent, looking at her.

"You're not going to say anything?"

"I promised." He sat in the corner of the seat, watching her. "However—" He sat up. "Since this is such a short trip and I have a very short time, I'll ask you now, would you honor me by having dinner with me this evening?"

"Dinner!" She laughed as if the proposal were absurd.

He called for her at a quarter to 8, or rather picked her up on a certain corner, because she said she had to tell her parents that she was going to have dinner with a girl friend. Rydal asked her which place she would like best in all Paris to have dinner in. With a roll of her dark eyes, as if he were suggesting a round trip to the moon for the evening's entertainment, she said:

"Ah, le Tour d'Argent, je suppose. Ou peut-être Maxim."

"An aperitif chez Maxim and dinner at the Tour d'Argent," Rydal replied, and put her into a taxi.

They ended the evening in a cabaret on the Left Bank. Her name was Yvonne Delatier. Rydal said his was Pierre Winckel—it being one of Rydal's theories, or rather his experience, that the majority of French people had unFrench sounding names, like Geneviève Schumann in Athens, whose family was as French as they came. Winckel sounded much more authentically French to him than Carpentier, for instance. However, here was a Delatier to spoil his theory. She was twenty and studying to become a nurse, but afternoons she worked for a travel agency on the rue de la Paix near the Opéra. It was plain she did not have much money. She had changed to her best, perhaps, but her pocketbook was a cheap one. Rydal wanted to press a thousand dollars on her, but he did not even begin to try it. He explained his affluence—he had to, since he had boasted about it—in the easiest way, saying that a grandfather in Normandy, whom he hardly knew, had left him twenty-five thousand new francs when he died, and the money had come in only that day. Rydal said he had a job in Saint-Cloud in an automobile showroom, but he was staying at a hotel in Paris just now to attend to some legal matters in regard to his grandfather's will. In the cabaret, they held hands. When the lights went out for the performers' entrances and exits, they kissed. She had to be home by 12:30 at the latest, she said. In the taxi, Rydal cleared his throat and asked without much hope of success, if she would care to visit his hotel in Montmartre. Laughing, she declined. That was life. He dropped her off half a block from her door, as she wished, and watched until she was safely inside.

She had asked him if he had spent much time in Italy, because he had a slight Italian accent. That was funny. He had her telephone number, and he had told her he would call her "soon".

C'est la vie. It had been a refreshing evening. He refreshed himself still more by putting two of the five-hundred-dollar bills into an envelope to send to Niko with a note of thanks for his hospitality in Athens.

Rydal set himself to awaken at 8, and woke up at twenty to. He reached for his telephone, and asked the operator to call the Montalembert for him. He would have called Chester last night, but he hadn't wanted possibly to attract the ear of the Montalembert operator by calling at a late hour. And earlier, he hadn't wanted to intrude on his evening with Yvonne by so much as a one-minute telephone conversation with Chester.

Chester was in, and sleepy.

"This is Joey," said Rydal. "I am sorry if I awakened you, but I wanted to tell you that if you leave for home today, I'll find out about it very soon, before your plane reaches New York. Do you know what I mean, Phil?"

Phil understood. He hung up in a pet, and Rydal lit a cigarette and lay on his back, thinking. He thought of Martha and Kennie in America, no doubt questioned by the police by now. What sort of person is your brother? He has a police record as a juvenile for sexual assault and breaking and entering at the age of fifteen. . . . Rydal turned over on his stomach and lay propped up on his elbows. *Rydal would never kill anyone,* Martha would say in her earnest way. *He's not a criminal,* Kennie would say to them. *It takes certain ingredients to make a criminal. . . . Yes, he's a graduate of Yale Law School, but why do you ask me? You could call the school and find out. . . . Judging from the papers, the caretaker at Knossos didn't know him by name. Why wasn't it somebody else he saw? Why my brother?* Rydal supposed he must write them. He frowned, thinking of the old hump, trying to explain why he had helped Chester in the first place. No, best not write. If the letter came from Paris, the police might get wind of the fact he was in Paris. At least, his brother and sister knew that he was still free, presumably not dead. No use writing to Martha, *I'm hiding out in Paris, and I have to, because I'm being framed,* something like that. *Framed* was neither quite accurate nor complete.

Rydal called the Montalembert just before 11, from a bistro on the Left Bank, not far from the hotel itself.

The hotel said that M. Wedekind had checked out.

Rydal didn't quite believe it. It sounded like a message Chester would have asked the hotel to tell anybody who called him. "Really? I spoke to him at eight. He checked out just a few minutes ago?"

"M-mm—just after nine, sir." The voice was definite.

"Thank you." Rydal left the bistro and walked towards the Montalembert. He glanced at every figure he saw on the street. When he came within twenty feet of the hotel door, he decided to go in.

He spoke to a man behind the desk, not the one who had been there yesterday. "I'd like to speak to Mr. Wedekind," Rydal said.

The man consulted a register list, then said to Rydal, "Mr. Wedekind has departed."

"Thank you," Rydal said. He now supposed it was true.

He went out on the pavement again, torn between telephoning various airlines to ask if Philip Wedekind was on any passenger list, and looking for him at some other hotel—the Voltaire, the Lutetia, the Saints-Pères, the Pas de Calais. They seemed too obvious, too much the hotels that all American tourists liked. The Georges V was Chester's taste, but too conspicuous. Some small hotel. Rydal sighed. There were pages and pages of hotels in the Paris telephone directory. There were hotels around nearly every corner in Paris. The thought of looking for him by visiting or telephoning them all was dismaying indeed. Yesterday he'd had good luck. He had hit the Montalembert on his third telephone call.

Would Chester leave the city so soon? Before any letter from the States could have arrived for him? He could, of course, have telephoned New York, but Rydal doubted that he would, because he wouldn't want Wedekind connected in any way with his shady colleagues in New York, and vice versa, any more than he had wanted Chamberlain connected.

One thing was certain, and Rydal felt a funny tingle of excitement, of pleasure, at the thought of it: Chester was on Paris soil at this moment. Maybe sitting at Orly, waiting for his plane, but he couldn't have left yet, Rydal thought.

Rydal called Orly.

The Orly girl was cooperative and patient, and took more than five minutes to check over passenger lists, but she reported no Philip Wedekind. Rydal thanked her.

Chester could have run into a friend, Rydal supposed. That was very likely in Paris. A friend could have put him up. But it was a bit unlikely that he would have moved out of his hotel to a friend's apartment at 9 on a Sunday morning. Chester might have taken a train to Marseille, with a view of taking a plane or a ship from there.

Rydal shrugged. He bought a newspaper and went into a café. He ordered a coffee.

His picture was on the front page of the newspaper. It was his passport picture. After his first shock at seeing it, he realized that it might have been in yesterday, after all, days ago, in fact, in Athens. If it had been in yesterday, Yvonne might not have made a date with him last evening. The picture was certainly like him in its straight-on view, it's serious expression. Rydal sat back in his chair and glanced around him. There was only a chunky man in cap and overcoat at the bar, his back to Rydal, and the man behind the bar and a woman who was mopping the tile floor. In the photograph, his hair was crew-cut and without a parting. About a year ago, he had started to part it on the left, as he had done most of his life, but before he left Niko's, he had adopted a right-hand parting, between a side and center parting. Not much of a help, but a little, he thought. But the photograph disquieted him. There wasn't much he could do to change his looks, short of dying his hair, and that wouldn't jibe with the Italian passport. The information below the photograph was interesting in a stale, rambling way. Rydal Keener was believed to be the killer or the kidnapper of William Chamberlain, who had disappeared on Friday, 19 January, from his hotel in Athens. Chamberlain had told the police several days ago that Keener was the slayer of his wife, Mary Ellen, whose body was found on the grounds of the Palace of Knossos. The police had been withholding the name of the slain woman until "elements of the story clarified themselves", but with the disappearance of Chamberlain, it was feared that the uncaptured suspect Keener had "struck successfully at his quarry, Chamberlain".

". . . Police state that Keener must know by now that Chamberlain has had ample time to inform the police of his (Keener's) crime, but according to Chamberlain, he is a vindictive and brutal type who will stop at nothing. American authorities report that Keener acquired a police record as early as fifteen for rape and for robbery . . ."

Ho-hum, thought Rydal. But his heart had begun to beat faster at that last sentence. Well, at least Keener was believed to be hiding out in Athens, where he had friends, Chamberlain said.

Rydal supposed he should buy a hat. He disliked hats.

He paid for his coffee and left the place. He had begun to feel uneasy about his hotel. Hadn't he mentioned its name to Yvonne last night? He had said, anyway, that it was in Montmartre. He felt he should check out today. Immediately. On the boulevard Saint-Germain, he got a taxi.

Less than one hour later, he was installed in a room at the Hotel Montmorency in a little street he had never heard of, up in the Clignancourt district. It was the sort of district and the sort of hotel, Rydal thought, that an Italian of moderate means and knowledge of the city might choose. On his passport, his occupation was civil servant. As soon as he was installed, he took the remaining money—his own American money—from the lining of his suitcase, and put it with Chester's new bills in his trousers pocket. He had more than thirteen thousand dollars, he supposed, though he did not count it. There might come a time when he couldn't get back to his hotel for his possessions, and money was always useful. He made one telephone call on a wild shot-in-the-dark chance to the Hôtel Lutetia, and asked for Mr. Wedekind. His hunch was wrong. There was no Mr. Wedekind. Rydal had one more idea: to haunt the American Express on Monday. There were other places one could receive mail, such as

Thomas Cook's, but the American Express seemed more likely, and he couldn't be in two places at once.

So, Monday morning, he went at 9 o'clock to the American Express office near the Opéra. If Chester did not show up today, he thought, he wasn't in Paris. Rydal spent a tedious morning. He had left his post at 9:30 for about fifteen minutes, in order to buy a hat at a shop nearby. Then he returned to his bench in the basement where the mail was given out, and hid himself beneath the hat and behind a newspaper.

Chester came down the steps just before noon. Rydal stood up, and immediately Chester saw him and turned. Unfortunately, there were three or four matronly women creeping down in a body just then, and a lot of jostling, impatient young people behind them, also on their way down, and when Rydal reached the top of the stairs, he had lost Chester. He looked quickly around the busy floor, at the lines for traveler's checks, at the information desk, then he went out on the street. He turned in a circle, looking.

No. He was gone.

Rydal cursed. Then he re-entered the building slowly. Chester hadn't been able to pick up his mail, and Rydal knew he would be anxious. He went down to the mail department again. There were telephone booths against one wall. He went into one of them, and closed the door and sat. From here, he had a view of all the mail lines. No one was waiting for a telephone booth. After a few minutes, when someone approached his booth, he took the receiver off the hook and pretended to be talking. He sat there for so long, he felt sure that Chester had decided to have lunch before he came back.

Chester came in at a little after 2. Rydal watched him closely, waiting his turn, glancing around him now and then in a way that

Rydal now saw was quite expert: a casual enough glance not to attract attention, yet his slow sweep took in the whole room. It hadn't taken in Rydal's glass-windowed telephone booth, however.

Chester was given a letter. He looked at the envelope on both sides, pushed it into his overcoat pocket, and walked towards the stairs. Rydal was a few feet behind him. Now there was going to be a little game of shadowing, something Rydal had never done. Shadowing must be so much easier, he thought, if the shadowee doesn't know the shadower. Rydal had to keep himself out of sight and Chester in sight. He was sorry Chester had seen the hat this morning.

Chester walked down the avenue de l'Opéra and went into a corner café, where he stood at the counter with a beer and read his letter. Rydal watched him through the café window from across the narrow side street. It was too far away for him to see the expression on Chester's face, but Rydal doubted if the news from home was pleasant. Rydal turned the corner and walked a few yards down Opéra before he turned again. He could still see both doors of the café where Chester was. After a few minutes, Chester came out and turned left, walking up the avenue again, his back to Rydal. Rydal followed him, keeping about a third of a block between them. There was quite a sprinkling of pedestrians on the pavement, so that if Chester looked behind him, his eye wouldn't necessarily fall on Rydal. Chester walked on around the Opéra to the right, then turned into a smaller street, and Rydal had hope: he might be going to his hotel. Rydal crossed the street and dropped farther behind. This street had less people in it. Chester vanished into a doorway on the left side of the street.

Rydal stopped, hesitated, thinking suddenly that Chester might know he was following him, that he might have ducked into the first hotel he came to, to throw him off. Rydal could see the name plaques on either side of the doorway, but he could not read them from here. He waited five minutes, then made himself wait another five, by his watch. Then he crossed the street, and went closer to the hotel, walking near the curb.

The hotel was the Élysée-Madison.

Rydal turned around, and the first thing he saw was a gendarme walking slowly towards him, his cape askew as if he had his hands on his hips underneath it. Rydal did not look at him after the first glance. He hated the new hat, which he felt was conspicuous, though it was a dull-brown felt.

The gendarme strolled on by him, but Rydal had the distinct feeling that the gendarme had stopped and turned to look after him. Rydal had ducked his face as much as he dared to into his upturned coat collar. And now he made himself go straight ahead, not look back. Yet an absolute panic had seized him to get to a telephone. He saw a bar-tabac half a block away and wanted to run to it. He managed to walk.

In the bar-tabac, he asked for a jeton. Then he looked up the hotel's number in the directory. His hands were perspiring. He realized he was scared, and the fact scared him more. He dialed the hotel's number.

"I would like to speak to M. Wedekind, if you please," he said in French, with the Italian accent that after three days had become habitual.

"Oui, monsieur, un moment," said a pleasant, female voice.

Rydal looked through the window of the booth and saw the gendarme standing on the pavement in front of the door. Rydal shuddered, and wet his lips. "Hello, Phil," Rydal said, interrupting

Chester's "Hello" in his haste. "Don't hang up. I have something very important to tell you."

Chester made a growling sound, then said, "What?"

"I want you to meet me tonight. Les Halles. Got it? In the flower section. It's a long pavement, you know, full of flowers and flower trucks. Plants. Got it? At nine o'clock."

"Why?"

"I'm going back to America." Rydal's throat was so dry, he sounded hoarse. He couldn't swallow. "Going back to America, Chester, and I want one last little payment. Ten thousand. All right? Last time around."

"Ugh!" with elaborate disgust. "When are you leaving?"

"Tomorrow morning early. By plane. So it's good-bye, Mr. Wedekind, and, for ten thousand more, I'll keep your little secret. *Secrets.* Is it a date tonight?—Hurry up. You know the alternative, don't you? I'm in a telephone booth—" His voice cracked. "—and if you don't want to make it, I'll just tell you know who that you're at the Élysée-Madison. I'm just around the corner, matter of fact. You couldn't possibly walk out without my seeing you." Rydal waited.

"I'll meet you," Chester said, and hung up.

Rydal hung up, and opened the booth's door. He bought a package of Gauloises. The gendarme was still there. Rydal could see him without looking at him. He opened the pack by pinching a little hole at a bottom corner. For Christ's sake, he thought, what's done it, the hat? The crazy hat? He lit his cigarette, and walked to the door. He did not look at the gendarme.

"Excusez, m'sieur. May I see your carte d'identité, if you please?"

"Ma quoi?"

"Carte d'identité, s'il vous plait."

"Ah, carta d'identità," said Rydal. "Si." He pulled the dark-green Italian passport from his inside jacket pocket. "Mi passaporto," he said, smiling.

The gendarme looked at it, and his eyebrows went up when he saw the passport photograph. The eyebrows came down again. Frank's retouching was at least *some* good, Rydal told himself hopefully. Frank had thickened his eyebrows, and had given the corners of his mouth an upward turn with a little shading. The gendarme was hesitating. He was a slender man of middle height with graying temples, a black moustache.

"Enrico Perassi. You come from Italy?"

"Si. Roma," said Rydal, though he knew the officer meant was that the country he had been in before coming to France.

"Greece," said the gendarme heavily, looking at the last page in which there were entries. "You have come from Greece just three days ago?"

"Si. I make a trip to Greece."

"For how much time?"

"Three weeks," Rydal replied promptly, remembering the dates in the passport.

"If you please, remove your hat, sir?"

"Hat?" Rydal repeated in Italian, smiling. He took his hat off.

The gendarme stared at him, frowning. Then he glanced at his clothes, at his new shoes, back at his face.

In that instant, Rydal felt his guard collapse. His left eye twitched. His mouth had become hard, unsmiling, defiant. Shame, guilt had annihilated him. For one flashing second, Rydal thought of the moment in his father's study, when his father had accused him of violence against Agnes. Then an instant later, it had passed, Rydal could smile slightly again, though his forehead was cool with sweat.

"Where are you staying in the city?"

"At—Hotel Montmorency. Rue Labat," Rydal said, pronouncing every letter in each name.

"You speak a good Italian? Speak some."

Rydal looked puzzled, as if he hadn't quite understood, and then, smiling, he rattled off, with an open-handed gesture that Italian evoked by itself for him: "Certainly, sir. Why not? It's the tongue of my birth. Very easy. Not like French. Ah, once I start, I probably won't be able to stop. Do you like Italian? You understand what I'm saying, signor?" He laughed and slapped the gendarme on the arm.

It was good, but it didn't do any good, essentially. The gendarme shook his head, handed Rydal back the passport, and said:

"If you please, I would like you to come to the préfecture for a few more questions. For just a few minutes." He already had Rydal by the arm, and was raising his other hand, with his white baton in it, for a taxi.

They arrived at a préfecture with little blue lamps beside the door. Here there was much talk between Rydal's gendarme and another officer about "Reedal Kayner" of Greece. Rydal's clothing was examined. His suit was Italian, but his shirt, well worn, was French. His tie was English (that was a bit odd, but possible, even though Enrico Perassi had never been to England according to his passport). His underwear was—of all things—Swiss. Rydal had bought it over a year ago in Zürich. They were going to go to his hotel, no doubt about that. His suitcase was American. His American passport was in the lining, out of the view of customs inspectors, but not out of the view of the French police. It was hopeless.

"All right," Rydal said in French. He was in a back room, stripped to his underwear.

The officers looked up from his great-grandfather's pocketwatch, which they were examining appreciatively.

"All right, it's true, I am Rydal Keener."

"Ah! You are—American!" said the second officer, as if this were more interesting than that he was Rydal Keener.

"And William Chamberlain is alive," Rydal said. "And I did not kill his wife."

"Ah, just a minute. Wait," said the portly second officer. He was going to get paper and sit down at the typewriter and take it all down properly.

The other gendarme, the one who had spotted Rydal, was almost strutting, walking up and down the room with a tight smile of satisfaction on his face.

Rydal recovered his trousers and his shirt. He first answered a lot of questions "Yes" and "No", and then he was asked to tell them what happened on Crete. Rydal said he had met the Chamberlains there. He admitted that there had been an attraction between Chamberlain's wife and himself. Chamberlain had been jealous, because his wife had told him she was in love with him, and wanted a divorce from Chamberlain. This seemed to go down well with the French police. Rydal said he had wanted to leave the Chamberlains, go back to Athens and wait for Mrs. Chamberlain to get her divorce, but Chamberlain had insisted that he stay with them. Then Chamberlain had attempted to kill him in the Palace of Knossos. Here Rydal could describe it exactly as it happened, and he thought his account sounded very convincing.

"Chamberlain was grief-stricken, I'm sure, when he found he had killed his wife. He ran away. I stayed for a few seconds by her body. I was stunned. Then I ran after Chamberlain. I found him again in Iraklion. That's only thirty kilometers or so away. I wanted to turn him in to the police, but he said if I did he'd say that I killed his wife because she wouldn't have me. Something like that. Do you see?"

"Um-m," grunted the first gendarme, who was now listening with intense interest. It was no doubt a story he would tell for a long time to come.

"Continue," said the man who was typing.

"We went to Athens together and there—"

"Together!"

"Tais-toi," absently from the typing officer.

"Yes. Mrs. Chamberlain wasn't identified at once, so it wasn't hard for Chamberlain to move about. He got himself a new passport in Athens, I'm sure of that."

"How so?" asked the typer.

"Because . . . he is here in Paris, and he is supposed to be dead or kidnapped in Athens. He couldn't possibly have entered France or even left Greece as Chamberlain."

"Um-m," said the listening gendarme.

"And where is he? Do you know?" asked the typer.

Rydal wet his lips. "I'd like very much a glass of water."

It was brought for him.

He still stood, talking. "I don't know where he is staying, but I have seen him here in Paris. He must have been here since Friday. I thought he would come to Paris, which is why I came here."

"Speaking of false passports, where did you get yours and why?" asked the listening gendarme.

"In Athens," Rydal said. "Rydal Keener was being sought . . . for murder. I had to get a passport. Don't you see? I am also trying to find Chamberlain." He said the last sentence with vehemence.

"In Athens, were you also constantly with Chamberlain?"

"On the contrary! He disappeared at Piraeus. From me, I mean. For a few days—Well, I was in love with his wife. I admit it. I was crushed by grief. I felt more grief than I felt hatred for Chamberlain. Do you understand? I might have told the Athens police immediately the story and said, 'Look for Chamberlain.' But don't forget he had threatened to accuse me if I accused him. It would have been my word against his, because we had no witnesses." Rydal finished his water.

"Where did you see him here in Paris?"

Rydal took a deep breath. "On the Champs-Élysées. This morning. I spoke to him, though he wanted to avoid me. I pretended to make—"

"Why did you not shout at once for the police when you saw him?" asked the officer who was typing.

"I suppose . . . I was afraid, the same old fear. I was afraid of what Chamberlain would tell the police about me. What I wanted to do is . . . just what I've done now. Speak to the police and—"

He was interrupted by a laugh from the gendarme who had found him. "And with all your efforts to appear an Italian!"

"Very well. All right. I was afraid," Rydal said, feeling uncomfortable. "But now it's said."

"One question here, please," said the typist. "I have left a space for it. Where did you stay in Athens? Did you get your false passport immediately? You were three or four days in Athens?"

"From Wednesday morning until Friday the nineteenth," Rydal answered. "I stayed with a friend. I don't care to give the friend's name. I don't think that would be fair, do you?" He looked the officer straight in the eye.

The officer shrugged and smiled at the gendarme.

"I was innocent. I am innocent, and I think I have a right to stay with a friend, who knows I am innocent. I don't care to involve my friend." He added more gently, "I think you can understand that."

"We shall return to that later," said the typing officer, poising his fingers over the keyboard again. "Now, where did you see M. Chamberlain, if you please?"

"On the Champs-Élysées near Concorde. This morning. I tried to frighten him into telling me his name and what hotel he is staying at. He refused. Then I threatened him—for a change. I told him that unless he paid me ten thousand dollars, I would go to the police and tell them the whole story and tell them that he was in Paris. He said he would give it to me. So we made a rendezvous for tonight at nine o'clock. I think Chamberlain will keep it."

"Where?"

"At Les Halles. In the flower market."

"Hmph!" grunted the gendarme. "A busy place. You think he will keep the rendezvous?" he asked hopefully, folding his arms.

"Yes." Rydal smiled. He thought Chester would keep it. It was time Chester was stopped. There was no way, really, to have a showdown without dragging the police in, and now they were in. He would have his share of blame thrown at him, too, for helping Chester hide the Greek agent's body. That had been a mistake, and people had to pay for mistakes. But it would be worth it to see Chester fall.

The typing stopped.

"Who were you talking to on the telephone in that bar tabac?" asked the gendarme.

Rydal answered slowly, "Nobody. I wasn't telephoning. I was pretending to telephone, thinking you might go away if I kept you waiting."

The gendarme nodded in a superior way, as if condescending to the stupidity of someone who thought he could be shaken off. "Dites donc!" He leaned forward, pointing a finger at Rydal. "You have had dinner Saturday night with a young woman named Yvonne . . . Yvonne . . ."

The other officer consulted a paper on his desk. "Delatier," he said.

"Yes," Rydal said.

"Yes. She called the police about you yesterday," said the gendarme. "She saw your picture in the paper. She said you had a lot of money."

"Not so much as I bragged to her that I had. I lied to her, I'm afraid." He still had the money, in his left-hand trousers pocket. They had slapped his clothes for weapons, examined them for labels, but they had not looked into his pockets—a wadded handkerchief in one, thirteen thousand dollars in the other.

The other officer was now on the telephone, reporting the finding of Rydal Keener to the main police headquarters, Rydal supposed.

"Would you place a call to the police of Athens and keep the line open, please? . . . Thank you."

19

At a quarter to 9 Rydal was driven by two police officers—one the gendarme who had found him—to Les Halles. Their car was a plain black Citroën. Rydal was very nervous, and at the same time simply tired. He was actually drowsy during the ride. He had not told the police Chester had shaved off his beard and moustache. They had asked, "He has a beard and a moustache?" and Rydal had replied, "Yes," at once, then had started to correct himself, and hadn't. He supposed he had thought it would make himself seem uncertain about it, make his story of seeing Chester in Paris seem untrue, if he had corrected himself. But that wasn't it, Rydal knew. Telling the police he was clean-shaven now seemed to be stacking the cards too much against Chester. This way it was more sportsmanlike. Maybe that was it. At any rate, he hadn't corrected himself. And he had been very emphatic, too, in saying that Chamberlain was clever about spotting the police, in plain clothes or not, so they had best keep a certain distance until they were sure they had him. "Oh, yes? How did he become so clever about police?" they had asked. Rydal didn't know, but he was. After all, Rydal thought, the police were going to keep their eye on *him,* mainly, and naturally they would see any person to whom he spoke, and who handed him anything—an envelope, a newspaper—that contained the ten thousand dollars. What would it matter if Chester had a beard and moustache or hadn't?

"Not too close," Rydal said as he saw the first flower-pots along the pavement ahead. "Let me out here. No, over there. To the left."

The car slowed down and swung to the left in the broad street. It was raining. The lights of the market made blurred yellow paths across the shining black streets, and the occasional shimmers of red lights reflected in them suggested to Rydal spilled blood.

"Into that little alley," Rydal said, annoyed now. "If he sees me getting out of this car, he'll know something is up."

"Very good, m'sieur, very good," the driver said with mock patience.

Rydal and the gendarme in plain clothes got out at the same time, from the right side of the car. The gendarme had his hands in his overcoat pockets, where there was no doubt a gun. He looked awfully much like a gendarme in plain clothes with a gun to Rydal.

"Let me go ahead," Rydal said to him. "Four meters—six meters ahead is not too much."

"Ah?" The gendarme wagged his head dubiously.

The other man was getting out of the car, too.

Rydal turned and crossed the street towards the pavement that was bordered with plants and flowers. Trucks presented their open back ends to the pavement, their floors full of plants and small trees with roots tied up in burlap, and in a few trucks a man or a woman slept on sacking, tired after a long day that had begun early in the country.

Rydal did not look for Chester at first. He walked along casually, hatless now, his head mostly down as he looked at the greenery.

"Hey, ivy here! Very cheap!" cried a woman's piercing voice. "Hyacinths in bloom! Take one to your girl! Take your choice, m'sieur!"

The leaves of rubber plants were glossy and bright in the market lights, and there was a pleasant smell of rich, rain wetted earth. The ivy seemed to glory in the cool moist air, the flowers looked bursting with happiness and vitality, and Rydal was sorry to think of any of them being taken into gas-heated Paris apartments. Rydal stopped and looked back, looked first at some chrysanthemums, then for the gendarme. The gendarme was fifteen feet or more behind him, one hand in a pocket now. Frowning, Rydal passed a hand across his hair, and went on.

He saw Chester, and his scalp prickled. Chester was about to turn at the corner on the broad pavement, and he was coming towards Rydal. Chester carried a newspaper-wrapped pot at the top of which some red blossoms showed. An intelligent prop, Rydal thought. Chester was twenty feet away, looking now at the plants on either side of him, then glancing straight in front of him.

Rydal slowed, idling. He stood erect, but looked down at a banked display of cacti in small pots on his right.

"Three for five francs, m'sieur," said the man. "This kind makes a pretty pink blossom."

Rydal hated what he was doing. He was balking. He wanted to take one gigantic leap, leap over the cactus display and through the brick wall behind it and disappear. *Remember Colette,* he thought. *Chester is a crook. He cheats honest men.* But there wasn't time to remember Colette, or to think about Chester's dishonesty. Rydal turned from the cacti and drifted on. Chester saw him now. Rydal half closed his eyes and gave a shake of his head, a faint shake which he finished with a tilt of his head to the left, a rubbing of his left ear, as if he had got water into it.

Chester passed by him.

Rydal walked on to the corner where he had first seen Chester. He was strangely relieved, as if he had successfully hurdled a dangerous crevasse that he had had to cross. But he listened tensely for a sound of commotion behind him. He yearned for the darkness around the corner. It was a darker street, a back street. At the corner, Rydal quickened his step slightly. For a few seconds, very few, he would be out of the sight of the gendarme. At the same time, he did not want to rouse the attention of anyone on this side of the block by running. Rydal gave himself about twelve steps, about five seconds, and then he dove, headfirst and horizontal, into the back of a truck. He held his breath, his eyes shut, expecting a voice. Nothing happened. He opened his eyes. The truck was empty and black, except for the little window in the back through which a driver could look when he drove. Rydal's hands felt dirt crumbs, moist newspapers, some small flower pots.

Just then a hurdy-gurdy started playing, very near. It played "La Vie en Rose".

. . . il me parle tout bas
je vois la vie en rose. . . .

Rydal crawled on his belly farther into the truck. Now his hands struck cloth, and he paused, afraid he had touched the cover of someone sleeping. It was just a pile of dark cloth for shading plants, perhaps, at the back of the truck on the floor. Rydal crawled into the corner and pulled it over him, over his head and feet. He lay still. He was just in time, for a flashlight shone then into the truck. He could see its glow through the cloth.

. . . ça dura pour la vie-e-e. . . .

Rydal almost smiled. He hoped not!

"Non," grunted a voice, and feet hurried off.

Rydal listened. Then he looked. There was only a dark wall across the pavement behind the truck. The only light came from the right, making a triangle at the left on the truck's floor.

Then suddenly a man's figure appeared, a man in a cap who shoved the dropped flap of the truck shut with a crashing, proprietary impact, and Rydal heard a bolt slide. Whistling, the man approached the front of the truck, his shoes clanked on the truck's metal steps, the engine started.

What luck! Rydal smiled and sighed.

The man drove like a demon. Rydal was tossed entirely into the air every few seconds. It crossed his mind that this man was running away from something, too. But Rydal could hear his whistling and singing over the noise of the motor. Rydal made his way to the rear of the truck and crouched behind the three-feet-high door. They were still in traffic, so that when the truck paused for a light, the head lights of a car behind glared against the back of the truck. Once at a stop, a street-lamp illuminated a street name brilliantly: rue de Belleville. Rydal couldn't have cared less.

The driver made a left turn that rolled Rydal against the truck's right wall. Rydal huddled behind the short door again. They were now in a district with less lights. The truck stopped for a red. Rydal jumped out. His rubber soles made a slapping noise on the street, but he doubted if the driver heard. Also, a man and woman walking under an umbrella saw him, but so what, Rydal thought. People rode trucks sometimes, drivers let off their workers here and there, and his clothing was not so good that he couldn't be taken for a truck-driver's assistant. Besides, it was dark. Besides, the man and woman walked on. Besides, he was free!

Rydal smiled into the rain as he walked down a street. It was just a *street,* in Paris. He didn't know its name. It was a medium-sized street, and a *sens unique,* he saw. A bar-tabac's slanting red cylinder glowed a hundred yards ahead. Rydal whistled "La Vie en Rose". He went into the bar-tabac, his coat collar up, his hair wet and purposely mussed, and such a cheerful expression on his face, he felt, that it would not be easy for people to see any resemblance to the earnest young man called Rydal Keener in the newspaper photograph. But it was unfortunate, he thought, that the police, due to wanting to capture Chester tonight, had not announced to the public that Rydal Keener had been apprehended. That would have given him the best protection of all. He bought a slug for the telephone.

Then he called the Hôtel Élysée-Madison, whose number he remembered.

M. Wedekind was not in.

"He has not checked out, has he?" Rydal asked.

"No, m'sieur."

"Thank you." No, of course he hadn't checked out. Not enough time had passed. Hardly fifteen minutes had passed since he had seen Chester. Yet hours ago, Rydal had thought Chester might have decided to check out just after his telephone call this afternoon. He wondered if Chester would be afraid to go back to his hotel for his possessions, thinking that he, Rydal, had told the police where he was staying? That was possible.

Rydal wondered, in fact, just what Chester would make of his giving him the warning at the flower market? Wouldn't Chester assume that the police had found Rydal Keener and were using him to catch Philip Wedekind? Or at very least that the police were watching him? Of course Chester would.

He walked on at a moderate pace, getting soaked and not caring at all. He walked in the general direction of the center of the city, which he knew by instinct. Now he recognized a couple of street names, Faubourg du Temple and then the avenue Parmentier, not because he had been here before, but because he had used to pore over maps of Paris and Rome and London as an adolescent. He knew vaguely he was in the north-east of Paris, because old "potatoes Parmentier" had been in the upper right of his folding *plan de Paris.* He grew bored with walking, and took a taxi to the Seine.

The driver asked him where on the Seine.

"Vicinity of Notre Dame," Rydal said in a careless tone.

Then he walked along the Quai Henri IV towards the Île Saint-Louis. He had walked along here more than a year ago, and he remembered being aware of the formal and cold atmosphere of the straight-fronted houses that faced the river. Formal, elegant, cold, unfriendly, he had thought. And neither they nor he had changed, really, but now the neighborhood seemed happy to him, even in the rain and in the dark. He was free. He could not go back to his hotel for the rest of his clothes or his notebook of poems or his few books, and he was being sought by the police at this minute, and he was without a passport or identification. But he had thirteen thousand dollars in his pocket, and he was free, as only a nameless person of his time could be free. It would not last long, he knew. But for these few hours, he would have it—freedom—he would savor it, he would rejoice in it, and he would never forget it. It was like being suspended in some element that did not really exist on earth, like the element in which angels flew, or spirits communicated with one another.

He looked at his watch. It was 10:15. He had been free for about an hour.

No, Chester would probably not go back to his hotel, he thought. Chester carried his passport at all times, and he probably carried all his money on him now. It would be typical of Chester to hazard taking a plane to the States using his Wedekind passport. In fact, what else could he do? Was he possibly at Orly or Le Bourget this minute? A passenger without luggage? Rydal rested his forearms on the parapet beside the Seine and looked at the illuminated façade of Notre Dame. Its design was complex, heavy, immobile, yet somehow floating, a work of art that seemed to him perfect, and it occurred to Rydal that it ought to be one of the Seven Wonders of the World, instead, perhaps, of the ponderous Pyramid at Gizeh. He was smiling, his eyes half closed as he looked at the cathedral's mysteriously weightless mass, and then a frown tightened his brows. Why had he let Chester go? Chester wasn't gone, of course, wasn't free, because Rydal knew his alias, and all he had to do was tell it to the police.

He pushed himself away from the embankment and walked on. At the Pont Neuf, he crossed to the Left Bank, and walked through the rue Dauphine to the boulevard Saint-Germain. He passed a gendarme as he crossed a street, and Rydal simply glanced at him, as any person might have, without a change in his speed of walking. But by now, Rydal thought, every gendarme on street patrol must have been notified of the "escape" of Rydal Keener. Rydal went into the first café he saw on Saint-Germain. He called Chester's hotel. It was a compulsion. He knew as he waited for the hotel to answer that if Chester was not in, he would go to the hotel and wait for him. He would wait indefinitely in the lobby, he knew. He would take a taxi directly there. And if he waited mysteriously in the lobby for an hour or two, Rydal had no doubt that the hotel personnel would notice him, would see that he was or looked like Rydal Keener, would call the police to come and take a look at him—and he would be back where he was before, only without the appointment with Chester.

"I should like to speak to M. Wedekind, if you please."

"Oui, m'sieur."

Rydal waited a whole minute. Longer, he thought. "He's out?" Rydal asked.

No one answered him.

Then Chester's voice said hoarsely, "Hello?" He sounded breathless.

"Hello," Rydal said. "Hello, Phil."

"Where are you?" coldly.

"Well, I'd say—somewhere near l'Abbaye on Saint Germain —Why?"

Chester did not speak immediately. "Are you with the police or what?"

Rydal smiled. "I'm not with the police. I'm absolutely free. And you? You sound distrait."

Only Chester's irregular breathing came over the telephone.

"Are you with the police?" Rydal asked. "Are they letting you pack up?"

"What kind of a trick is this?" Chester said in an angry tone that was familiar to Rydal.

"No trick, Chester. I was with the police and now I'm not. Suppose I come to see you?" He hung up before Chester could answer.

Rydal ran to a *tête de taxis* near the Brasserie Lipp.

The taxi-driver didn't know the hotel or the street.

"Near the Opéra!" Rydal said. "Drive to the Opéra and I'll direct you when we get there."

He sat up on the edge of the seat during the drive, feeling very happy, as if he were on a lark of some kind. He felt also as if he had surrendered to the totally irrational, as much as if he were blind drunk and embarking on a most unwise action, such as driving a car fast on the unprotected hairpin turns of the Saint Gotthard pass on a dark night. There were many factors in his visiting Chester now, Rydal thought. Chester was terrified, first of all, and Rydal was looking forward to seeing him with his own eyes in that condition. No more, perhaps, would Rydal ever see Chester with that paternal sternness—Rydal had, for obvious reasons, to call it paternal—on his face that he had seen the moment just before he gave Chester the *no* in the flower market of Les Halles. At Rydal's shake of the head, he supposed, Chester's courage had collapsed. He had probably fled back to his hotel, at any rate fled from Les Halles. And there was just the possibility that tonight he would beat Chester up. Say, no more than two good blows to the jaw. That would satisfy Rydal. Straightforward blows, none of the knee or the fist in the stomach stuff that Chester had tried with him on the boat from Crete. One paste in the mouth, on the mouth that had so often kissed Colette's. No, that was a bit primitive, Rydal thought. None of that, he warned himself. No fisticuffs, just a few words. He glanced out at the lights of the Tuileries—it was like a glimpse into the seventeenth century—and Rydal suddenly saw a scene of mercy between himself and Chester, saw himself touching a shaking shoulder and saying to Chester—What? Some brilliant idea that would come to him, of course, in regard to Chester's escaping from the police. Rydal was smiling slightly. He did not want to help Chester at all. Not at all. In reality, quite consciously and definitely, Rydal detested him.

"Make a right at the next corner, please," Rydal said to the driver. "Two streets up and it's on the left." He had the money ready.

Rydal got out of the taxi in front of the hotel and walked in. It was a small, ornate lobby. Rydal went to the desk and asked the man to tell M. Wedekind that M. Stengel was on his way up. The name popped into his head. It didn't matter. The man spoke to Chester, then said he could go up.

Chester opened the door, pale and visibly shaking—or perhaps it was a shudder that Rydal saw. His shirt collar was unbuttoned, his tie slid down.

"I'm alone," Rydal said. He went into the room. The room was in disorder, even the bed rumpled, as if Chester might have tried to hide in it after he came back from Les Halles tonight.

"I suppose you've come for the money," Chester said.

"Oh—Well, as I've said before, I'm not averse."

"This time you're not getting it."

"Oh," Rydal said in a polite tone, and with an absence of interest that was genuine. He looked at Chester.

The only color in Chester's face was around his eyes, and it was pink. He had picked up a nearly finished glass of Scotch from somewhere. The inevitable bottle was on the inevitable bureau.

"What happened to your police friends?" asked Chester.

"I gave them the slip."

Chester sipped his drink. "They picked you up?"

Then Rydal was suddenly angry, felt a fury that was like a brush of flame. He waited until it had passed. "No. I dropped by and talked to them."

"What?" Chester said, frowning. "Don't give me that crap.—What're they waiting for?"

Rydal looked at him, and he didn't need Chester to tell him that all his money, his "assets" in the States were gone now, seized by the American police or perhaps absconded with by Chester's scared pals. Only a loss of money could have broken Chester down so. Losing Colette hadn't had this much effect on him.

"What kind of game are you playing, Rydal?" Chester asked.

Rydal shrugged. "It must have dawned on you I haven't told the police your name or the name of this hotel, or they'd be here."

"All right, you're asking me to pay for that. Is that right?"

Rydal had an unpleasant reply in mind, but the bickering irked him. Chester would have paid now for his not telling the police his alias, or would pay if Rydal promised not to tell it for twenty-four hours, or something like that, so Chester would have time to get to America. "Why don't you get out of the country?"

Chester looked at him suspiciously. "You came here to tell me that?"

"Certainly not. I could have told you that on the telephone. I came here to *see* you." Rydal smiled, and lit a cigarette.

Chester's pink-rimmed eyes stared at him. "What did you tell the police?"

"I told them what happened at Knossos. What happened in Crete. I said that's where I'd met you. Mr. and Mrs. Chamberlain. And then I told them you'd vanished in Athens. The Athens part didn't hold water very well, but when I told them I had a date with you tonight, they weren't too fussy about the rest of it. They wanted to get you."

"And? Why didn't you let them?" Chester's voice was hoarse again, and there was a note of self-pity in it, which probably alcohol had brought. "Rydal, I'm a ruined man. Look at that! At that letter!" He gestured towards the papers on the night table, which in the general disorder of the room, Rydal had not noticed before. "I haven't a cent in the States! I'm MacFarland—in that letter. I'm wanted for murder—" His voice stopped, the tone dangling.

"I can imagine. I'm not interested," Rydal said.

"Tell me what you want. Let's have it. If you told the police to come here—"

"If I'd told the police to come here, they'd have been here sooner than I. Do you know what I want, Chester?" Rydal asked, walking towards him. He said slowly, "I'd like a photograph of Colette. Have you got one?"

Chester had taken a step back. He frowned. "Yes. Yes, I've got one," he answered, angry but reconciled, stunned, hopeless. He went as if in a daze to his jacket that was thrown over a chair and groped in the inside pocket of it. He pulled out a mass of papers and money. A small card fell to the floor.

Rydal moved to pick the card up, and caught also a five-hundred dollar bill that was fluttering down.

"It's the only one I've got left," Chester said in a maudlin voice. "The others—are in the States."

"Pity." Rydal snatched the photograph from his fingers and looked at it. He smiled. It was in color. Colette looked straight at him in a full-face view, her reddish hair fluffy, her mouth smiling. Looking at her lavender eyes, Rydal could hear her voice speaking to him: *I do love you, Rydal. I do.* Had she ever said it in those words? No matter, she was saying it now. Rydal put it into his jacket pocket, the left breast pocket, the handkerchief pocket. "A pity you had to kill her," he said to Chester.

Chester put his hands over his face and wept. He sat down on the bed, his face sunk in his hands.

Rydal had had enough. "Pull yourself together. Either go to the police or pack up and fly to the States." Chester looked as if he hadn't the energy to do anything but give himself up to the police, if that. Then Rydal realized there was a small matter he might bargain about. It concerned the Greek agent's body in the Hotel King's Palace in Athens. In return for Chester's not mentioning his services there—No, Rydal shied away from it. It was dishonest, cowardly. And he had to smile at his own resurgent sense of honor, risen again like a phoenix, out of where, out of what? "Which do you choose to do?" Rydal asked.

Chester was now staring into space, his shoulders hunched. "It's best if I get to the States. Get back home. Got to start over again." Chester hauled himself up and went to the bureau for the bottle. Then, with the bottle, he looked around the room, like someone half blind, for his glass.

Rydal saw it first and handed it to him. "Your fortitude is admirable," Rydal said in a tone his father might have used in one of his devastating speeches, "but just how long do you think you can keep it up in the States? What's Philip Wedekind going to do first? Start selling phony stock to gullible old ladies or—"

"Ah, Philip Wedekind can disappear as soon as I hit home ground," Chester said.

The drink in his hand had raised his confidence, for the moment. Rydal felt the warm anger in his face again. "And then—then, when you're caught as Mr. X, and they find out you're also Chamberlain and MacFarland and so forth, you'll give out with the old story again? Rydal Keener killed my wife, Keener blackmailed me, and, way back, Keener killed the agent in the hotel in Athens. Is that it, Chester?"

Chester did not answer, did not even look at him. He didn't have to. Rydal knew that was it. What else could it be, from a man like Chester? Chester dragged himself across the room to the closet.

"I'm wasting my time here and yours, too," Rydal said. "We could put everything off a little while longer, maybe I could buy a French identity card, maybe you could get to the States. But what's the use? Why don't you get on the telephone, Chester? I know the French police would like to—"

Chester was facing him with a gun in his hand.

Rydal was surprised, but not frightened. "What's the use of that? It'll just make a noise and you'll have the whole hotel up here."

Chester came closer, his face and his hand with the gun very steady now.

Chester had nothing to lose, Rydal realized. Chester wouldn't mind at all killing him. Rydal grabbed for Chester's wrist, struck it but failed to get a grip, as Chester fired. In sudden anger, Rydal hit him hard on the jaw with his fist. Chester fell. Rydal went to the door and out. He took the stairs down to the floor below, saw by the indicator that the elevator was on its way up, and he pressed the down button. The elevator went on up, past his floor.

"What was that?" asked a woman's voice in French in the hall above.

"A gunshot?" said a man's voice.

The elevator stopped on the way down, and Rydal got in. He was so tense, his tension seemed to hold his brain immobile. He thought only: *don't hurry.*

His objective was merely the dark street outside, and he felt a kind of triumph and relief when he got there. The man who had ridden down in the elevator with him walked quietly away in the opposite direction on the pavement. Rydal walked one street, then two. He felt confused, shocked—as if what had just happened was complicated and inexplicable.

Rydal felt suddenly very sad and old. He raised his head, took stock of where he was—at the corner of the boulevard Haussmann and chaussée d'Antin—then proceeded purposefully to find a telephone.

He called from a brasserie. He did not know the location of the police station the operator had connected him with, but the man he spoke to knew the name William Chamberlain, and Rydal told him Chamberlain could be found at the Hôtel Élysée-Madison under the name Philip Wedekind.

"Very good! May I ask your name, sir?"

"Rydal Keener," Rydal said.

"Rydal Keener! Where are you? If you do not tell us, this call can be traced, anyway."

"Save yourself the trouble. I'm in the Café Normandie, boulevard Haussmann and—near the Opéra. I shall wait for you."

So ended his freedom.

20

At that moment, Chester was hurrying along the same street, the boulevard Haussmann, but in a direction away from the café where Rydal sat. He wore an overcoat and a hat, and his passport was where it always was, in the inside pocket of the overcoat, but otherwise he carried no possessions. *I dropped a lightbulb . . . I dropped a lightbulb. . . .* He had said it to the woman who stuck her head out of her door into the hall, two doors away from his, just as he was looking out of his own door. *J'ai laissé tomber une—une lumière?* What had he said? Anyway, though she still looked puzzled, she hadn't done anything about it. He'd got out of the hotel, that was the main thing. *Coolness,* Chester, that's what counts, said a distant and tired voice, an automatic voice within him. He had taken the elevator down calmly, as usual. Gone calmly through the lobby, which he had half expected to be full of police, summoned by Rydal. He had certainly expected to see Rydal in the lobby. In fact, he couldn't understand what Rydal was up to, running off like that. Unless Rydal was going to call the police from some safe spot, like a public telephone booth, call them and inform and not give his own name. Chester had thought that was the most likely, and so he had lost no time in getting out of the hotel. *J'ai laissé tomber tine*—Chester shook his head nervously. Stop that nonsense. Rigmarole going around in his head. He had to get out of Paris. He wanted to go to Marseille. Or to Calais, or Le Havre, where the boats left from. Whichever city a train was going to first. It would take too long to get to an airport, and airports, he thought, were more easily watched than railway stations.

There at last was a hack stand across the street.

Chester got into a taxi and told the driver, "Gare du Nord". It was the busiest gare in Paris, Chester thought. At least he had always come in or taken off from there, when he wasn't flying.

There was a train to Marseille at 6 a.m., a slow train. And there were several trains to Calais, but Chester chose Marseille.

He left the station and went into a bar nearby, and ordered a Scotch. The Scotch steadied him wonderfully. It made him realize the stupidity of waiting for the train, if Rydal had reported him to the police. Yes, indeed. And he'd better assume Rydal had. Rydal was in some kind of suicidal mood. Hadn't he proposed that *both* of them go to the police and tell all? The absurdity of it! Chester indulged himself in one more Scotch.

Then he went out and, after trying three taxi-drivers, got one who was willing to take him as far as Lyon for the fifty-dollar bill that Chester showed him under a light. Chester said he had just heard that a ship he was supposed to sail on was leaving Marseille in the morning, and he had to make it.

Chester felt quite safe in the taxi. He felt hidden, invisible, in the darkness. The taxi-driver was chatty at first, asked him how he happened to be in Paris without luggage—Chester said he had just come up for a two-day last-minute visit and had been staying with a friend in Paris—but then the driver settled down to his business, and they did not speak any more.

They arrived in Lyon at 5 a.m., Chester gave the driver fifty francs besides the fifty dollars he had given him in Paris, and then, seeing an all night café—or perhaps one that had opened very early—Chester decided to sit it out there until daylight. He felt he had got a slight jump on the police, and that Lyon was not a likely place for them to be looking for him. At 8:30, he had a shave in a barber's shop, then he bought a ticket for a 9:30 train to Marseille. On the train, he slept. His companions in the compartment were two men engrossed in newspapers, enviably rested and fresh-looking in clean shirts and neat suits.

In the early afternoon, the train spilled its passengers out in a large, grey railway station, and Chester, without pausing for a newspaper or a drink, kept walking until he was out of it. He felt very conspicuous in railway stations, as if every man behind a newspaper on a bench was in reality a police agent on the lookout for him. The streets had a downward slope, Chester presumed towards the water, which he did not see even after several minutes of walking. At last he came to a broad, busy avenue, which he saw was the Cannebière. He had heard of the Cannebière, the main avenue of Marseille. Looking down it, he could see a short span of water, the Mediterranean. Chester turned in the direction of the water. The Cannebière was lined with shops of all kinds, haberdasheries, bar-tabacs, pharmacies, and there seemed to be three or four glass-fronted restaurants or bars to every block, the kind which in summer would have tables and chairs spread out on the broad pavement, he supposed. He liked the bustling activity of the street, the variety of characters he saw among the people—workmen with shovels over their shoulders, women with a little too much make-up, cripples peddling pencils, a couple of British sailors, men with trays of trinkets slung on cords around their necks. He imagined he could smell the sea.

He had thought by simply going down to the water, he might find an outward-bound ship, a passenger ship or a freighter. All he saw at first was an open rectangle of a harbour full of small fishing boats tied up at the wharf with furled sails, and a few more coming in. A placard advertised an afternoon excursion to the Château d'If.

"Where are the big boats?" he asked a fisherman.

"Oh, out there," the man said, waving an arm to the right. He had metal-framed front teeth, like Niko in Athens. "This is the *old* port."

"Thanks." The vieux port. Chester had heard of it.

He walked down the right side of the old port. Fishermen were mending nets, coiling rope. He narrowly missed being hit by a basketful of crayfish shells which a woman flung from the door of a small restaurant. She was yelling something that Chester couldn't understand. His walk netted him nothing but a pretty view. He saw a grey battleship, which might have been British or American, but nothing that looked like a passenger liner. He walked back to the Cannebière. He had noticed some travel agencies on the Cannebière on his walk down.

No boat was leaving that day. A Swedish freighter was leaving tomorrow for Philadelphia, but the man in the travel agency was not able, when he telephoned the ship, to speak to the person who would know if there were cabins for passengers on the freighter. The only passenger liner the man mentioned was an Italian boat Chester had never heard of, not one of the big ones, coming in tomorrow and sailing the day after tomorrow. Chester did not want to wait that long.

He thought he had best try flying. He telephoned the Marignane airport and learned that there was no room on any flight today.

"And tomorrow?" Chester asked.

"A flight at two in the afternoon, sir. Do you wish to make a reservation?"

"Yes. For the two o'clock, please. Wedekind. *Double vé . . .*"

He could pay for his ticket at a certain agency on the Cannebière, he was told. Chester said he would buy it at once. He did, with francs he obtained from a bank which was also on the Cannebière. After that, he strolled up one of the streets to the east. He assumed it was to the east, since the Cannebière seemed to run from north to south to the water. Marseille seemed rather like a dirtier Paris, and the town looked even older. He dropped into a café for a Scotch, had two, then drifted on, upward. He came to an outdoor market, all empty of produce and shoppers now, where women and men were sweeping up cabbage leaves, scraps of paper, and damaged oranges and potatoes. The town was shutting up. That meant the bars and restaurants would soon be in full swing.

At 6:30, Chester was in the men's room of the Hôtel de Noailles, changing into a new white shirt he had bought, doing the best he could to clean his nails and to smooth his hair without a comb. He was well on the way to being drunk, he realized, but he felt absolutely in command of himself, even confident, with his airplane ticket in his pocket, and with plenty of money on him. He intended to telephone Jesse Doty tomorrow just before he went to the airport. Jesse's letter had sounded quite shaken and worried, even defeated. "Am destroying subscriber lists. . . ." A word from him would give Jesse courage. Just a confident tone, saying, "We've weathered some bad times before, old chap, and . . ."

Chester made his way back to the bar of the hotel, where a Scotch he had sipped only once awaited him on the counter. In the paper bag that had held his new shirt he had his soiled shirt, a good heavy silk one that Colette had bought for him in New York at Knize's. In a few minutes, he thought, he would go and see about a room for the night here. He liked the looks of the Hôtel de Noailles. He wondered what Rydal was doing at this moment? Were they looking all over Paris for him? Chester chuckled to himself, saw the barman looking at him, and stopped. He stared into his drink. He had been imagining the French police, numerous and lively, rushing into his hotel room last night and finding it empty. Looking the Paris streets for him all last night in the rain—lots of luck!—when he had been riding down to Lyon in a taxi. Maybe they'd think he had jumped into the Seine. Chester hoped so. Yes, he must have presented a pretty dismal picture to Rydal last night, the picture of a man not far from suicide. Well, people had another think coming in regard to Chester MacFarland. Philip Wedekind. *Well, Mr. Keener,* the French police would say, *where is this Wedekind you're talking about? You say he's the same as Chamberlain? Prove it. Where is he?*

Chester changed his mind about staying at the Noailles. Maybe best not register at a hotel tonight, not if Rydal had spread the name Wedekind around. A whorehouse, that was the place to hide in. No trouble to find in this town, either, as he had already been accosted three times before 6 p.m. Whorehouses had hidden many a man in trouble. Yes, indeed.

"Un autre, s'il vous plaît," said Chester, sliding his glass forward.

"Oui, m'sieur."

During the second drink, Chester consulted with the barman about a good restaurant for dinner. The barman recommended the Noailles. But in the course of the conversation, he suggested a few others, and Chester chose the Caribou out of the lot, mainly because he could remember its name best. The Caribou was—Chester couldn't retain the street name—down a bit towards the vieux port and to the left.

It was close to nine before he got there. He had stepped into a restaurant at the upper corner of the vieux port, because a woman hawker out in front had fairly pulled him in, and, once in, he had decided to sample Marseille bouillabaisse, touted as the very best in the city by the woman. Chester thought his appetite equal to the task of two dinners that evening. At this little restaurant, he somehow acquired two children, who tagged after him despite his giving them five francs apiece to disappear. The children went with him to the Caribou. The children had directed him there. The maître d'hôtel or a waiter at the restaurant made the children go back out of the door, and showed signs of refusing Chester service, but Chester said as solemnly as he could:

"I am awaiting someone. A table for two, if you please."

And he was shown to a table.

From here on, Chester was aware of very little. Warm candlelight. A sort of balcony in the place from which mounted heads of caribou or moose or elks looked down on him. A plate of food consisting of two round slabs of dark meat—what was it? he had forgotten what he ordered—a bottle of wine that was white when it should have been red. Chester was sure he had ordered red. A very cold and unsympathetic brunette woman, quite pretty, at the table next to him, who refused to answer him when he spoke to her. There was string music, from somewhere.

And from somewhere, deep within him, hope, confidence, even laughter struggled up to the surface. He was quite drunk, that was certain, but he wasn't going to pass out, and he felt he could walk. He deserved to be drunk, after what he had been through. He took out his ball-point fountain pen and started to compose a telegram, or his message on the telephone tomorrow, to Jesse, and discovered he couldn't write well enough to read, or at least read tomorrow. No matter.

The next thing Chester was aware of were wet cobblestones in his face and pains in his feet. His feet were being struck, three times, four. A man's voice shouted to him in French. Chester looked up the red stripe of a trousers leg into a gendarme's smiling face. Chester's hair, wet and matted with mud, hung over his eyes. He struggled to get up aching from head to foot. He fell again. The gendarmes laughed. There were two of them. Chester realized that he was barefoot, trouserless, also. He was *naked* under his overcoat! He looked around for his clothes, as he might in a room he had undressed in, but he saw only a gutter down which clear water ran, cobblestones, a few trees with peeling bark along the pavement, the gendarmes.

"Your name, m'sieur?" one asked in French. "Card of identity?" His voice shook with laughter.

A bird twittered, pure and clear, from the sunlit top of a leafless tree.

Chester felt for his passport. It was gone. His pockets were empty. There were not many in the overcoat to look in. He had not a thing, not even a cigarette.

"Look here, I don't know how I got here," he began in English. He swayed on his bare feet, as if the pain in his head were pulling him this way and that with its weight.

The young moustached gendarme who had spoken to him stepped off the curb, tucked his baton under his arm, and searched Chester's overcoat pockets. He was still smiling uncontrollably, and the other gendarme, an older man, was rocking back on his heels with laughter. A window went up above them.

"Why don't you keep our streets clean of such trash!" shrieked a woman in a white nightgown. "A fine time to wake a person up!"

"Ah, you know, Marseille has many distinguished foreign visitors," replied the young gendarme. "What would we do without tourists? This one has spent every sou here!"

Somehow the words were brilliantly clear to Chester, clear as the throat of the bird that was still singing in the treetop. *Why don't you look for the people who robbed me?* Chester had the sentence half formed in French, and then it dissolved in a wave of self-pity. He began to curse, good round curses in English. He cursed through his tears. He threw off the hands of the gendarmes. If they wanted him to walk, he could walk, and without their assistance.

The gendarmes toughened up in a flash, and the white baton crashed on Chester's head. His knees buckled. They caught him.

Then off they went, round a corner, Chester with his head lolling, catching dazed glimpses of his two white feet flapping like plucked birds below him, bruised and bleeding, he was sure, from the cruel, cold pavements beneath them.

"F'Christ's sake, haven't you got a taxi?" he roared.

"Dum-te-dum-te-dum," sang the young gendarme, walking sprucely along on his left, and the one on Chester's right guffawed.

They flung him into a straight chair in a building that smelled of dead rats, sweaty wood, and stale tobacco.

"Votre nom—votre nom—votre *nom!*" A hatless gendarme leaned towards him with pencil and paper.

Chester told him what to do with himself, but he seemed not to understand it.

"Your—*name!*" he said.

"Oliver—Donaldson," Chester said heavily. Let them chew on that for a while. Oliver Donaldson, Oliver Donaldson. He mustn't forget it. "A glass of water," Chester said in French.

Somebody gripped his jaw and turned his face this way and that. There was much conversation among three of them, muttered, and Chester couldn't understand it. Chester glared back at all of them. Some were smirking at his attire.

"Philippe Wedduhkeen?" one of them said.

Chester sat stonily, bare feet planted as firmly on the floor as if he were fully clothed and wore jackboots.

Another, rushing so that he nearly tripped, shoved a small photograph in front of him. It was his passport photograph.

Cries of "Si!—Si!—Mais *oui!*"

"No," Chester said, and, as if this were a signal for a Bacchanal or a riot to begin, all the gendarmes seemed to leap in the air, to shout, to caper about, slap one another's backs, and dash in all directions. Chester had had quite enough, and he stood up to fight. He remembered catching two of them at once by the fronts of their tunics. He thought he succeeded in bashing their heads together. Then something hit him on the head.

When he lifted his face, some of the blanket lifted with it, stuck with blood. Chester touched his nose, and, frightened by what he felt, took his fingers away. He was lying on a cot in a cell. A bright beam of sunlight fell on his head, but he was not warm. His body shook with a chill. His teeth chattered, and he clenched his jaw to silence them. He frowned intensely at the grey stone wall before his eyes.

The realization of his position, his capture, his semi-nudity, his wretched physical state, was like dropping to the end of a rope with a terrible, almost neck-breaking jolt. It was something quite new to him. He had never sunk so low. It was like some awful pit he might never be able to climb out of. These thoughts, or sensations, were neither mental nor physical entirely, but a mixture of both. His brain seemed a tiny thing that was miles away from him. He remembered the photograph of himself. They had called it Philip Wedekind when they shoved it in front of his face. But it wasn't on record as Wedekind. Rydal would have had to tell them that. That photograph could have come only from the Department of State in America. It was not the photograph that the Greek agent had had in his notebook. It was the passport photograph of Chester MacFarland. He pushed himself up from the cot. Rydal Keener had done it all. Rydal Keener had caused him to kill Colette. Rydal

Keener who was in Paris. Chester swore he would have his blood, if it cost him his own life.

Someone was coming into his cell. A gendarme with a tin bowl of something. A gendarme smiling slightly, and it was not a nasty smile.

Chester sat up and stood up, and so slowly the gendarme didn't know at first what he was doing, Chester flipped open the gendarme's holster and took out his gun.

The bowl of soup fell on the floor.

Chester gestured with the gun for the gendarme to stand against the back wall, and then there was a noise at the cell's door, and Chester fired at the gendarme who had brought the soup. He thought the gun did not go off. Chester was struggling with the safety catch, when a bullet hit him in his side. As he fell, another bullet struck him in the cheek.

21

It seemed that Chester had, or developed in his last moments, a wretched fear of death. He had talked, wept, and "confessed" with his last strength to a man of God who happened to be a Catholic, whom the police had rushed to his cell. Rydal heard the news at noon in Paris, in a police station in Cluny where he had been held since the police picked him up in the café in the boulevard Haussmann. Chester had not been in the Hôtel Élysée-Madison when the police went there to find him. He had escaped without taking any of his belongings with him, it appeared, and a check of Paris hotels, air fields, and railway stations had produced nothing. Then news had come from Marseille that Chester had been found in a gutter, stripped of money, papers and all his clothing except an overcoat. This Rydal had been informed of around 10 a.m., when he awakened in the cell where the police had put him. At about the time Rydal heard Chester had been found, Chester was dying, Rydal realized later. The news of his death came at noon.

Chester, with his last strength, had admitted to the priest and to the police clerks and officers who were standing by that he was William Chamberlain and also Chester MacFarland, which was his real name. He had told—and it must have been in gasped fragments, for Rydal heard about the blood coming from his mouth due to a wound in the lung—of the murder of the Greek agent in the Hotel King's Palace in Athens. The gendarme who spoke to Rydal had it down on paper, sent by wireless from the Marseille police. He read to Rydal:

". . . 'Rydal Keener was in the hotel corridor. He saw me with the body. I said to him, if you say anything about this, I will say you did it. I paid him to keep silent. I wanted him with me so I could watch him. Rydal Keener is not guilty of anything, but I made him help me hide the body in the service closet in the hotel corridor. It is not true that he blackmailed me. Not true.' That is correct?" asked the gendarme.

Two other police officers were watching and listening in Rydal's now open cell.

"Go on," Rydal said.

"'I am guilty of swindling. I am guilty of fraud. I am guilty of the ruination of many men in the United States. I employed Rydal as my spy, my bodyguard, and then, when he made advances to my wife, I became angry. I tried to kill him at Knossos, because he knew too much. The vase fell on my wife instead. I then told Rydal that if he tried to accuse me, I would inform the police that he had killed her while trying to kill me. I don't want to die. I am afraid to die. I am only forty-two. Am I dying? Hold my hand, hold my hand . . .' The rest is . . . babbling," the gendarme finished.

The reading shook Rydal profoundly and for a few seconds bewildered him—as if it might all be untrue. It was like hearing of his own father breaking down, hearing of something unbelievable. And yet he knew Chester had expressed those ideas, which the French had put into idiomatic French, and smoothed out into long sentences. And Chester had said all he could possibly say to clear him. *Rydal Keener is not guilty of anything.* Chester had actually been kind, more than kind. Rydal blinked. Tears had come in his eyes.

"Is what he says true?" the gendarme asked Rydal finally.

"That's . . . substantially true." Rydal was trembling, and tears were ready to burst out again. He watched the gendarme, who was writing something at the bottom of the paper. In the early part of Chester's statement, he said that he knew Rydal Keener must have "told everything" in Paris, but that was not so. Rydal had not mentioned MacFarland. Rydal had not changed his story that he met the Chamberlains in Crete. The police had discovered MacFarland by seizing Philip Wedekind's mail at the American Express in Paris, they had told Rydal. They had cabled the New York police to find a man called Jesse Doty, and that was how the police had connected Wedekind with MacFarland.

The gendarme—not the one who had read the statement, but one who had questioned Rydal the night before, following the boulevard Haussmann rendezvous—asked Rydal, "Is it true that you saw MacFarland in the hotel corridor with the body of the Greek agent?"

"Yes."

"You had known MacFarland before?"

"No," Rydal said.

"You met him at that moment in the corridor? Quite by accident?"

"Yes."

"And he threatened to accuse you if you should betray him?"

The question had a faintly skeptical note, as well it might. "He had also a gun in his pocket," Rydal said. "The agent's gun. He wanted me to help him carry the body to the service closet. And then—after I had done this—I felt myself guilty of being an accessory after the fact."

The gendarme nodded. "Ah, yes. This must be noted, however. Your attitude. Of course." He studied the papers in his hands.

Rydal knew he had told a half lie. But Chester had told a whole one, one that fairly cleared him. Chester's lie would save him. It was a case of both of them lying, in a sense. Rydal had lied by omitting the murder story in Athens, saying he had met the Chamberlains only on Crete. To the police, that omission would appear as an effort to hide the fact he had been an accessory. Only he himself, Rydal thought, would ever know or believe that he had omitted that Hotel King's Palace incident as much to save Chester from a murder charge as to save himself from the charge of being an accessory. Rydal did not know as yet, couldn't know with the five gendarmes in the tiny cell with him, how his lie would sit on his conscience.

The gendarme looked at Rydal thoughtfully. "It is your attitude in Athens after the death of Mrs. MacFarland that is not clear. You were forty-eight hours in Athens. You have said that you obtained your false passport from the same source that MacFarland obtained his Wedekind passport, and you learned from this source that his new name was Wedekind. Yet you did nothing about it. He was stopping at the Hotel El Greco. If you had told the police his name—" The gendarme shrugged. "But on the contrary, you remained silent and obtained for yourself a false passport."

"At that point," Rydal said, "I was in a worse position than before. He had said he would accuse me of killing his wife, and he did accuse me to the police in Athens. The police were then looking for me. As I pointed out before, there were no witnesses to what happened. It would have been my word against his, and the Knossos ticket-seller had seen me running from the palace grounds."

"Ah?" doubtfully. "But MacFarland was so afraid, as Chamberlain, that he changed his name to Wedekind. Wasn't he afraid of you?"

"Yes," Rydal agreed firmly. "He knew I . . . I detested him because he had killed Colette. His wife. He knew I was upset. He was afraid I would go to the police in Athens and tell them what really happened. I could have gone farther back, you see, and told them about MacFarland, too. It was no wonder he wanted to disappear from me."

"But you did not make a move."

"Monsieur—I was in love, and she was dead." Rydal said it with conviction. It was true. It was true enough. Impossible to explain, to the bureaucratic mind, the intricacies of his emotions in regard to Chester, in regard to Colette.

"You will have to be more formally interrogated than this," said the gendarme. "I shall see if it can be arranged this afternoon—late. Meanwhile, I am afraid you must stay here."

They all left his cell, and locked it again. Rydal sat down on his cot. He stared at his old brown suitcase that had been in the Hotel Montmorency. At least they had fetched that for him and given it to him, and his passport was in it still.

The interrogation that afternoon took place at dusk in a building several streets away. Some eight men were present, jurists, gendarmes, clerks. The facts were treated like hard stones, picked up and examined and tossed down. The result was a zigzagging and inaccurate pattern, it seemed to Rydal, and yet in every crucial area, he was cleared. He did not by any means emerge a hero, nor did his behavior appear very intelligent, but none of his actions was labeled criminal. None except the least of them, to Rydal, the obtaining of the false Italian passport, merited even a mild term of opprobrium in the view of the assembled officials. For this he was to pay a fine to the Italian government. He was released with a request to go to the French Consulate General to have his passport put in order; that was, a stamp saying he was legally in the country.

Rydal spoke to the gendarme who had questioned him in the cell. "I suppose MacFarland will be buried in Marseille? Or were there any arrangements made for his body to be taken to the United States?"

The gendarme gave a big shrug with arms outstretched.

"Would you find out for me, please? Could you call Marseille?"

Back at the station where Rydal had stayed overnight, the gendarme called Marseille. Chester's body was to be buried the following morning early in a potter's field outside Marseille. For an instant, Rydal saw it, a wooden box carelessly dropped into a pit, probably in a drizzling rain, probably under the bored eyes of an officer or two, the minimum of witnesses required by law, impatient to get away. No friends, no mourners, not a single chrysanthemum, the traditional flower at French burials. Chester deserved more than that.

"Why are you interested?" asked the gendarme.

"I thought I might go to the funeral—or whatever it is," Rydal said. He had to go. No question. Rydal looked at the gendarme's puzzled face. "Yes. I'm going," he said.